MURDER IN THE AFTERNOON

It was early afternoon when Lucy pulled into a vacant parking spot in front of Slack's store and shifted the Subaru into park. Thinking of last night's award ceremony, she was determined to get her confiscated video camera back. She couldn't recapture Toby's big moment, but she certainly wasn't going to miss the one and only opportunity she'd have to videotape the girls' ballet recital.

Squaring her shoulders, she marched into the store. It was something of a letdown to discover that nobody seemed to be around. Lucy peered down the aisles and called out a hello, but there was no answer. She wondered if the store was closed, and began to feel uneasy. Perhaps she should come back another time.

What other time? she reminded herself. She needed the camera now. Spotting Slack's office door slightly ajar, Lucy decided to give it a try. She knocked smartly, which made the loose glass rattle.

The unlatched door swung slowly inward.

And there she found Morrill Slack slumped forward on his desk, motionless.

Lucy ran to him and reached for the phone to call the ambulance. The receiver was unpleasantly sticky, but it was only after she'd hung up that she noticed blood on her hand. Forcing herself to focus, she saw the entire desk was splattered with blood.

Slack's head, she realized with a growing sense of horror, had been brutally bashed in . . . and it very much looked as if her video camera had been used to do the job.

Books by Leslie Meier

MISTLETOE MURDER

TIPPY TOE MURDER

TRICK OR TREAT MURDER

BACK TO SCHOOL MURDER

VALENTINE MURDER

CHRISTMAS COOKIE MURDER

TURKEY DAY MURDER

WEDDING DAY MURDER

Published by Kensington Publishing Corporation

TIPPY-TOE MURDER

Leslie Meier

Kensington Books
Kensington Publishing Corp.
http://www.kensingtonbooks.com

To Greg
Love always

KENSINGTON BOOKS are published by

Kensington Publishing Corp.
850 Third Avenue
New York, NY 10022

All Kensington Titles, Imprints, and Distributed Lines are available at special
quantity discounts for bulk purchases for sales promotions, premiums, fund-
raising, and educational or institutional use. Special book excerpts or custom-
ized printings can also be created to fit specific needs. For details, write
or phone the office of the Kensington special sales manager: Kensington
Publishing Corp., 850 Third Avenue, New York, NY 10022, attn: Special
Sales Department, Phone: 1-800-221-2647.

Kensington and the K logo Reg. U.S. Pat. & TM Off.

First Printing: October 1996
10   9   8   7

Printed in the United States of America

ACKNOWLEDGMENTS

I am grateful to the wonderful women who inspired and helped me when I was writing TIPPY TOE MURDER, most especially Melody Hall of La Melodia Academy of the Dance in Harwich Port, Massachusetts.

Also, I am indebted to Roberta Tambascia of Independence House in Hyannis, Massachusetts, for sharing her insights about domestic violence with me, and to Honora Goldstein and Rachel Carey-Harper, cofounders of The Clothesline Project.

And, of course, the ladies in New York: superagent Meg Ruley and editors Pam Dorman and Paris Wald. Thank you!

Acknowledgments

I am grateful to the wonderful women who inspired and helped me when I was writing *Tippy-Toe Murder,* most especially Melody Hall of La Melodia Academy of the Dance in Harwich Port, Massachusetts.

Also, I am indebted to Roberta Tambascia of Independence House in Hyannis, Massachusetts, for sharing her insights about domestic violence with me, and to Honora Goldstein and Rachel Carey-Harper, cofounders of The Clothesline Project.

And, of course, the ladies in New York: super-agent Meg Ruley, and editors Pam Dorman and Paris Wald. Thank you!

Prologue

The day she disappeared, Caroline Hutton took her dog for a walk around Blueberry Pond, just as she always did.

Although she was worried and distracted, she managed to control her wayward thoughts by concentrating on the here and now.

She followed the flight of a herring gull soaring high above her. Wouldn't it be wonderful, she thought, to fly on strong white wings?

She took deep breaths of the clean air, and soaked up the warm sunshine. In her memory she stored the image of the pine trees surrounding the pond, dark-green spikes against the brilliant blue sky.

She enjoyed the exuberance and energy of her golden retriever, George, named after the famous choreographer George Balanchine. She smiled when he leaped into the pond, landing with an enormous splash, and paddled around for his morning swim. When he clambered out and braced himself for a good shake, she took a few steps backward. She laughed as he came toward her, spraying water every which way. When he loped off down the dirt road with his nose to the ground sniffing out adventure, she followed him.

Although she was well over seventy, she walked easily, with the grace of a dancer. Years of discipline and training had given Caroline Hutton, Caro to her friends, strength and an extremely straight back.

Spying them from her kitchen window, Lucy Stone smiled to herself. A glance at the clock confirmed what she already knew; it was twenty past eight. Caro walked her dog along the old logging trail behind her house at this time every morning; only blizzards and hurricanes deterred her.

Lucy paused a moment, taking a break from her chores, and watched as the old woman and the dog walked down the sunny road, golden with fallen pine needles, and came to the edge of the woods. Later she would remember that one moment they were there together in the sunshine, and then they stepped into the dark shadows and disappeared.

One

Instructions for Ballet Performance Friday, June 14, Tinker's Cove Academy of the Dance (otherwise known as the pink sheet)

Where's Caro? That's what Caro's oldest and dearest friend, Julia Ward Howe Tilley, was asking herself later that morning. She turned off the flame under the shrieking kettle and peered out the kitchen window, looking for Caro's little blue Honda. Caro stopped by every morning after exercising George to share a cup of tea and a chat.

Perhaps something was wrong, she fretted. The car might have a dead battery, or Caro might have a touch of the flu. In either case, however, she would have expected her to call.

Miss Tilley (only her very closest friends dared to call her Julia) reached for the phone and dialed Caro's number. Although she let the phone ring ten times, and then hung up and dialed again, letting it ring ten more times, there was no answer.

Where was Miss Hutton? Gerald Asquith, president of Winchester College, pressed the button on his intercom and asked his secretary if there had been any message from her.

"No, sir, none at all," she answered.

"Well, that's rather unusual," said Asquith. "Isn't she scheduled for a two o'clock meeting?"

"Yes, she is," agreed the secretary. "Do you want me to call her?"

"No, that's all right," he said. The purpose of the meeting was to discuss a rather large bequest Miss Hutton was planning to make to the college, and Asquith didn't want to appear too eager. On the other hand, it was very unlike Miss Hutton to be late.

Maybe she'd had trouble with her car, maybe she'd had a flat tire en route. That was the most likely explanation, he decided, making a note to call her the next day. That would send just the right message; he would appear concerned but not anxious.

Kitty Slack, Caro's neighbor, was surprised on Tuesday morning when George appeared at her kitchen door looking for a breakfast handout.

"Go home," she told him.

The dog cocked his head and scratched the screen door, adding a whine for emphasis. But when Kitty opened the door to let him in, he refused to enter. Instead, he turned right around and headed home.

Kitty followed him across the driveway that separated the two properties and knocked at Caro's kitchen door. The door was unlocked, so she went in, calling her neighbor's name. There was no answer as she went from room to room. She even checked the cellar and garage.

Everything was just as it ought to be. The car was in the garage, the clean dishes stood in the dish drainer, the towels were neatly folded in the bathroom. It seemed that Caro must have stepped out just for a minute. But if that was the case, why was George whining so?

Kitty picked up the phone and rang the police station.

"Tinker's Cove Police," recited the bored young dispatcher. When she took the job she thought it would be exciting, but she soon discovered nothing much ever happened in Tinker's Cove.

"This is Mrs. Slack," said the old woman, hesitating. "I don't really know if this is a matter for the police."

"Why don't you talk to Officer Culpepper?" suggested the dispatcher, transferring the call. Barney Culpepper was good with old ladies and children.

"Well, good morning, Mrs. Slack," said Culpepper, his voice booming through the telephone line. "What can I do for you?"

"I don't know if I should be bothering you with this, but I do think something is wrong."

"It's no bother. What's the problem?"

"I'm afraid something has happened to Caroline Hutton. Her dog George came over to my house a little bit ago, and I can't find any sign of her. Something must have happened to her. She wouldn't go off and leave George, would she?"

"Are you at her place?"

"Oh, yes."

"Stay there and I'll be right over to take a look around."

"Well, all right," she agreed, "But I really ought to go home. Morrill will be wanting his dinner."

"I'll be there in two shakes of a lamb's tail, Mrs. Slack."

Kitty replaced the receiver and stood awkwardly in the kitchen. She didn't know what to do with herself in another woman's house, so she finally went over to the window to watch for Officer Culpepper.

When the phone rang, a few minutes later, she picked up the receiver.

"Hello," she said stiffly, uncomfortable about answering someone else's phone.

"Miss Hutton? Gerald Asquith here."

"I'm not Miss Hutton. I'm her neighbor, Kitty Slack."

"Oh. Can you put her on?"

"I'm sorry, but she's not here."

"Where is she? She missed an important meeting yesterday."

"I don't know where she is, but I think there's someone you ought to speak to," said Kitty, looking up as Culpepper arrived and handing him the receiver.

Culpepper had just finished talking with Asquith and was folding his notebook shut when Tatiana O'Brien appeared at the kitchen door.

"What's the matter?" she demanded, shocked at finding a police officer in Caro's kitchen. "Where's Caro?"

"Dunno yet," Culpepper told her. "All we know right now is that she's not here."

"Not here? That's ridiculous." The young woman tossed her glossy long black hair back over her shoulder in a graceful gesture. "I'm supposed to have lunch with her today."

"Maybe you'd better tell me all about it," said Culpepper, opening his notebook to a fresh page.

"There's not much to tell. We were going to discuss the show. It's a week from Friday, you know, and there are only a few rehearsals left. I called to ask her opinion on a few things, and she invited me to lunch."

"You're sure she invited you for today?"

"Absolutely." Tatiana's bright blue eyes flashed. She was not used to being doubted.

Culpepper tapped his notebook against the back of his hand and considered the situation. He knew Tatiana taught ballet to most of the little girls in town, and her show took place every year just as predictably as the Fourth of July parade.

"I can't imagine what's happened," said Kitty. "I think poor George is hungry."

All three looked at George, who was sniffing at his empty food dish. He gave a hopeful wag of his tail and then collapsed on the floor, putting his chin down between his paws.

"I better inform the chief," said Culpepper, reaching for the phone.

On Wednesday, Chief Oswald Crowley took a call from Hancock Smith, the chairman of the board of selectmen.

"Crowley, what's all this I'm hearing about Caroline Hutton? They say she's missing. What are you doing about it?"

"I'm following the usual policy, that's what I'm doing."

"Enlighten me, Crowley. What's the usual policy?"

"Well, sir," drawled Crowley, "the usual policy is business as usual unless there's a ransom note or some indication of violence. Chances are this lady went off on a little vacation and forgot to tell the neighbors."

"You mean you're not doing anything at all?"

"I wouldn't say that. No, sir, I'd say we're monitoring the situation. Waiting for developments."

"That's not good enough, Crowley. I'm warning you, you'd better get on this fast or I'll have your fat ass, understand me? Let's start questioning her friends and neighbors, conduct a search. The poor old woman could be lying in the woods somewhere. A lot of very influential people are interested in this, Crowley. I just got a call from the state rep's office. And one from Asquith over at the college. And Miss Julia Ward Howe Tilley is expecting me to return her call as soon as possible. Are you getting the picture?"

"You're coming in loud and clear, Hancock, but what I wanna know is where's the money gonna come from?"

"What money?"

"Money for man-hours, that's what money. There's no line item in the budget for tracking down missing old ladies."

"Just do it. We'll figure that out later."

"Okay," said Crowley, shrugging and picking his teeth with his fingernail. "But remember, when she shows up in two weeks with a bright-orange Florida tan, you're the one who authorized this nonsense."

Hearing a commotion outside, Kitty Slack went to investigate and discovered two uniformed policemen wearing surgical face masks and rubber gloves tipping the contents of Caro's garbage cans onto a large sheet of plastic. As she watched they began sorting carefully through the pile of trash.

Working in her garden a bit farther out of town, Miss Tilley was startled when she heard the sound of sirens. Looking up, she was distressed to see several cruisers and an ambulance speeding down the road.

In her farmhouse, nestled in the mountains out beyond the town, Lucy Stone heard the sirens come closer and closer. She went out on the porch and saw a procession of official vehicles go bouncing down the old logging road.

"Hey, Mom, what's up?" asked Toby, her ten-year-old son.

"I dunno, let's go and see," said Lucy, who remembered chasing fire engines with her father. She was so small, and the seats in his Buick were so big, that she went sliding every time he took a turn. Those were the days before seat belts, of course. She was just about to share her memory with Toby when she realized he was already quite a ways ahead of her.

"Not so fast," she called. "Wait for me!" Now six months pregnant, Lucy was finding it hard to keep up with Toby.

Toby slowed just enough to remain in sight. When he reached the clearing that contained Blueberry Pond, he paused and waited for his mother. Together they surveyed the scene.

A K-9 patrol consisting of one officer and a large German shepherd was checking the edge of the woods, and a group of uniformed policemen were launching a small boat in order to drag the pond. Lucy spied her friend, Officer Barney Culpepper, among the group and waved at him. As soon as the boat was afloat, he approached them, crunching across the pebbly beach in heavy black rubber boots.

"What's going on?" asked Lucy.

"We're searching for Caroline Hutton," he said, pulling out a handkerchief and mopping his sweaty forehead. "We gotta check all the places she was known to go. Haven't turned up anything so far. Seems like one minute she was here, next thing anybody knew, she wasn't."

"Like in a magic show?" asked Toby.

Culpepper scratched his chin. "Yeah," he finally agreed. "Just like that," he said, snapping his fingers.

Gerald Asquith unfolded his paper on Thursday morning and saw the question everyone was asking, in stark black letters two inches tall: *"WHERE'S CARO?"*

" 'Search for missing prof continues,' " he read, scanning the front page. A grainy photograph of several men in a small motorboat, one of them holding a grappling hook, was prominently featured.

He switched on the TV, and immediately he saw a long line of volunteers walking slowly through the woods, searching for Caro.

Driving to work, he heard several callers offer their ideas about Caro's whereabouts on WMVL talk radio.

"This is Susan from Portland. I bet she was raped and killed by some sexual psychopath. They'll probably never find her body. Maybe he ate it, like that Jeffrey Dahmer."

"That's an interesting idea, Susan. Next caller, you're on the air."

"My name's Irma and I live in Tinker's Cove. I think she was probably kidnapped by Satanists. Didn't they find signs of Devil worship in the woods over near Gilead last summer? Pentagrams and altars and sacrificed animals? Everybody said it was just kids, but I wonder. Maybe they've graduated from animals to humans."

"Well, Irma, let's hope nothing like that is going on. It's almost summer and we wouldn't want to scare away the tourists, would we? Next caller?"

"Yeah, this is Jim from Lakewood. I was reading in the paper just the other day about how these aliens from outer space abduct people. There was an interview with a fella who said he was taken away by these weird little dudes with bug eyes and floated around in their spaceship for a coupla weeks. They brought him back, and he can remember some of it, but not everything. He said they usually zap your memory, but in his case the zapper must not've worked too good. Don't laugh, I read it in the paper. Aliens. Happens all the time."

TWO

No food or drink is allowed in the Auditorium during rehearsals or performance.

As she drove down Main Street, Lucy Stone couldn't help noticing how deserted it seemed. After Caroline Hutton's disappearance last week the town had been overrun with state and local police officials, volunteer searchers, and reporters and TV camera crews. All the excitement soon fizzled, however, when the intense investigation failed to produce any trace of Caro.

Now, the search had been called off "pending further developments," as Chief Crowley explained in a final news conference. Caro was no longer headline news; she hadn't even made page 3 in the morning paper but was only mentioned in a two-inch follow-up story on the same page as the obituaries.

Lucy pulled the little Subaru into one of several vacant parking slots in front of Slack's hardware store and struggled out. The car had certainly not been designed for a woman who was six months pregnant. She crossed the sidewalk and then paused for a moment outside the store to read a handwritten notice that had been tacked on the door. PRESS *NOT* WELCOME, it read. Then she planted her feet firmly and yanked the sticky door open.

She hardly ever shopped at Slack's. The place was an

absolute relic and the prices were outrageous. But today she didn't have the time or the energy to drive thirty miles to Portland just to buy a bag of fertilizer.

The store was a fixture on Main Street. In fact, some people believed Tinker's Cove had been named after the first Slack, a tinsmith named Ephraim. While some Chamber of Commerce members would have eagerly seized on such a link to the past, cultivating an old-fashioned atmosphere for the benefit of the tourists who arrived in droves every summer, Morrill Slack never even considered it. His store was old-fashioned because he was too cheap to modernize it.

Nothing newfangled here, thought Lucy, glancing around. This was not the sort of hardware store that sold salad spinners. Nails were still kept in wooden kegs and sold by the pound. Little wooden drawers behind the long counter were filled with nuts and bolts, and customers had to ask for what they wanted. Pity the poor soul who didn't know a wood screw from a machine screw or a female fitting from a male. If you didn't know exactly what you wanted, and weren't prepared to pay retail plus for it, Morrill Slack certainly wasn't going to waste his time helping you.

"Hi, Lucy," said Franny Small, the round-faced little cashier. Everyone in town knew Franny; whenever illness or tragedy struck, Franny followed, bringing a foil-covered dish of Austrian ravioli. Franny was thirty-five years old, lived with her mother, and had worked in the store for years.

"Gosh, it seems so quiet in town it's almost spooky. Where'd everybody go?"

"After that bomb scare at Kennebunkport on Saturday they all cleared out real fast," said Franny. "It's kind of a relief, really. I got sick of being interviewed, especially since I didn't have anything to say. Of course, they were all after Mr. Slack 'cause he's Caro's neighbor and all, but they didn't get much from him, that's for sure. He finally put a sign up. Did you see it? Told me not to let any reporters in the store."

"No reporters interviewed me," said Lucy, "but the police did. Barney Culpepper came by, along with that state detective, Horowitz, but I couldn't tell them much. I saw Caro a week ago Friday, walking George as usual. I slept in a bit on the weekend, so I don't know if she went walking or not. Last Monday was the first time I missed her. They've had search parties and dogs all over the woods and down to the pond, but they haven't found any sign of her."

"And now they've stopped searching," said Franny.

"I'm sure they've got bulletins out," speculated Lucy. "They're probably contacting police departments all over the country."

"Don't bet on it," said Sue Finch, appearing from behind the paint display and setting a quart of white enamel on the counter. "Got to paint the Adirondack chairs," she explained, smiling a greeting to Lucy.

"What do you mean?" asked Lucy. "Why don't you think they'll keep looking for her?"

"She's an old woman with one foot already in the grave. Old women are practically disposable."

"Sue, that doesn't sound like you!" Lucy was shocked.

"I've been volunteering over at the women's shelter in Portland and I guess it's getting to me." Sue shrugged and pulled a rather elegant French purse out of the leather backpack she used as a shoulder bag. Sue had a natural flair for clothes and accessories that Lucy admired but had long ago given up trying to emulate. It took too much energy.

"It's an epidemic," she continued angrily. "Women beaten, raped, killed, and by the time the police and the courts do anything, it's almost always too late."

Franny fumbled taking the bill Sue proffered, and her face suddenly lost its color. While Franny was occupied ringing up the paint on the antique cash register, Lucy shot Sue a warning glance, then placed her order.

"Franny, I need a bag of five-ten-five for the garden. Have you got any?"

"Sure. Let me have Ben put that in the car for you. You shouldn't be lugging around heavy bags of fertilizer."

"Thanks," said Lucy, reaching around to rub her aching back. In answer to Franny's call, a scruffy, skinny teenager appeared from the back room. He was dressed in the uniform of his tribe: long, baggy shorts and an oversized Guns 'N Roses T-shirt. He was wearing an extremely expensive pair of athletic shoes, the same style that Lucy's son Toby had unsuccessfully begged her to buy for him. An officially licensed Red Sox cap sat on his closely shaved head.

"Whatcha want?" he asked Franny. There was a hint of defiance, or maybe just defensiveness, in his stare.

"Mrs. Stone wants fifty pounds of fertilizer—it's the green bag over there. You can put it in the silver Subaru out front."

"I'm supposed to be sweeping the back room," he said, shifting his weight impatiently from one foot to the other.

"This will only take a minute," said Franny mildly. "You can hardly expect Mrs. Stone to lift it, in her condition."

The women were amused to see a blush spread over Ben's pimply cheeks, and watched as he shuffled over to the neatly stacked bags of fertilizer and hoisted one onto his shoulder. When the door finally slammed behind him, Franny spoke.

"He's Mr. Slack's grandson," she said, tilting her

head toward a door containing a pane of frosted glass marked "Office" in peeling black letters. "He's been coming in to help out for the past two weeks. The old man's thrilled to pieces that he's taking an interest in the business. Let's see, that'll be six ninety-five."

"Are you sure?" asked Lucy, raising her eyebrows. "It was only two ninety-nine in the K mart flyer."

"I don't know what K mart is charging," announced Morrill Slack, who had suddenly appeared in the office doorway. Dressed in a sober black suit and a snowy-white starched shirt, he looked like an apparition from the past. "I do know that my price is six ninety-five, take it or leave it."

The old man took his heavy gold pocket watch out of his vest pocket and stroked it lovingly with his large, flattish fingers before flipping open the lid to check the time. He shut it with a snap and held it in his hand a moment, savoring its heft before replacing it carefully in his vest pocket.

"Well, do you want the fertilizer or not?" he demanded abruptly, impatiently clicking his dentures back and forth with his tongue. He glared through his wire-rimmed glasses at Lucy and Sue. "You've already taken up quite enough of Franny's time with your gossiping."

"Oh, I want it," said Lucy hastily. "Ben's already put it in the car. I really appreciate the service."

"He's a fine boy," observed the old man as he returned to his office.

Franny allowed herself a moment of rebellion and rolled her eyes for her friends' benefit before ringing up the transaction.

"See ya, Franny," said Sue. She took Lucy's elbow and steered her out of the store. "Have you got time for a cup of coffee?"

"Sure," said Lucy, stepping nimbly to avoid the heavy door.

"Good, 'cause I'm dying to know what that was all about."

"What do you mean?"

"Why'd Franny act so funny when I mentioned working at the shelter?" They paused at the curb, waiting for a lobster truck to rumble by, then crossed to Jake's Donut Shop.

"Franny was a battered wife," said Lucy as the two settled down at a table.

"Franny?" exclaimed Sue. "I can't believe it. I never even knew she'd been married."

"It was a long time ago, fifteen years or more. Bill and I had just moved here. It was quite a scandal. He died falling down the stairs, and some people thought Franny gave him a push."

"Franny? I can't believe it. Was there a trial?"

"I don't think so. I don't remember why. Maybe it was an accident. I know he drank a lot. I'm kind of fuzzy on the details, but I do know most people thought he got what he deserved." She paused to consult the menu. "I can't decide what to order. Doc Ryder'd kill me if he ever found out I was even in this place."

"Lucy, don't change the subject. Tell me about Franny's husband."

"Honest, Sue, I told you everything I know. It was a long time ago. How many calories do you think a Bavarian creme doughnut has?"

"Forget calories," advised Sue with the nonchalance of a perfect size eight. "Pregnancy's the one time you ought to be able to indulge. Do you have any cravings?"

"Not really. Mostly I'm just tired. I'm not twenty-five anymore. It's harder as you get older. My back's been bothering me this time."

"Then you need Jake's Tiger Milk shake," advised Sue. "You can hardly taste the brewer's yeast."

"I'll have a glass of grapefruit juice," Lucy told the waitress.

"And I'll have iced coffee," said Sue.

"So what's this about working at the women's shelter? It doesn't seem like your sort of thing."

"I know. I guess my consciousness got raised a little late," agreed Sue. "Somehow hitting all the sales and snapping up the bargains lost its luster. I wanted to do something, well, I really hate this word, meaningful."

"Why don't you go to work?"

"Raising two kids, cooking three meals a day, and keeping a clean house doesn't give you much of a resumé," she said, pausing while the waitress placed their orders on the table. "I thought this might help me get something more interesting than cashiering at the IGA."

"Or answering the phones at Country Cousins," said Lucy, referring to her former job at the giant mail-order company. "Bill swears I got pregnant just so I could quit."

"That's ridiculous."

"No. He's right. But next time I'm going to sign up for a course. It's gotta be easier on the back."

The two women shared a laugh and sipped their drinks. Sue poured some milk into her iced coffee and watched it swirl through the dark liquid.

"I don't really like it with milk, but I can't resist seeing it change color like that," she admitted. "Lucy, you love a good mystery. What do you think happened to Caro?"

"I don't know. It's scary, isn't it? I think about her all the time. She was so nice, you know?"

"Do you think she was murdered or something?"

"According to Barney Culpepper there's no sign of

any foul play. The police think she either went away of her own accord, on a trip or something, or she killed herself. He said they're not seriously considering suicide, since no body's been found."

"Sounds to me like they're just making excuses. Do you think they're really looking for her?"

"I think they've done as much as they can. A case like this really needs a full-time investigator."

"Someone like you?" asked Sue with a mischievous smile.

"I don't think so," said Lucy slowly. "Bill's been difficult enough lately. He'd have a fit if I started playing detective again."

"Are you two having problems?" Sue's tone was sympathetic.

Lucy shrugged. "You know how it is. We didn't plan this pregnancy—it just happened. I know he's worried about money. I mean, he's a carpenter and this will be our fourth kid. It's more than that, though. There's no time anymore just for us. Little League practices, ballet lessons, PTA meetings. There's always something. I can't blame him for losing his temper now and then."

"Does he hit you?" asked Sue in a low voice.

"No!" exclaimed Lucy. "He wouldn't do that."

"I'm warning you, Lucy, it's a continuum." Sue drew an imaginary line with her fingers. "At one end there's verbal abuse, then there's physical abuse, and finally there's ultimate abuse. That's when he kills you."

"I think I'm safe enough," said Lucy. "That crisis center seems to be making you awfully cynical."

"It's been an eye opener," said Sue, shaking her head sadly. "There's so much abuse. It's crazy. It's out of control. One of the advocates told me more women were killed by husbands and lovers during the Vietnam years than soldiers were killed overseas, and it's getting worse."

"I can't believe it," said Lucy. "Except for Franny, I don't know any battered wives."

"Oh yes you do."

Lucy thought for a minute and then leaned forward. "Who?"

"I can't tell you. But believe me, there's plenty of women afraid for their lives and for their children, right here in Tinker's Cove."

Sue paused and slowly shook her head.

"The kids, that's the part that really gets me. Have you seen that story in this morning's paper? Some poor woman gone to jail rather than hand her kid over to an abusive father. The judge, male, of course, won't let her out until she tells where the kid is. It makes me so mad. They call it a war against women, but if we fight back they slap us in jail. It's not fair."

Surprised at her own vehemence, Sue cracked an apologetic smile. "I tend to get carried away on this subject. Oh, well, I gotta go, Lucy. I didn't realize it was so late. The plumber's coming at eleven and I don't want to miss him."

"That's okay," said Lucy. "I'll get the check."

She watched her friend leave the coffee shop, and then made her way slowly to the cash register. She knew she had no business feeling light-headed, she'd just had a glass of juice, but for a moment the floor tilted crazily beneath her. Home ought to be a safe place, a haven.

"Is everything okay?" asked the cashier, a motherly woman with her gray curls confined in a hair net.

"I must have stood up too fast," said Lucy, reaching in her purse. Where would she go, she wondered as she waited for her change, if she couldn't go home?

Three

There is no charge for the performance—donations welcome.

The store was quiet after Sue and Lucy left. Franny perched on her stool behind the counter and leafed through a pile of old invoices. She could hear an occasional *humph* from Mr. Slack in his office, and she heard Ben knocking around in the back room, where he was supposed to be sweeping.

Franny wasn't as happy about Ben's coming to work in the store as his grandfather was. In the past she'd pretty much had the place to herself, but now that the boy was coming in, the old man was constantly popping out of his office and interfering.

Through the years, although she was officially only a cashier, she'd gradually taken over the running of the business. She was used to having things her way, and she resented Ben's presence.

To give him his due, the boy really seemed to take to the business. He had a way of stroking various items, as he put them on the display shelves or stowed them in drawers, that reminded her of his grandfather.

Perhaps it was one of those family traits that get passed along, but it was unnerving to see the teenager working his big hands the same way the old man did. He even had an oversized nut and bolt he kept in his pocket. He fiddled with them just the way Slack fondled that precious gold pocket watch of his.

Most upsetting of all, now that Ben was working in the hardware store, his friends had started hanging around. Franny could feel her stomach hardening and twisting into knots when they arrived, pushing and shoving one another and tripping over their huge basketball shoes. It was a wonder they didn't knock over a display rack or topple one of the neatly stacked pyramids of paint cans. They seemed to be everywhere at once, and she couldn't possibly keep an eye on all of them.

Actually, she was a little afraid of them. While they dressed like kids, she knew they were actually young men. They were bigger than she was and full of rough male energy.

From what she observed it seemed Ben was their leader and they were reporting to him. She was sure they were up to no good. Their whispered conversation was full of winks and nudges, and they constantly checked over their shoulders to see if they were being overheard. She tried to keep her distance, but if she had to approach them to help a customer, she noticed they would move away or fall silent. Whenever Mr. Slack appeared, they disappeared.

Returning to the invoices, Franny went through them one more time. She couldn't understand it. According to the paperwork, the store had received enough batteries to last through the summer, based on her best estimate using last year's figures. They'd gotten twenty boxes each of AA and D batteries, the most popular sellers, and ten boxes each of the other sizes.

Last week she'd noticed the display rack was nearly empty, and she'd asked Ben to fill it.

"Can't," he'd said, avoiding her eyes. "They're all gone."

"There should be plenty in the storeroom," she'd insisted, looking curiously at his two buddies, who were lounging by the paint display. They seemed to find the conversation extremely amusing. "Go check again."

"There's no point. I'm telling you, they're all gone. Look, I'm taking a break now," he'd said, signaling his friends to follow him outside.

Sure enough, she couldn't find any batteries in the storeroom, either. She was sure they hadn't been sold; she would have noticed the unusual number of sales and ordered more. Where had they gone?

It was very disturbing, especially since she'd been having such a hard time lately making up the bank deposit. That was always the first task of the day. She would take the previous day's take out of the safe and add up the checks and cash, square them with the total sales figure, and fill out the deposit slip. Then Mr. Slack would put the whole business in a blue vinyl zippered pouch and take it to the red-brick bank across the street.

For the past few weeks, however, she hadn't been able to get the figures to match, even though she was especially careful whenever she made change. Every morning the cash was five or ten dollars short. She checked and rechecked her figures. She knew she wasn't making mistakes in addition, and she wasn't giving out the wrong change.

Only one answer seemed possible to Franny, especially when she realized the trouble began after Ben came to work in the store. Franny suspected the boy loved the business just a little bit too much and was appropriating some of the merchandise and cash for himself and his friends.

Franny found this behavior shocking. Why didn't he simply come right out and ask his grandfather for whatever he wanted? She was sure the old man would give it to him. In fact, he seemed to get more than enough from his parents. Fred and Annemarie spoiled him rotten, showering him with faddish clothes and video games, even a car. Franny didn't approve.

"Franny, there's something I'd like to see you about. That is, if you're not too busy," said Slack, standing in the open doorway.

"Sure, Mr. Slack. What's the problem?"

"We had better go into the office," he said. He turned and Franny followed him, taking a seat in the plain wooden visitor's chair. She watched as he seated himself in his creaky old swivel chair, rubbed his long nose with his flat fingers, and pushed his glasses up where they belonged. He sucked his wrinkled cheeks in, popped his top denture loose, and shoved it back in place with his tongue. It made a satisfying click.

"What's the problem, Mr. Slack?" repeated Franny, growing impatient. She wanted to get back to those invoices.

"You know perfectly well, Franny. These figures don't match up," said the old man, pointing to the ledgers on his desk. She could see that he was very angry. Each papery cheek had a bright red spot the size of a quarter, and the wattles under his chin were shaking.

"I know," agreed Franny, relieved that he'd brought up the subject. "The cash is short by a hundred and forty dollars, and the inventory is off, too."

"Do you have any explanation?" The old man's blue eyes may have faded some, but he could still work up a pretty nasty stare through those wire-rims.

"I think it's shrinkage, sir," she answered. "Someone's stealing from the store."

"And who might that person be?" Slack was really mad now; Franny could hear his dentures clicking furiously.

She hesitated before answering. She was sure Ben was the thief, but she was reluctant to accuse the boy.

"I don't know," she mumbled.

"Well, I do. And Franny, I expect complete restitution by Friday, or your position here will be terminated!"

Franny felt as if she'd been kicked in the stomach. Too shocked to speak, she felt her eyes filling with tears.

"I will not tolerate thievery!" The old man pounded on his desk with his fist, making her jump. He was truly in a state, and Franny was afraid he might have a stroke or a heart attack. She decided the best thing to do would be to leave him alone to calm down, so she crept back to the cash register.

After all these years, how could he think she was a thief? she fumed, angrily brushing away the tears that wouldn't stop coming. If anything, he'd been stealing from her. She'd been working in the hardware store for fifteen years, and always at minimum wage. You would have thought it would break him, the way he carried on when Congress raised it to four twenty-five.

It was painfully clear that she'd stayed too long in Slack's musty old store, allowing a temporary job to become permanent. She'd always meant to look for something that paid better, but she'd kept putting it off. Too lazy. Too afraid of the probing questions an interviewer might ask. And, she admitted to herself, she enjoyed being in the center of town and chatting with the customers. Business was never exactly brisk, but it was steady, and she never felt rushed or pressured the way the girls who worked in the mall did.

She heard the old man shuffling around in his office and glanced at the clock. It was noon. He soon appeared, carefully setting his ancient straw Panama on his head and straightening his jacket.

"Don't forget what I told you, Franny," he warned as he struggled with the door.

Franny involuntarily held her breath as the door finally gave way, only to slam shut, barely missing his heels. It would serve him right, she thought, if it did catch him. The door had warped years ago, but he'd stubbornly refused to hire a carpenter to fix it. She watched as he marched stiffly past the plate-glass windows. An upright Yankee businessman. A cheapskate.

What am I going to do? she asked herself. She had to straighten it out as soon as possible; she didn't want to lose her job. What if he started talking about her, bad-mouthing her all over town? Who'd hire her then?

A tap on the glass door roused her from her thoughts, and she smiled weakly at Fred Earle, the postman. He pushed the day's mail through the slot and gave a friendly wave before going on to the next store. Franny picked up the assortment of bills and advertisements and began sorting them. One catalog caught her eye; it was for security equipment.

As she looked through the pages featuring motion sensors and video cameras, an idea began to take shape in her mind. It was only Tuesday, and she had until Friday. Perhaps she could catch Ben shoplifting on videotape and give Mr. Slack the evidence he needed. She knew just where she could get a video camera. Lucy Stone had one, and she lent it to anyone who asked.

A video was the answer.

Franny straightened her shoulders; her eyes gleamed with excitement. She'd show them. Franny Small was going to fight back.

Four

Little ones are encouraged to nap before the performance.

Returning home, Lucy was surprised by the sense of relief she felt. It was probably some sort of nesting instinct gone haywire, but lately every time she left home she couldn't wait to return. The sturdy old farmhouse had always been a source of comfort to her, and she and Bill had worked hard to make it attractive, but never before had she felt so attached to it.

I'm getting to be like a turtle, she thought, wanting to carry my house on my back. Instead, when she'd left that morning she had stuffed the loose knob from the newel post in her bag.

Whatever could I have been thinking? she wondered as she replaced it. The house was unusually quiet; today she could enjoy the rare luxury of having it all to herself. Bill was at work, Toby and Elizabeth were at school, and four-year-old Sara was playing at a friend's house.

The baby inside her gave a kick and she laughed. Don't worry, I didn't forget you. What'll we have for lunch, kiddo?

Rummaging in the refrigerator, Lucy resolved to eat a healthful, well-balanced meal of moderate portions. She pulled out a bowl of leftover spaghetti, sprinkled it with Parmesan cheese, and began eating it cold. When that was finished, she made herself a peanut butter and jelly sandwich, then rounded off her meal with a handful of chocolate-chip cookies and an enormous glass of milk.

Feeling rather drowsy, she lumbered off to the couch in the family room so she could put her feet up for a little while. She resolutely set aside the mystery she was reading and dutifully opened the latest book on painless childbirth, but she found she couldn't concentrate. The slim volume soon slipped from her fingers as she drifted off to sleep.

Her sleep was not peaceful, however, but filled with disturbing dreams. In one dream she was lying on the same couch, but the newborn baby was at her side. Her attention was drawn to the ceiling, where she was horrified to see light fixtures sprouting like flowers in a time-lapse film. She had a dreadful sense that things were out of control. She had to get rid of the extra chandeliers that were growing constantly larger, taking up more and more space, but she didn't know what to do.

The scene suddenly shifted and she found herself standing in the nursery doorway. Flames flickered around the crib of her neatly swaddled child. She snatched the little bundle up and held it tightly against her breast, overwhelmed with relief that her baby was safe.

Without warning, she was perched on a high bridge, where the infant inexplicably slipped from her arms and drifted slowly away from her through the air. The white receiving blanket unfurled and floated away, baring the baby's tiny arms and legs. She stood watching, arms outstretched, as the naked infant continued a slow descent toward the river beneath the bridge.

At first the river was only a thin, shiny ribbon of silver, but it grew wider as the baby fell closer. When the tiny body finally met the water, there was a huge slow-motion splash as it disappeared, the entry point marked only by a spreading circle of ripples.

Unable to turn away, she watched until a white shape rose slowly from the depths to remain floating a few inches beneath the surface of the water. The features gradually became clear. They were not those of her baby. It was the round, wrinkled face of Caroline Hutton.

Lucy woke with a start, shocked to see she'd slept for more than two hours. She heard the childish voices of Toby and Elizabeth, home from school—arguing, as usual. She staggered into the kitchen to greet them, still groggy.

Brother and sister were too busy shoving each other away from the cookie jar to notice her, but they stopped struggling when they heard her voice.

"How was school?" she asked, filling the water kettle.

"Okay," mumbled Toby, his mouth full of cookies. His growing body seemed to require constant refueling.

"Do you have much homework?"

"Are you kidding? School's almost over. Today we watched a video."

"All day?"

"Almost. We had art and gym and stuff."

"Oh. How about you, Elizabeth?"

"I helped Mrs. Wright clean out the closets."

Eight-year-old Elizabeth, Lucy knew, was helpful and competent.

"Where's Sara?" asked Elizabeth. "Don't we have a dance rehearsal?"

"She's over at Jenn's. Mrs. Baker's bringing them both to the rehearsal. You'd better start getting ready. We have to leave in a few minutes.

Lucy rubbed her eyes, made a cup of hot decaf, and asked herself for the umpteenth time if the pregnancy was a mistake. After all, she and Bill were lucky to have three healthy children. And until she had to quit her job answering the night phones at Country Cousins, they'd been financially secure. Now she had less money, less energy, less patience, less everything.

Well, not quite less of everything, she admitted, gently scratching the itchy, tightly stretched skin over her enlarged tummy.

Despite her long list of complaints, Doc Ryder kept reassuring her that she was exceptionally healthy. He dismissed heartburn, backache, shortness of breath, exhaustion, and swollen feet with a wave of his hand and advised her to remain active.

"Don't be afraid to exercise," he told her. "Your grandmother probably plowed the back forty before lunch, had the baby, and plowed the front forty before cooking supper.

Lucy blinked, remembering a stately, buxom matron who never left the house without her hat and gloves. "My grandmother did no such thing and you know it," she hissed. "She stayed in the hospital for two weeks and was waited on hand and foot."

"Most of my mothers only stay for twenty-four hours after delivery," said the doctor. "They can't wait to get home."

"At seven hundred dollars a day, who can blame them?" Lucy remembered snapping at him. Setting her empty cup in the sink, she called Elizabeth.

"Mom, I have to have my hair in a bun," the little girl informed her. "Tatiana said so."

Lucy knew better than to risk disobeying the temperamental dance instructor, so she meekly brushed Elizabeth's silver blond hair and twisted it into a sloppy bun that ended up being more bobby pins than hair.

"That's the best I can do," she told Elizabeth. "We've got to go or we'll be late. C'mon, Toby. I'll drop you at Eddie's house.

* * *

The high school auditorium was a confusing whirl of activity when they arrived about twenty minutes later. Lucy paused for a moment in the doorway, waiting for her eyes to adjust to the dim interior after the bright sunlight outdoors.

Tatiana, dressed in tights and leotard, her dark hair twisted into a perfect chignon, was giving directions to several teenage dancers who were sprinkling rosin on the stage. The noise, as the girls' high-pitched voices reverberated against the painted concrete-block walls, was deafening. The rows of seats were full of mothers and their little ballerinas, all dressed in a rainbow of leotards.

Lucy was happy to see her youngest, four-year-old Sara, seated beside her best friend, Jenn, in a nearby row. Jenn's mom, Karen Baker, waved Lucy over.

"Thanks for getting Sara dressed," said Lucy, sliding in beside her. "How'd you get her bun so perfect? I really botched Elizabeth's."

"I used gel. Works like magic."

"Oh," said Lucy. "I wish I'd thought of that."

"It's your first year," said Karen. "As long as you do exactly what Tatiana says, everything will be okay. This is the big show, you know, and she gets nervous. Did you get the pink notice?"

Lucy nodded.

"Do exactly what it says. No underpants, strings tucked in, rouge and lipstick, and absolutely no bangs," recited Karen. "Oh, and no crossed straps on the costumes, either. Have you sewn the straps on yet?"

Lucy shook her head.

"Sew them on straight," advised Karen; then, noticing Lucy's terrified expression, she laughed. "Honest, it's not so bad. And it's worth it in the end. The girls love performing." Karen lowered her voice. "With everything that's happened, I just hope the show goes on."

"What do you mean?"

"I heard Tatiana's real upset about that woman who disappeared—Caroline Hutton. Tatiana was her student, you know." Karen nodded sagely. "So far, everything's gone smoothly today. Keep your fingers crossed. There they go."

The mothers watched as the ballerinas took their places backstage and the rehearsal began. As the notes of a Viennese waltz swirled through the auditorium, Lucy watched the little dancers perform. She was impressed. Although she'd been dropping the girls off for Saturday rehearsals for several weeks, this was the first time she'd seen what they were doing. It was an ambitious show, and although the rehearsal was rough in spots, Lucy could see it was going to be a success.

The older girls were amazing, she thought, up on their toes, leaping and turning, their faces taut with concentration. Their efforts made Lucy appreciate how difficult ballet really is, especially the toe work. She was awestruck at the discipline and hard work these girls had invested in years of lessons and practice.

The music ended in a crescendo, all the dancers were assembled for the finale, and Tatiana began bringing each group forward to rehearse their curtsies. When the three high school girls who were Tatiana's star students finally stood alone center stage, Lucy found herself applauding them furiously. Feeling tears pricking her eyes, she blinked hard, trying to hold them back.

"Never mind. It always gets me, too," Karen confided, handing her a tissue. "Come on, we have to go around backstage to get the girls."

Lucy followed her through a maze of hallways, finally

locating her daughters in a cluster of other small ballerinas.

"You were perfect," she told them. "I've never seen anything so beautiful." Shepherding them through the crowd, Lucy resolved to study the pink notice very carefully.

Pulling into the driveway a few minutes later, she was horrified to discover it was almost five-thirty and she hadn't given a thought to dinner. She was taking a package of hamburgers out of the freezer when she heard the screech of tires on the gravel driveway. Bill was home.

"Hi," she said, as he came in, letting the screen door slam behind him. Noticing his flushed face, she asked, "Tough day?"

"Hot. I was putting down roofing."

"Why don't you take a quick shower? I'll have some burgers ready in a minute."

"Burgers, again?" he complained, pulling a can of beer out of the refrigerator.

"How about a Coke?" suggested Lucy.

"What do you mean?" he growled. "I worked hard all day and I want a beer. Got a problem with that?"

"I don't," said Lucy, awkwardly bending to pick up Mac, their large black tomcat, who had wandered into the kitchen, attracted by the aroma of cooking meat. She opened the door and gently tossed him outside. "Don't forget you're coaching tonight."

"Oh," he groaned, collapsing heavily onto a pressed-oak chair. "I forgot. Oh, what the hell," he shrugged, popping the tab. "I've been looking forward to this beer all afternoon."

"Fine example you are. For our youth, I mean," said Lucy, gently brushing a lock of hair off his forehead.

Bill pulled her onto his lap. "I'm a good guy. I come home every night, don't I? I give you my checks. I help with the kids. What do you want?" There was a tone of self-pity in his voice that Lucy hadn't heard before.

"I've got everything I want," she said, standing up and kissing the top of his head. "But I better get those burgers cooked or you'll be late for the game."

"You know, Lucy, I remember when dinner was a special part of the day. We used to eat with forks."

"I remember that, too," said Lucy, flipping the hamburgers. "The kids were younger then. That was before ballet lessons and Little League."

"How about tomorrow? Could we have mashed potatoes and gravy?"

"No." Lucy shook her head sadly.

"Why not?"

"Awards Night at the school. Toby's getting a perfect-attendance award."

"No kidding," said Bill, taking a pull on his beer.

"Supper," called Lucy. "Come and get it!"

As the three children seated themselves at the table, Lucy passed around the hamburgers and a plate of carrot sticks. Toby, dressed in his baseball uniform, reached for the ketchup. The girls waited their turns impatiently.

"I kind of like these simple suppers," admitted Lucy. "The kids never ate the cooked vegetables anyway. I think they like this better."

"I guess," said Bill, taking an enormous bite. "So, how was your day?"

"About usual," answered Lucy, thinking guiltily of the hours she'd spent napping on the couch while Bill was hammering down asphalt shingles in the hot sun. "Everybody's still talking about Caroline Hutton. Why do you think she disappeared?"

"She was old. Old people are always wandering off. You read about it in the papers all the time. They'll find her sooner or later."

"Those people have Alzheimer's. Caro doesn't, and she's in great shape, too. I'd love to find out what really happened to her," said Lucy.

"What could happen in a place like this?" asked Bill sensibly. "Lucy, I'm sure the police are doing everything they can. This doesn't have anything to do with you."

"Of course it does. This is where I live," said Lucy, reddening.

"You've got enough to think about with this baby coming," reminded Bill. "Mind your own business."

Lucy resented this comment, but she didn't want to fight in front of the children. She kept silent, staring out the window.

"Hey, Toby, I hear you're getting an award," said Bill, using his jovial paterfamilias voice.

"It wasn't anything. I didn't even know I had perfect attendance," admitted Toby.

"What do you mean? I'm proud of you. I never had perfect attendance." Bill got up from the table and laid his plate on the counter. "Almost finished, Toby? Tonight's the night I bet you get a home run off that Rockbound Insurance pitcher. I heard he's only got one pitch, and it's not even fast."

"Go get 'em, slugger," said Lucy, giving Toby a quick hug. She knew he hadn't gotten a good solid hit yet this season and was nervous every time he went up to bat.

"Are you coming to watch the game, Mom?" he asked hopefully.

"I don't think so, honey. I've got a lot to do at home tonight. Next time, okay?"

"Okay," he said, lowering his head and following his father out the door.

"Mom, when's the baby coming?" asked Sara.

"In about three months. Not very long."

"Will the baby want to play with my toys?"

"No, stupid. Babies don't do anything but eat and sleep, do they, Mom?" said Elizabeth.

"Don't insult your sister. If you're done with supper, how about putting out some food for the cats," suggested Lucy, turning to brush Sara's bangs out of her eyes.

"Don't worry about the baby," she told the little girl. "Just think, pretty soon you won't be the youngest anymore. You'll be a big sister, too."

Sara scooped up a blob of ketchup with her finger and sucked it thoughtfully. Then she hopped down from the table. "I'll help Elizabeth feed Softy, Mac, and Diana," she volunteered, proudly naming the family's three cats before running off.

Lucy sat at the table for a minute, slowly shaking her head. She knew it would be hard for Sara to adjust to the new baby, and she felt sad about it. Guilt, she thought, the mother's curse.

As she scraped the dinner plates and set them in the dishwasher, Lucy's thoughts turned again to Caroline Hutton. She realized that although she knew all about Caro, she didn't really know her. She'd seen her around town, she knew where she lived and what car she drove, she greeted her when they met, but she'd never exchanged more than a few words with her. Of course, Lucy was grateful for the fund Caro had established for the purpose of encouraging young dancers. It was thanks to that money, which was administered by the town recreation department, that she could afford ballet lessons for both girls.

Caro also helped promising local dancers attend Winchester College's dance program, and one or two had even gone on to join prestigious dance companies. Lucy occasionally picked up the college alumni magazine in the free bin at the library, and she'd been struck

by the many fond references the graduates made to
Caro. She was obviously one of those rare teachers who
was truly committed to her students.

It seemed incredible to Lucy that a woman so many
people cared about could just vanish, and she felt a
surge of indignation.

People matter, she thought, snapping the dishwasher
door shut with just a bit too much force and switching
it on. A person shouldn't be allowed to disappear with
a perfunctory search and a news conference. What was
it Chief Crowley had said? Lucy pawed through the pile
of old newspapers stacked in the corner of the kitchen
and found the story she wanted, the press conference
announcing the suspension of the investigation. There
it was, in black and white. "This is one mystery we'll
probably never understand," the chief was quoted as
saying.

I don't know about that, thought Lucy. I bet someone
who cared, someone who liked to get to the bottom of
things, could find out what happened to Caro. The way
to start, she decided, would be to have a chat with her
friend, Officer Barney Culpepper. The police probably
knew more than they were telling.

Lucy caught herself. I've been reading too many mysteries, she decided. Bill's right. I've got enough on my
mind. The kids, the baby, they had to be her first pri-
ority. She took the pink notice off the refrigerator,
where she'd stuck it with a magnet when the girls first
brought it home. She read it through, took a deep
breath, and called the girls.

"Put on your costumes so I can sew on the straps,"
she told them.

"Straight, not crossed," warned Elizabeth.

"Straight, not crossed," she repeated, as if it were a
solemn oath.

Five

Straps on costumes to be worn straight—not crossed in back.

The mild spring evening was inviting, so Lucy went out to sit on the back porch while she sewed. Settling herself on the creaky old glider, she carefully stitched the elastic straps on. That done, she still had to attach the frilly strip of sequins and ruffles that was supposed to conceal the elastic.

It was pleasant, sitting outside, listening to the shrieks of the girls as they played on the swing set. It had been an especially warm day for mid-June and Lucy didn't even need a sweater. She knew it would be hours before the sun set; these long evenings were a luxurious contrast to the dark, short days of winter.

As she worked, Lucy wondered why she didn't sew more. It was relaxing, taking neat little stitches, pulling the thread through the fabric. Perhaps she would make something for the baby, she thought. It might be fun to try her hand at counted cross-stitch, or even smocking. Maybe the baby would be a little girl, and she could make all sorts of pretty little dresses for her.

Completing Sara's costume, Lucy held up the tiny pink tutu to admire it. Back in January when the costumes were ordered, Lucy had agonized over the seventy dollars the two costumes cost. Now the price was but a memory, and she had to admit they were adorable. Tatiana always chose tutus for the littlest girls, with these ridiculous bits of netting attached to satin bodices, and trimmed with sequins, ruffles, and ribbon rosebuds. I would love to have worn one of these when I was a little girl, she thought, remembering how disappointed she had been when an older cousin got married and neglected to include her as a flower girl.

She put aside the first costume and began work on the second. Hearing a car turning into the driveway, Lucy looked up and was surprised to see Franny Small's little blue Dodge.

"Hi, Franny. What brings you all the way out here?" she called cheerfully, hoping that Franny hadn't decided that the Stones needed a dose of Austrian ravioli. Lucy suspected that one, perhaps even two of Franny's foil-wrapped offerings were buried deep in the bottom of the freezer.

"Oh, it was such a nice evening I thought I'd take a drive," explained Franny, sitting down on the rickety aluminum chair that completed the back-porch furnishings. Lucy longed for white wicker with flowered chintz cushions, but they couldn't afford it.

"Actually," Franny continued, "to be honest, I want to ask a favor. Could I borrow your video camera?"

"Gosh, I'd love to lend it to you," answered Lucy regretfully, "but I want to use it myself on Thursday. It's the dress rehearsal for the big ballet show, and it's the only time Tatiana allows cameras." Seeing Franny's crestfallen expression, she asked, "What do you want it for, anyway?"

"Oh, Lucy. Mr. Slack thinks I've been stealing from him, and it's the only way I can think of to prove that I'm innocent."

"Why would he think that?"

"Because the money comes out short every day, and there's merchandise missing."

"But it can't be you!" exclaimed Lucy a shade too vehemently. She didn't want Franny to think for a minute that she doubted her honesty.

"Well, if it isn't me, and it isn't him, it must be his grandson," reasoned Franny. "He'd rather believe it's me than Ben."

"Oh," said Lucy slowly. "That makes sense."

"I'm pretty sure it's Ben. There was never any problem before he started working at the store. The inventory figures on batteries are way off, and his friends come into the store all the time, and they all have those big portable radios. They use batteries, don't they?"

Lucy nodded, thinking of the small fortune it cost to keep Toby's little Walkman operational.

"Even worse," Franny continued eagerly, "have you noticed all that writing on the Bump's River Road bridge?"

"You mean the graffiti?"

"The rude words painted all over it. I think Ben stole cans of spray paint and gave them to his gang," concluded Franny, pursing her lips in disapproval.

"I wouldn't call them a gang. They're just small-town boys. They get bored and get into mischief. How long has Ben been working in the store? Shouldn't he be in school?"

"I think he got suspended or something. Probably for drugs," said Franny, whispering the last word.

"He seems awfully young to be involved in drugs," said Lucy. "Besides, they're expensive."

"He's sixteen, he drives a better car than I do, and he has access to plenty of cash. A hundred and forty dollars is missing," argued Franny. "And you should see the clothes he wears. His shirts say things like 'Party

Naked' and 'Public Enemy,' and one has leaves all over it. I think they're marijuana leaves."

"That's just the style. All the kids wear them," explained Lucy, thinking back to the good old days when shirts had stripes and little alligators. "Toby wanted me to buy a shirt at the mall that said 'NWA' and I almost did until he mentioned it meant 'Niggers with Attitude,'" laughed Lucy. "And the shoes. He wants Pumps or Airs or something that cost over a hundred dollars."

"Did you get them for him?" asked Franny.

"No," said Lucy. "We compromised on something a bit more reasonable."

"Not Ben. His parents buy him whatever he wants. He's been spoiled since day one. Even Mr. Slack says so. I guess that's why he was so pleased when the boy agreed to work in the store. He thinks he's taking an interest in the business. Mr. Slack was real disappointed when Fred went into real estate."

"Fred's done awfully well," said Lucy. "We bought this house from his outfit, Yankee Village. We have our insurance with him, too. He isn't pushy the way you expect a salesman to be. He's very polite."

She often saw Fred Slack around town, usually clutching a roll of plans under his arm as he climbed into his Wagoneer. He always gave her a hearty greeting and a big smile. It was impossible not to smile back. He sported a bright-red walrus mustache and favored outrageously preppy clothes, often wearing slacks covered with spouting whales or ducks. His ruddy face and round belly seemed to indicate a hearty indulgence in life's pleasures. He was nothing like his father, thought Lucy.

"Mr. Slack doesn't think much of Fred," said Franny. "Or his wife."

"Really? He doesn't like Annemarie?" Lucy was amazed. Everyone in Tinker's Cove agreed that Annemarie Slack was absolutely perfect. She had renovated and decorated a condemned old captain's house on Main Street, saving it from demolition and transforming it into a showplace that was featured in *Nor'East Life* magazine. Annemarie was a gourmet cook, entertained lavishly and frequently, managed her own graphics firm, and was frequently seen on her knees weeding the perennial bed. Worst of all, with her classic features and blond pageboy, she was extremely attractive. Sue Finch had once remarked that Annemarie Slack made Martha Stewart look like an underachiever.

"Mr. Slack told me Annemarie is a painted hussy," giggled Franny.

"He actually said that?" laughed Lucy. " 'A painted hussy'?"

"Yes," gasped Franny. "With bleached blond hair!" She was laughing so hard she had to hold her stomach. "I'm sorry," she apologized to Lucy, once she regained control of herself. "It must be the strain. He told me he'll fire me if I don't make restitution by Friday."

Privately Lucy thought that getting fired from the hardware store would be the best thing that could happen to Franny, but seeing her suddenly stricken expression, she found herself offering her the camera.

"You can only have it tomorrow and Thursday morning," she told Franny. "I absolutely must have it back on Thursday afternoon."

"Lucy, I promise I'll bring it to you on my lunch hour Thursday. I won't let you down."

"I know, Franny. Are you sure this is the best way to handle this? What if you do get Ben on tape? What'll happen to him?"

"He'll get what he deserves, I hope," said Franny self-righteously. "It will be good for him. I don't think he's ever heard the word no."

"Kids need so much attention," said Lucy, watching

as the girls tried to catch one of the cats. "Come on," she called to them. "It's getting late."

Franny nodded approvingly as the two little girls ran to obey their mother. "See? If that was Ben, he wouldn't mind you. He'd make a point of ignoring you."

As she walked Franny to the car and watched her carefully place the camera on the floor behind the driver's seat, Lucy felt uneasy. If Slack was so blind that he refused to admit his grandson was stealing, he probably wouldn't appreciate having it pointed out to him. Even if she did manage to capture the young delinquent on tape, Lucy was afraid the evidence would backfire on Franny somehow.

"Say, Franny. What's happened to George? You know, Caro's dog?"

"Barney Culpepper took him. Says he's a good dog, and shouldn't have to stay in the pound."

"Any news of Caro?"

"Not a word," said Franny, shaking her head. "It's scary, isn't it?" She looked up at the mountains behind the house. "There's an awful lot of woods around here for a person to get lost in." She gave a little shiver, then put the key in the ignition and started the car.

She had just pulled out of the driveway when Bill and Toby turned in.

"Hi, guys," Lucy greeted them. "How'd the game go? Did you win?"

Toby didn't stop to answer but rushed right past her and stormed into the house, slamming the screen door for emphasis. Thank goodness Franny didn't see that, thought Lucy.

"Your team lost?" she asked Bill.

"Nope," he said, putting his arm around her shoulder. "We won. Five zip."

"So what's the problem?"

"Toby didn't play very well. In fact, he struck out. Four times."

"Oh," said Lucy with a sigh.

"If anybody else had been coaching, he probably would've spent the game on the bench. I kept sending him up. I figure he'll never get a hit if he doesn't go up to bat. But now he says he wants to quit the team."

"Isn't there something you can do to help him? Practice here at home?"

"It's the damnedest thing, Lucy. Here in the yard he's a great hitter. Never misses. It must be nerves or something. He just can't relax when he goes up to bat. It's killing me," admitted Bill, sitting down heavily on the glider. "What's this?" he asked, picking up one of the tutus.

"Those are the girls' costumes. Aren't they adorable?"

Bill looked skeptical. "How much did those cost? More than a good glove?"

"I don't know," said Lucy, shrugging up beside him. "How much does a good glove cost?"

"Twenty, thirty dollars."

"Just look at that sky," said Lucy, indicating the billowing mass of dark clouds that were gathering, blocking their view of the mountaintops. "I think a storm is brewing."

Six

No chewing gum.

"For goodness sake, Franny, watch what you're doing!"

Startled by her mother's voice, Franny looked up from the morning newspaper she had been so absorbed in, and realized she had poured too much milk on her Cheerios.

"Never mind, Mom," she said, as her mother leaped for the roll of paper towels. "I'll clean it up."

She was too late. Her mother, Irma, efficiently mopped up the overflow and reduced Franny to preschool status in one deft motion. "If only you would be a bit more careful, Franny," she commented.

"I was just looking to see if they've found Caro, but there isn't anything."

"There's more to that than meets the eye, I'll bet," said Irma over the rim of her coffee mug.

"What's your theory?" asked Franny. She knew her mother loved to gossip and spent most of the day on the telephone, chatting with a large circle of friends.

"It's shocking, that's what it is. A woman disappearing in broad daylight like that. Makes you wonder if any of us are safe. I'm calling Niemann the Key Man first thing this morning and getting all the locks changed. And Franny, I want you to be extra careful.

No more leaving the car unlocked—or the house, for that matter.

"But, Mom, we've never bothered with locking the door," protested Franny. "I know I'll end up locking myself out."

"We never had to till now. But I'm not taking any chances. They got Caro, and that dog didn't even bark."

"Who got her?"

Irma looked carefully over both shoulders, then leaned forward over the table and whispered to Franny, "Satanists."

"What?" Franny nearly choked on a mouthful of cereal.

"It's more widespread than you think," said the older woman, nodding. "Didn't you read those articles Ted Stillings wrote last summer? Young people go off in the woods and, well, all sorts of obscene nonsense goes on. The police over in Gilead found the evidence in the woods. Altars, bloodstains, carvings on trees."

"It's a fad, Mom. That's all it is. The kids see these rock videos and experiment a little."

"They sacrifice things, Franny. The story said there was blood."

"Animal blood, Mom. It's not right, but kids have always done stuff like that. Blowing up frogs with firecrackers, taking potshots at squirrels and birds, even strangling cats."

"I'm not such an old fuddy-duddy that I don't know the difference between a little boy with a BB gun and a Satanic ritual," insisted the older woman.

"Ben at the store wears a Satan T-shirt," said Franny thoughtfully.

"There!" crowed Irma.

"You don't really think he had anything to do with Caro's disappearance, do you?"

"I wouldn't be surprised," said Irma, getting up and running water into the kitchen sink. "There are supposed to be ways you can tell. Some of them have three sixes tattooed under their hair, or other symbols. Does Ben have any tattoos?"

"Not that I know of," said Franny.

"I bet some hunter will find whatever's left of poor Caro out in the woods somewhere, all carved up and tied to a tree, or laid out on some altar." She turned, and Franny was shocked at the intensity of her expression.

"Honestly, Mom, I don't think we have too much to worry about. I'm gonna be late if I don't hustle." Franny gave her mother a quick peck on the cheek, grabbed her purse, and dashed out the door. Sometimes Mom was just too much, she thought as she drove to the store. She wanted to get the video camera set up before Mr. Slack arrived.

There was no sign of him, however, when she arrived and unlocked the door as usual. The cheap electric clock that he had put up when he sold the old Regulator to a shrewd antique dealer indicated it was only a quarter to nine. She knew she had fifteen minutes before Mr. Slack arrived, precisely on the hour.

Hauling out a rickety old ladder, Franny climbed up and set the camera behind a dusty advertising cutout that had stood on top of a display cabinet for as long as she could remember. She climbed down, studied the faded image of the earth dripping with red house paint, and satisfied herself that it concealed the camera. She grabbed an X-acto knife from a rack, went back up, and cut out the center of the "o" in the "Cover the Earth" printed along the bottom. She angled the display a bit so the camera had a clear view of the cash register, pushed the on button, and stepped carefully down.

She had barely gotten the ladder put away when she heard the bell on the door jangle. Mr. Slack had arrived.

"Franny, I believe we're expecting a delivery today."

"That's right."

"Be sure and let me know when the truck arrives," he told her, marching stiffly into his office and shutting the door. A minute later he reappeared with the cash envelope for the register. "There's exactly seventy-seven dollars and fifty cents in that envelope," he informed Franny.

"I know," she nodded in agreement. Every morning for the past fifteen years she'd started the day with one roll each of pennies, nickels, dimes, and quarters, twenty-five single, five five-dollar bills, and one ten. What was the old man trying to prove? she wondered.

Franny set up the cash drawer, changed the date on the printer, and checked to see that the sign in the door read OPEN. There were no customers, so she took the feather duster out of the broom closet and began dusting the merchandise. She had worked her way through the pots and pans, the dishes, and the vacuum cleaner bags all the way to the electric drills when the Hasco truck signaled its arrival with a sharp squeal of its brakes.

"The truck's here," she told Mr. Slack. He pulled himself shakily to his feet, and Franny watched anxiously until he had his legs firmly beneath him. Then he marched stiffly to the front of the store, where he surprised Stan, the Hasco driver, by greeting him cordially for the first time in the eight years he'd been driving the route.

"Good day to you, Mr. Slack," answered Stan, casting a curious glance at Franny.

"Stan, I think it will be just fine if you put the boxes

along that wall. I'll be checking the invoices myself today," said Slack.

"No problem," answered Stan, handing the old man a thick sheaf of computer printouts. He went back out to the truck but soon returned, wheeling in a dolly loaded with boxes.

"I'll count the items in the boxes and you check them off, okay?" Franny asked Mr. Slack.

"That will be fine," he answered, carefully unscrewing his fountain pen.

"What have we got here?" murmured Franny, opening the first box. "Okay. Six Phillips-head screwdrivers, six-inch, item number one-six-oh-nine-six, and six more eight-inch, number one-six-oh-nine-eight. Got that?"

Mr. Slack began looking through the papers, but soon shook his head in frustration.

"I need my other glasses, Franny. I'll be right back." While he made his way back to the office, Franny found the correct sheet and put it on top of the pile of papers. When he returned she showed him where the screwdrivers were listed, and the old man carefully checked them off.

"Now we've got hex wrenches, six assorted on a card, item number one-seven-oh-one-six. Got that?"

"You're going much too fast, Franny. Haste makes waste, you know. Now what was that number?"

"One-seven-oh-one-six," repeated Franny slowly.

"It's not here."

Franny glanced at the invoice, found the notation, and pointed it out to him. Then she went back to the carton.

"A dozen half-inch steel tape measures, twelve-foot, item one-five-oh-one-two, and a dozen half-inch tapes, twenty-four-foot, one-five-oh-two-four, and six three-quarter-inch tapes, twenty-four-foot, one-seven-five-two-four."

"You'll have to repeat that, Franny," said Mr. Slack.

Franny looked at the wall of cartons Stan was building along the side of the store and sighed. She could do this much faster herself, but Mr. Slack would never let her. He didn't trust her and he had to assure himself the invoices were correct.

"I'll try to go slower," she said, looking up as Stan reappeared carrying a clipboard.

"Would you sign this, Mr. Slack?"

Slack took the clipboard and began reading the attached papers.

"You don't have to read it," advised Stan. "Just sign it."

Mr. Slack's bristly gray eyebrows shot up. "I never sign any without reading it."

"It doesn't mean anything, except that I was here and you took the delivery. If there are any problems, you can sort it out over the phone. Isn't that right, Franny?" he demanded impatiently.

"Oh. So Franny has been signing the papers without reading them?" The old man sounded like a prosecution lawyer asking the crucial question, the one that would condemn the defendant beyond any reasonable doubt.

"Sure, everybody does," affirmed Stan.

Another nail in my coffin, thought Franny. "Why don't you get a cup of coffee, Stan? I'm sure Mr. Slack will have signed the papers by the time you get back."

"Okay. I usually stop at Jake's anyway. But I gotta be back on the road by ten-thirty."

"Mr. Slack, we'll never be able to check all these boxes in ten minutes. Why don't you write a qualifier? Something like, 'Delivery received, contents unverified,' and sign it?"

"That's a good idea, Franny," he said. Truth be told, his rheumatism was acting up and he wanted to sit down. He took the clipboard into his office and sat down at the desk. When Stan returned he raised an eyebrow at the beautifully penned statement, complete with Slack's stylized Palmer-method signature.

" 'Bye, now," said Franny. She smiled. "See you in two weeks."

Turning to Mr. Slack, she offered a suggestion.

"Mr. Slack, we could save time if you told me the items and I checked them off. I'm a lot more familiar with the invoice codes, and you could sit on this little stool."

Using Franny's method, they worked much faster, mostly because Franny looked over Mr. Slack's shoulder to see the contents and checked off each box while the old man hunted for the numbers on one or two items. What makes old people so slow, wondered Franny, struggling to keep her impatience in check. Someday she would be old, no doubt, and would appreciate the tolerance of young folks. By noontime the old man was clearly exhausted. He usually spent the morning at his desk going over the figures, slipping in a few catnaps between the columns. He hadn't been this active in years.

He went home for lunch promptly at noontime. A little later Ben wandered in. Franny grabbed her purse and was out the door in a flash. She had only a half hour before she had to go back, a stingy thirty minutes of freedom.

She drove her car down to the fish pier and parked there to eat the egg salad sandwich her mother had packed for her. The sky was white with clouds, and without any breeze the cove was a flat, oily gray that matched her mood. The oppressive weather didn't seem to bother the gulls, greedy as ever as they squabbled over bits of old bait, then flew off to follow a rusty old lobster boat as it chugged out into the bay to check traps. Glancing at her watch, she realized with a start that her half hour was almost gone.

Back at the store, the afternoon dragged by slowly. Mr. Slack turned over the job of checking the merchandise to Ben, and he and Franny made short work of the remaining cartons. Then Franny began stocking the shelves with the new merchandise, making sure she stayed out of Ben's way as much as possible. She wanted to give him every chance to incriminate himself while the camera was rolling.

As the afternoon grew closer to three o'clock, Franny began to worry. The tape was good for only six hours, she knew, and she wanted to turn the camera off before it began recording over the previously taped images. It was just a little after three, however, when Ben announced he "had to see some guys" and left the store. Franny wasted no time in dragging out the ladder and climbing up to retrieve the camera.

She started guiltily, nearly falling off the ladder, when she heard Slack's voice demand, "What are you doing, Franny?"

"You almost gave me a heart attack," she stammered, turning to face him and nervously patting her chest with a fluttering hand. "This display is so old and dusty, I was just looking to see if I could spruce it up a little bit."

The old man studied the sagging cardboard poster. "Take it down," he ordered.

"What?" Franny was horrified. If she moved the poster, the camera would be revealed before she had a chance to view the tape. And while she knew she hadn't done anything wrong in setting up the camera, she was sure Slack wouldn't see it that way. "Why don't we wait until the paint rep can give us a new one," she suggested, casting about desperately for an escape. "Don't you think the store will look bare without it?"

"No, I don't," said Slack impatiently. "Do as I say, Franny. Give me the poster."

For a moment, Franny froze, feeling exactly like a truant caught out of school. Then she lifted the poster. The camera was in plain view.

"What's that?" demanded Slack, squinting through his glasses.

"A video camera. I wanted to show you the real thief. I set it up behind the poster," she explained, showing him the hole she had cut. "A lot of stores use them."

"Never mind all that," he said, brushing aside her explanation. "Where did you get it?"

"I borrowed it from Lucy Stone," she explained, trying to remain calm. Her stomach was churning; she dreaded the old man's anger.

"You're incorrigible, Franny," he said in his quavery voice. "Now you're involving your friend. How foolish do you think I am? I know what those cameras cost. My son, Fred, has one. And you want me to believe that Lucy Stone lent you one." He shook his head in disbelief.

"But she did, Mr. Slack. Just call and ask her."

"I'll do no such thing. I know perfectly well that Lucy Stone could not afford an expensive camera like that, any more than you could, unless you'd been stealing from me."

The light in the store suddenly dimmed, but Franny could see two spots of color appearing in the old man's cheeks. She could even smell his stale breath as he leaned toward her.

"Mr. Slack, won't you at least look at the tape?" she pleaded, holding out the camera.

"For shame!" he thundered, snatching the camera out of her hands. "You're a thief and a liar, Franny!"

"Mr. Slack, Lucy needs the camera for her daughters' ballet," said Franny, struggling to keep her voice even.

"Take your lies and get out. Now!" he roared. Lowering his voice, he added, "Your services are no longer required." He pointed to the door with his long, flat finger. He was quivering, absolutely shaking with rage. His color wasn't good, Franny observed, and he was gasping for breath.

She didn't want to leave the camera with him, but she decided she'd better go. Lucy could come back for it later. She walked softly over to the counter and bent down to take her purse out from the shelf beneath the register where she kept it. Trembling, fighting off nausea and dizziness, she mustered every shred of dignity she possessed and walked straight to the door, looking back only once as she braced herself to push it open. Once she was outside, she couldn't help giggling nervously. What a day. What a horrible old man. As he stood there with his mouth gaping open, struggling to catch his breath, Franny thought he looked just like a glassy-eyed codfish flapping on the pier. Oh, well, there was a definite bright side to all this, she thought as she walked to her car. Now she'd never have to look at him, or smell him, or have anything at all to do with him ever again.

Seven

Put makeup on at home.

Lucy spent Wednesday morning working in the garden, pulling out weeds and picking lettuce and sugar snap peas while Sara played nearby, arranging her doll babies in a toy carriage and feeding them dandelion soup. It soon grew too muggy and hot to work, so Lucy retreated to the house. She drew a tall glass of water from the cooler of bottled spring water that stood in a corner of the kitchen, sat down at the table and dialed the police station.

"Lucy, how's every little thing?" asked Culpepper. "Nothing's wrong, is it?"

"Oh, no. Everything's fine. I haven't seen you for a while and wondered if you might be coming out this way one of these days."

Lucy didn't agree with the prevailing opinion that a married woman should have only female friends. She had taken an immediate liking to Barney Culpepper when he stopped to fix a flat tire for her soon after she'd moved to Tinker's Cove. She had gotten to know him better when they were both members of the Cub Scout Pack Committee. He often dropped by for a cup of coffee and a chat; he liked to gossip just as much as she did.

When Lucy found Sam Miller's body in the Country

Cousins parking lot the previous Christmas they had teamed up to find the killer, but not before Culpepper had almost become a victim himself.*

"Well, I do have a dog complaint out near you," Culpepper said. "What are you having for lunch?"

Lucy considered the contents of her pantry, usually depleted by this time of the week. "Tuna?"

"Sold. I'll see you around twelve."

After looking out the window to check on Sara, Lucy decided to get a head start on supper and began slicing a cabbage for coleslaw. She'd just finished adding the dressing when she heard the crunch of tires on the gravel driveway.

Lucy waited on the porch while Sara ran across the lawn to greet the huge police officer. He caught the little girl under her arms and tossed her high into the air above his head and she screamed with delight.

"Put her down," begged Lucy. "If you get her too excited she'll never take her nap."

"Oops, sorry," apologized Barney. Lucy couldn't help thinking he looked like an oversized puppy who'd received a scolding.

"That's okay. Come on in. I've got a couple of sandwiches all ready for you. You, too Sara."

"So, Barney," began Lucy once they were all settled at the round oak table. "What's the real story about Caro's disappearance?"

"What you see is what you get," Barney said, finishing his first sandwich in a few bites. "Don't you read the papers? Crowley's suspended the investigation."

"I can't believe it. Nobody's looking for her?"

"Lucy, she could be anywhere. We can't search the whole state, the whole country, the world. Can you

*See *Mail-Order Murder*

imagine the fuss the Taxpayers' Association would make at the town meeting?"

"Well, you can't pretend nothing's happened. A woman's disappeared!"

"The case is still open," said Barney. "She's been officially declared a missing person. The state police put out an APB with her description. They'll send out flyers to post offices and police stations. There's even an eight hundred number people can call if they see her. But to tell you the truth, nobody thinks she's in any sort of trouble. There was no sign of violence, and there hasn't been a ransom note. She also withdrew five thousand dollars from her savings a few days before she disappeared."

"What does that mean?" asked Lucy, jumping on this new piece of information. "Was she being black-mailed?"

"No, Lucy. I think she probably went on vacation and forgot to tell anyone."

"Barney, I can't believe that. She would never leave George."

"That's the part that bothers me," admitted Barney. "He's an awfully nice dog. He's really gotten to be part of the family."

"It was nice of you to take him in." Lucy smiled at him across the table. "Come on, Sara, aren't you going to eat your sandwich?"

"I want more tomato chips," said the little girl. "Please."

"That's po-ta-to chips," corrected Lucy. "You can't have any more until you eat your sandwich."

"That's not fair," whined Sara.

"That's the law," said Barney, using his official tone of voice. Lucy was amazed to see Sara obediently begin eating the sandwich.

"God forgive me, Lucy, but I almost hope she doesn't

come back. Eddie's grown so attached to that dog it would break his heart to give it up."

"You could get another dog for him. A puppy."

"Yeah, you're right. Listen, Lucy. I wouldn't worry about Caro too much. These old ladies do odd things, they get notions in their heads. We had one old bat call the station the other day saying spacemen were living in her attic and they were driving her crazy with their Morse code. It turned out her smoke alarm was beeping 'cause the battery was running down."

"From everything I've heard about Caro, she was pretty sharp."

"Well, that's where someone like you could be helpful. Why don't you ask around and tell me what you hear? I'm not supposed to, but whenever I get a free minute I pull out the case. I only wish I had time to do more. Which reminds me, I guess I better get back to work. You haven't had any trouble with the Johnsons' dog, have you?"

"Nope."

"Good. Thanks for the lunch." He stood and put on his hat, then turned to Sara. "I'm glad to see you cleaned your plate. Now I won't have to arrest you."

Sara's eyes grew very big, but when Barney winked she decided he might be teasing and gave a cautious little laugh that stopped abruptly the minute he left.

"Time for your nap," said Lucy, lifting the little girl down from her booster chair. "I'll be up in a minute to tuck you in."

Five thousand dollars was a lot of money, thought Lucy as she cleared the lunch table. What was it for? Maybe Caro did go on a trip after all. But Lucy still didn't believe Caro would abandon George.

She remembered the last time she'd seen them on

the logging trail. Caro had thrown a stick for the dog, and he'd happily retrieved it, tail wagging. When he brought it to her, she fell to her knees and gave him a big hug. Lucy had been moved by the gesture.

What did she need five thousand dollars for? Lucy yawned and followed Sara upstairs. If only she weren't so tired all the time, maybe she could figure it out. These days, no matter how much sleep she got, it never seemed to be enough.

The roar of the school bus as it accelerated for the climb up Red Top Road woke Lucy and she stood up, stretched, and braced for battle. She heard the screen door slam, and then heard the familiar sounds of Toby and Elizabeth scuffling as they fought to be first at the cookie jar again today. This was getting ridiculous.

"You don't need to fight. There are plenty of cookies. You may each take four, and don't stuff them in your mouth, Toby. Sit down at the table."

Elizabeth and Toby exchanged glances and took their seats, expecting a scolding. Lucy poured them each a glass of milk, and then noticing Sara standing in the doorway, still sleepy from her nap, she poured a third glass. She sat down, took Sara in her lap, and began outlining her strategy for the evening.

"Tonight is awards night at the school. It's at six, so we'll have an early supper at five. Don't go too far from the house, okay?"

Elizabeth and Toby nodded.

"After supper, you'll change into your good clothes—not before, because you might spill something on them, like ketchup. Okay?" Elizabeth and Toby nodded again.

"I laid your good clothes out on your beds, and I want you to try them on right after you finish your snack."

"Do we have to?" groaned Toby.

"You have to. You haven't worn them since Easter, and I'm worried they might not fit."

"What'll we do if they don't fit?"

"We'll improvise. Now off you go."

Lucy washed the glasses and set them in the drainboard, then she slowly climbed the stairs.

"Don't come in—I'm not ready," warned Toby.

"I see London, I see France," chanted Elizabeth.

"That's enough," said Lucy, slipping a dress over Sara's head and buttoning it up the back. She turned the little girl around, and leaned back to study the dress. "You look very nice. Now let's see if your Mary Janes still fit."

The little patent leather slippers were tight, but Sara could still cram her feet into them. Elizabeth's, however, were hopeless.

"Hang on, I think there's a pair of white sandals in that bag of clothes Pam Stillings gave us." Lucy pulled a rumpled brown grocery bag out from the back of the girls' closet and fished around inside it. "Here they are," she said, triumphantly producing a pair of barely worn white summer sandals.

"I can't wear those, they're disgusting," protested Elizabeth. "They're hand-me-downs."

"They're very nice, and it's just for one night. Try them on."

"Why can't I wear my sneakers?"

"Sneakers look terrible with a dress."

"I'll wear pants."

"I'd like you to wear a dress. Doesn't Sara look nice?"

"Sara's only four, and I'm eight. You want me to look like a baby."

"You won't look like a baby in the sandals. Especially if you don't wear socks. People will think you're wearing stockings."

"Really?"

"Sure. All the girls will be jealous."

"Amy's mom lets her wear stockings, and heels. Every day."

"In third grade? I don't believe it."

"Well, she does, and she has pierced ears, too."

"Next thing you'll be telling me she wears black cocktail dresses with sequins," muttered Lucy, lifting Sara's dress carefully over her head.

"Everybody wears black. I'm the only girl in the third grade who's not allowed to wear black," protested Elizabeth, reviving an old argument.

"Black is for grown-ups, and even grown-ups don't wear it after Memorial Day," advised Lucy. "Unless they're tourists from New York."

"Mom, you have all these little rules that nobody's ever heard of except you."

"Yeah, Mom. I'm not gonna wear this shirt," Toby chimed in. "I'll look like a geek."

"You already do," Elizabeth said cattily.

"That's enough," repeated Lucy, losing her patience. "Now, what's the matter with that shirt?" she asked, turning to Toby.

"It's got an alligator. Nobody wears those anymore."

"No?" Lucy remembered Lydia Volpe, her friend who taught kindergarten, relating how she used to teach the children to salute the flag by telling them to put their hands on their alligators.

"No. It's all wrong. Can't I wear a T-shirt?"

"No, you can't. It's this or your long-sleeved button-down oxford."

"I guess I'll wear this, but everybody will laugh at me."

"You'll be surprised. Everybody will be dressed just like you. Take these off for now and change, and you can go out and play."

Checking her watch, Lucy hurried downstairs to set

the table and start supper. She had just switched on the oven when she heard Bill's truck.

"Hey, Lucy, I was thinking," he began as he came through the kitchen door. "We ought to tape the ceremony. Where's the video camera?"

"Bill, you're not serious, are you? We've got so much tape of the kids, and besides, it'll embarrass Toby."

"What do you mean? We have hardly any videos of the kids, thanks to you. You're too cheap to buy blank cassettes, and when you do break down and decide to invest two ninety-nine, you push the wrong button."

"That was just once," Lucy said. "I got confused."

"And I never got to see Sara in her starring role as the Easter Bunny," reproached Bill, wrapping his arms around her.

"I'm sorry," said Lucy, slipping out of his embrace and opening the freezer. "You'll just have to rely on your memory tonight. I loaned the camera to Franny."

"What? Why'd you do that?" demanded Bill.

"It's complicated. But she promised to give it back before the dress rehearsal tomorrow."

"I wish you'd checked with me first," grumbled Bill. "After all, it was *my* parents who gave us that camera. Are those fish sticks?"

"Yeah. Fish sticks, potato puffs, and coleslaw. Home-made coleslaw."

"You know I hate fish sticks."

"It won't kill you to eat them this once," snapped Lucy. Realizing the conversation was in real danger of becoming a fight, she took a deep breath and explained, "I needed something quick and easy for dinner. The ceremony's at six. You better take your shower now if you want one."

Bill turned to go, but then he stopped in the doorway and turned to face her. "You know, Lucy, you're really pushing it," he said. There was just the hint of a threat in his tone, but it made Lucy uncomfortable and she didn't answer. She avoided his eyes and busied herself opening the packages of fish sticks. A moment later she heard him stomping up the stairs.

Conversation at dinner limped along as Lucy and Bill avoided speaking to each other by questioning the kids about their day at school. For once Lucy didn't have much of an appetite, but she noticed that Bill managed to eat an awful lot of fish sticks for someone who claimed to hate them. When the phone rang, she welcomed the reprieve and ran to answer it.

"Hi, Lucy, it's Franny."

"Hi, there. What's up?"

"Lucy, I don't know how to tell you this, but Mr. Slack caught me with the video camera, and he confiscated it."

"What?"

"He took it. He said I couldn't possibly afford it unless I'd been stealing from him and therefore the camera must rightfully be his."

"Didn't you tell him it belongs to me?" exclaimed Lucy, then bit her tongue as Bill looked up.

"I did, but he didn't believe me. I'm so sorry. I never thought this would happen. He fired me."

"Oh, Franny, I'm so sorry. Don't worry about the camera. I'll just drop by the store tomorrow and tell him it's mine. I hope he believes me, I have to tape the dress rehearsal."

"I think that's the best thing to do. He'll probably come to his senses by then. I'm awfully sorry."

"Never mind."

No sooner had Lucy hung up than Bill began questioning her. "What was that all about?" he demanded.

"Kids, you'd better get changed," she told them, and waited until they were safely upstairs before explaining.

"This is too much," he exploded angrily. "You didn't

even check with me before loaning it to someone we hardly know."

"Bill, half of that camera's mine and I loaned it to one of my friends."

"You didn't loan half of it, you loaned the whole thing, and she's lost it." Bill's voice grew louder and he pounded the table with his fist. "Tomorrow you'd just better get the whole thing back."

"I will. Now calm down. This is supposed to be Toby's big night," pleaded Lucy. "I have to get dressed."

By the time everyone was buckled in place in the car, the kids had realized their parents were fighting. They were unnaturally quiet in the back seat; Lucy and Bill didn't speak in the front seat.

Lucy clamped her hands tightly together and wished the butterflies in her stomach would settle down. She couldn't resist glancing anxiously at Bill from time to time. He was clearly angry, and he expressed it by driving too fast, turning too sharply, and tailgating the car ahead of him. Lucy didn't say anything, afraid she would only make matters worse.

Eight

No jewelry.

Driving briskly along Route 1, Caro Hutton felt, well, *exhilarated* was really the only word for it. After the boring daily routine, the rut she'd fallen into, she was finally having an adventure. It was about time, she thought. How had she settled so easily for a life in which walking the dog was the high point of the day?

The problem was that once she retired, every day was the same. She rose early in the morning, did some stretching exercises, and walked George. Then she visited with Julia, drove home, and tidied the house. Once those chores were completed, the day stretched emptily before her except for the occasional meeting or luncheon.

When she was teaching she used to look forward to having unlimited time to visit with friends and pursue her interests, but now that she actually did have the time, she found herself making excuses. She couldn't call a friend right now, she would reason; everyone was probably busy and would resent an interruption. Projects she had planned now seemed too ambitious. Building a gazebo, for example, seemed such a big job. What if she fell off the ladder? Wouldn't she feel like a fool then!

So she would read the newspaper, and then probably

she would pick up a book. When she tired of reading, she would turn on the TV. She refused to watch soap operas, but some of the talk shows were really quite interesting. People who communicated with the spirit world, people who had sex-change operations, women who had other people's babies—this was a strange new world indeed. Caro found she couldn't resist the tearful confessions and scandalous revelations that filled the afternoon airwaves.

Perhaps one day she would be on one of those shows, she thought, glancing at her small companion. I was a kidnapper, she would tell the audience. I chose to disappear and start a whole new life, a life I never thought I could have, she would say to Oprah, or Phil, or even Geraldo. Their eyebrows would rise in astonishment as she outlined the plans she had made and the precautions she had taken.

It was simple, she would tell them. I first got the idea when I read about a woman who went into a shopping mall and never came out. She just disappeared, leaving her husband waiting in the parked car. It's easy for a woman of a certain age to disappear, she would explain, because no one is really interested in finding her.

Of course, her young companion was a different case. Someone was very interested in finding her, but if everything went according to plan, he wouldn't. Glancing at the little girl seated beside her, with her blond bangs and freckled nose, and skinny, knobby knees, Caro felt a stab of emotion so sharp that it was almost physically painful. Even though it had been a very long time since she'd felt a similar sensation, she recognized it as love. Oh my, she thought.

"Are we almost there?" asked the little girl, stirring restlessly.

"Almost," she answered, flipping the turn signal and heading off the highway. "Now, what's your name?"

"Lisa," recited the child obediently.

"Good. And who am I?"

"You're my grandmother."

"And why aren't you with your parents?"

"My parents are taking a vacation in Europe, so I'm spending the summer with you in Maine."

"Perfect. Be sure to say it exactly like that. Any mistakes will mean big trouble."

The little girl nodded soberly. Then she shivered. She was dressed only in shorts and a thin shirt.

Caro pulled the car over to the side of the road and braked. She reached for the stadium blanket she kept in the back seat and arranged it over the little girl.

"How old are you?" she asked.

"I'm seven."

"Somehow you seem older," she said. "Is that better? It's not much farther, I promise."

She pulled back onto the road and followed the familiar route, surprised that even though she hadn't been in this part of the state for many years, very little had changed. She felt reassured. The plan was good. She had gone over it time and time again. It would work, it had to work.

She brushed aside thoughts of George—the dear, stupid, doggy beast. She knew her absence would shatter him, temporarily, until he forgot her. But the neighbors were all kind, and she didn't doubt for a minute that someone would adopt him. Besides, who was more important—an animal or a person? Her fingers tightened on the steering wheel and she glanced at Lisa. She smiled. The little girl was fast asleep.

Nine

Hair in bun with hair net.

At ten to nine, Kitty Slack was already tired. She'd been up since five and was beginning to run out of energy, so she sat herself down for a minute on the hall stairs. She perched Morrill's straw hat on her knees and waited.

As soon as she heard the latch on the downstairs bathroom door click, she jumped to her feet. Morrill emerged, took his hat and set it on his head, gave her a formal peck on the cheek, and marched stiffly out the door. Watching from behind the velvet drapes in the front parlor as he proceeded down the walk, Kitty wondered what life would be like without him. It wasn't the first time she'd entertained such thoughts.

From her vantage point at the bay window, she watched Morrill shrink smaller and smaller as he proceeded down the street. Soon she couldn't see him at all. Then her attention was drawn to a silver Subaru, which was being parked on Main Street, right in front of the old granite mounting block. She saw Lucy Stone get out, and rubbed her own aching back sympathetically when Lucy bent over awkwardly to release a small child from the back seat.

Lucy stood for a moment on the sidewalk and regarded the house. Then, her decision made, she took the child by the hand and began walking up the drive to the back door. Kitty met her there.

"Lucy Stone, what a nice surprise!" exclaimed Kitty as she opened the door. "And who's this?"

"This is Sara," said Lucy. "Sara's four."

"Well, do come in and visit," urged Kitty. "I hope you don't mind sitting in the kitchen. It's really the coziest room in the house."

From what Lucy had seen through the heavily draped windows as she walked up the drive, she didn't doubt it. "The kitchen is the heart of the home," she said, taking a seat on a battered old wicker sofa.

The sofa was arranged, along with a rocking chair, in a sunny corner of the kitchen. Geraniums lined the windowsill, a basket of knitting sat next to the rocker, and a pile of well-thumbed magazines and travel brochures rested on a lamp table.

"Are you going on a trip?" asked Lucy.

"No, just dreaming," said Kitty as she lifted an aluminum percolator off the stove. "Would you like some coffee? I usually have a cup around now."

"No, thanks," said Lucy, eyeing the inky brew. Sara had cuddled up beside her and was looking about curiously.

"There's a basket of toys under the settee," said Kitty. "Why don't you pull it out and see what's there." She nodded approvingly when Sara jumped down, seated herself on the braided rug, and began investigating the basket. "How many children do you have?" she asked Lucy.

"This will be my fourth," said Lucy, patting her tummy.

"Four! Aren't you lucky! I didn't have Fred until rather late in my marriage. I was thrilled to finally have a baby."

"And a son, too. Your husband must have been pleased."

"I think he was, in his way," recalled Kitty. "Of course, like many people his age he didn't believe in showing affection. He was afraid that sparing the rod spoiled the child. People don't think that so much anymore."

"Sometimes things change for the better," observed Lucy, wondering how to broach the subject she wanted to discuss. "I don't quite know how to begin," she said, leaning forward, "so I guess I'll just plunge in. I came here to ask you to tell your husband that the video camera he took from Franny Small yesterday really is mine. I need it back to tape my daughters' ballet rehearsal. Tatiana only allows cameras at the dress rehearsal, and it's today. At three-thirty."

Kitty's face was blank. "I don't know what you're talking about."

"My video camera," said Lucy, taking a deep breath. "Franny borrowed it to prove to Mr. Slack that she isn't the one stealing from the store. He caught her with it, and fired her. He also confiscated the camera, and I want it back."

"He fired Franny? When did all this happen?"

"Yesterday," said Lucy. She could practically hear the wheels turning in Kitty's head as she put two and two together.

"Thank you for telling me, Lucy. This explains why Morrill was so upset last night."

"Didn't he tell you what happened?"

"He did say something about it being Annemarie's fault. That's all."

Lucy was amazed at this lack of communication between husband and wife. "How long have you been married?" she asked.

"More than fifty years," said Kitty. "I can hardly believe it myself. Times were hard all those years ago. It was during the Depression. My folks were sure happy when Morrill started showing an interest. It meant one less mouth to feed."

"They forced you to marry him?"

"Oh, no. I didn't mind. I figured taking care of this nice house would be lots easier than haying and milking on my folks' farm."

"Kind of like getting a better job?" Lucy was fascinated.

"Yup," said the old woman, breaking into a broad smile. "Of course," she said, slapping her knee and cackling, "I don't think Morrill has any intention of letting me retire."

Lucy joined in Kitty's laughter. She couldn't help admiring her. Kitty was clearly a survivor, and Lucy suspected it was her sense of humor that got her through.

The laughter stopped abruptly when Lucy realized Sara was no longer playing quietly on the rug.

"Where's she gotten to?" exclaimed Lucy, dashing through the swinging door into the dining room, past the long mahogany table, which still held the remains of Morrill's solitary breakfast. Lucy cast an anxious glance up the tall staircase and frantically checked the front and back parlors.

She found Sara in the study, lifting a bell jar off a pair of stuffed bluebirds. The birds were sentimentally nestled together on a branch of flowering apple. The flowers were made of blown glass, and the whole arrangement was probably priceless. It looked as if it belonged in a museum.

"Sara! Don't touch!" scolded Lucy, replacing the glass dome. "You mustn't go wandering about in other people's houses."

"No harm done," said Kitty. "I bet Sara would like a cookie."

Back in the kitchen, she sat Sara at the scrubbed pine table, gave her an enormous molasses cookie, and poured a glass of milk for her. "I bake cookies, but I rarely have a young visitor to eat them," said Kitty. "These used to be my grandson Ben's favorites. I only have one grandchild, but he's a good one."

"You must be proud of him," said Lucy politely. "He was very helpful to me the other day. He put a bag of fertilizer in my car. Finish up, Sara, we have to go."

"So soon?" Kitty would have preferred a longer visit.

"I'm afraid so," said Lucy, lifting Sara out of the chair. "I'll be stopping at the hardware store this afternoon. Do you think you could talk to your husband before then about the camera?"

"I'm afraid not, Lucy. I've learned it's better if I don't interfere."

Disappointed, Lucy led Sara to the door. "Well, thank you for the visit. What do you say, Sara?"

"Thank you for the cookie," whispered Sara.

Lucy was on the doorstep, turning to go, when she noticed Caroline Hutton's was the house next door. She spoke without thinking.

"You're Caro's neighbor! Have you heard anything?"

The old woman shook her head. "I can't believe Caro would go off without telling me. We had an arrangement. I have her house key and I always take her mail and water her plants when she goes away."

Lucy noticed she had crumpled her apron and was nervously kneading it in her hands.

"There's food in the refrigerator, and a gas furnace. I don't know what to do."

Lucy understood Kitty's anxiety. Her own mother had found the responsibilities of home ownership overwhelming when she was suddenly widowed. With Lucy's encouragement she soon decided to move to a small apartment in a retirement community.

"Would you like me to go over with you?" asked Lucy, patting the old woman's hand.

"Would you?" Kitty's eyes lit up. "I'll get the key."

As she watched Kitty scurry off, Lucy carefully arranged her features. Kitty didn't need to know how eager she was to search for clues in Caro's house.

Ten

There will be an opportunity to photograph each class before the dress rehearsal.

While Lucy waited for Kitty, she watched Sara turn circles on the lush grass lawn. Huge old trees shaded the Slacks' backyard, making it an ideal place for children to play in the summer. She wondered if Fred had been allowed to invite his friends over for noisy games like Cowboys and Indians or Capture the Flag.

"Doesn't she get dizzy doing that?" asked Kitty.

"That's why she does it. She likes getting dizzy. Come on, Sara. We're going next door."

Crossing the driveway, Lucy took note of the neat exterior of Caro's house. It was much smaller than the Slacks' house, of course, but it had a character all its own. It was a modern, architect-designed dwelling with bleached cedar siding, an oversized brick chimney, and a huge picture window. It didn't look anything like the other houses in Tinker's Cove.

"How did she get permission to build a house like this?" asked Lucy.

"It's older than you think. It was built in the fifties, before we had the historical commission. Morrill doesn't like it much; he says it looks like a gas station."

"It sure is different," said Lucy, waiting while Kitty

unlocked the sliding glass door. Heavy homespun drapes concealed the interior.

Once inside, Lucy decided the house was surprisingly elegant. It was uncluttered, serene, vaguely Oriental. The living room was sparsely furnished, but it contained a state-of-the-art entertainment system, neatly housed in polished teak.

A small hall led to two bedrooms, simply furnished in Danish modern. The master bedroom was distinguished by a shaggy rya rug; otherwise it was almost identical to the smaller guest room.

"The police searched, but they didn't find anything. This house doesn't have any hiding places," said Kitty.

"It's so neat," exclaimed Lucy, thinking of her own slapdash housekeeping.

"It was always like this. Never anything out of place. The kitchen's this way."

In the sleek, galley-style kitchen Lucy helped Kitty empty out the refrigerator. It was well stocked with salad greens and other perishables; it was not the refrigerator of someone who was planning to take a trip.

Lucy followed Kitty downstairs to the cellar. It was just as tidy as the rest of the house. The walls were lined with shelves containing flowerpots, paint cans, and a few oversized stock-pots. There was a washer and dryer, and a huge furnace that sprouted ducts like tentacles. It had probably been installed when the house was originally built. A pilot light burned fiercely behind the grate.

"I don't like gas," clucked Kitty. "It's awfully dangerous."

"It should be turned off," advised Lucy. "The weather's warm now and the pipes won't freeze."

Kitty looked at the furnace skeptically.

"I think you just flip this," said Lucy, pointing to a red emergency switch. "Shall I?"

"I'm sure you know best."

At Lucy's touch the furnace sputtered, then fell silent.

"Much better," said Kitty.

Returning upstairs, Lucy found Sara seated on the sofa, turning the black pages of an old-fashioned photo album.

"What did I tell you, Sara?" she demanded, taking the book. "You mustn't touch other people's things."

"I'm sorry," whispered the child, pouting and studying her new sneakers.

"That's okay," chuckled Lucy, undone by Sara's adorable expression. "Where did you find this?"

"There." Sara pointed to a drawer in the coffee table.

Lucy pulled the drawer open and spotted a second album; this one had a carved wooden cover. She took it out and carefully turned a few of the fragile pages. She thought of her own family albums and how she had sat with her mother, asking the same questions over and over. "Who's that? Where's that? When was that picture taken?" Each photograph was a document indicating relationships, friendships, times, and places. Family albums contained a wealth of information.

"Put it back, Mommy," reminded Sara.

Lucy began to replace the albums, then hesitated. The temptation was too great. They might contain a clue that would explain Caro's disappearance.

"Mrs. Slack," she began.

"Lucy, I see the cesspool truck's at my house. I'd better run if I'm going to catch him before he drives all over the lawn."

"Go on," urged Lucy. "I'll lock up here."

"You're a dear," exclaimed Kitty, hurrying off. Sara followed her to the door and stood watching as the old woman ran awkwardly across the driveway.

Promising to work things out with her conscience

later, Lucy closed the drawer and tucked the albums
into her African basket shoulder bag. She took Sara's
hand and glanced around to make sure nothing was
disturbed. Then she left the house, carefully locking
the door behind her.

Eleven

*Pictures and videos are to be taken during the dress
rehearsal* ONLY!

It was early afternoon when Lucy pulled into a vacant
parking spot in front of Slack's store and shifted the
Subaru into park. It was just like Morrill Slack to con-
fiscate the camera, she thought. He obviously didn't
have any respect for Franny, or anyone he considered
his inferior, even his wife. He lived in the past, when
a small group of men like himself controlled almost all
the wealth in Tinker's Cove and the rest of the popu-
lation eked out a meager living as hardscrabble farmers
and fishermen. He had little knowledge of the modern
world, in which videos were almost as common as snapshots.

Thinking of last night's award ceremony, Lucy was
determined to get the camera back. The evening had
started out miserably enough. In fact, when she'd taken
her seat in the school auditorium she'd doubted she
would get through it. Bill's face was stony, the girls were
fidgety, and Toby looked quite nervous up there on
the stage. It was crowded, noisy—and very hot, thanks
to the greenhouse effect created by evening sunlight
pouring through the windows.

The school principal stood up; the room quieted
down. He ordered the shades drawn and assigned sev-

eral sixth-grade boys to do the job. The school band began playing "The Star-Spangled Banner" and everyone stood up.

As the band struggled through the difficult song, Lucy glanced at Bill and their eyes met, just as a particularly sour trumpet note sounded. She giggled, he broke into a grin, and they began to enjoy the evening.

It was almost embarrassing, they agreed later, that Toby won so many awards. They had expected the attendance award, of course, and were pleasantly surprised when he won a book prize for an essay on prejudice. When he was called up to receive the fourth-grade mathematics award, Bill squeezed her hand. When he also received the science award, and a certificate for outstanding scholarship, they could barely contain their pride.

Their son was the very picture of a humble scholar as he went back and forth from his seat to receive his awards. When the principal described him as an extraordinary young man, Toby blushed mightily, shuffled his feet, and hung his head. It was only afterward, when Ted Stillings snapped his picture for the paper, that he allowed his pride to show. Standing on the sidelines, observing his glowing face, Lucy wished she could have recorded the ceremony.

She couldn't recapture Toby's big moment, but she certainly wasn't going to miss the one and only opportunity she'd have to videotape the girls' ballet recital.

Checking her watch, she saw it was just a little bit past one and she still had to buy blank tapes. Then she had to pick up Sara at Sue's house, where she had temporarily parked her. Lucy didn't want any distractions while she coped with Morrill Slack.

She hoped there wouldn't be any difficulty. Her swollen feet were killing her and she wished she were back home taking her usual after-lunch rest on the couch.

She also had a wicked case of heartburn; she probably shouldn't have had that second cup of decaf this morning. Her back ached and, as almost always, she had to pee. She was in no mood to tolerate any nonsense from a cranky old fart like Morrill Slack.

Squaring her shoulders and bracing her legs, she yanked the stubborn door open and marched into the store. It was something of a letdown to discover that nobody seemed to be around. There was no sign of Slack, or even Ben, in the place. Franny's usual spot at the cash register was empty. Lucy peered down the aisles and called out a hello, but there was no answer. She wondered if the store was closed, and began to feel uneasy. Perhaps she should come back another time.

What other time? she reminded herself. She needed the camera now. She didn't even have time to go over to the Slacks' house. Spotting the office door slightly ajar, she decided to give it a try. After all, the old guy might be hard of hearing. She knocked smartly, which made the loose glass rattle. The unlatched door swung slowly inward. There she found Morrill Slack slumped forward on his desk, motionless.

Lucy ran to him and reached for the phone to call the ambulance. The receiver was unpleasantly sticky, but it was only after she'd hung up that she noticed blood on her hand. Forcing herself to focus, she saw the entire desk was splattered with blood. Slack's head, she realized with a growing sense of horror, had been brutally bashed in and it very much looked as if her video camera had been used to do the job. It was lying next to Slack's head on the desk, and bits of tissue and bone clung to it. Lucy's gaze shifted back to the old man. One pale blue eye was still open, and stared dully through the cracked lens of his eyeglasses. Her last thought, as she fainted dead away, was that he looked like a fish on ice.

Twelve

No reserved seating.

It was only minutes later when Lucy came to, flat on her back on the floor. She struggled to sit up, but overcome by dizziness and nausea, she collapsed again.

The next thing she was aware of was the booming voice of Barney Culpepper.

"Don't touch anything except Mrs. Stone," he ordered a pair of uniformed EMTs. "You guys contaminate this crime scene and I'll never hear the end of it."

"Don't raise your head, Mrs. Stone," said one of the EMTs. "We're just going to slide you onto this stretcher and take you for a little ride to the next room. Oopsydaisy, there we go."

The sudden movement made her head whirl and she groaned.

"Be careful with her," she heard Barney bellow.

"I'm okay," she reassured him once they had her settled in the store. "I must've fainted."

"Do you have any chest pains?" asked the EMT, slipping a blood pressure cuff around her arm and inflating it. "Any pain at all?"

"No. Yes. My head hurts."

"Good. Your pressure's okay. I'm going to give you

this lollipop to suck on. When you feel like it, you can sit up."

Lucy concentrated on sucking the pop and tried not to think about the gory scene in the next room. "Is he dead?" she asked Barney.

"Afraid so, Lucy. Just try to relax," he answered.

Lucy let out a quavery little sigh and took stock of her situation. Nothing hurt, except for her head, and nothing was broken. A flurry of activity inside told her the baby was fine. Her hand was still blood-smeared, and she wanted to wash it.

"Is there any place I can clean up? I have to get the girls to the dress rehearsal. And I need that camera."

"There's no hurry, Lucy. Number one, the dress rehearsal's been canceled until further notice. There's a sign on the auditorium door. And number two, you're not going to have that camera for a long time. It looks like it's the murder weapon and it's gotta go to the state crime lab. If there's a trial and it's submitted as evidence, it could be years 'fore you get it back. If I was you, Lucy, I'd just get another one. They've come down in price quite a lot."

"Yeah. And they're a lot lighter now, too," agreed one of the EMTs. "Yours musta been pretty heavy to do all that damage."

"Nah," said the other EMT, shaking his head. "Did you see how thin his skull was? Cracked just like an egg."

"Do I have to stay here?" asked Lucy, suddenly desperate to leave. She sat up and swung her legs over the side of the stretcher.

" 'Fraid so," Barney said. "The investigating officer will want to ask you some questions. You can't go till he says so."

"What about Toby and Elizabeth? I was going to pick them up at school."

"I'll call Marge," said Culpepper, referring to his wife. Lucy caught the nod he gave the EMTs before strolling out to his cruiser, and felt suddenly uneasy.

"Am I a suspect?" she demanded as soon as he returned. "It must look pretty suspicious, being found in the same room with a dead man. And it is my camera."

"Aw, Lucy, 'course you're not a suspect. All I know is we're supposed to sit tight until the staties get here. Looks like that's them now."

A steady stream of official vehicles began arriving outside, and soon the store was filled with investigators. Lucy sat quietly, watching their comings and goings, until Barney told her an officer would take her fingerprints.

"You can't be serious," she protested feebly as an officer noted the condition of her hands and proceeded to scrape off a sample of the blood. After that her fingers were inked and rolled one by one against a card. Only then was she given a towelette to clean her hands. Lucy was using it when she heard a familiar voice.

"Mrs. Stone, I see you're in the thick of things once again," observed a slight man in a tan raincoat.

Looking up and seeing Detective Sergeant Horowitz's familiar face, his long upper lip reminding her of a rabbit, she attempted to smile.

"I didn't do it," she said.

"That's what they all say, at first," he replied, shaking his head. His hair had thinned since last December, when he'd been in charge of investigating Sam Miller's death. That episode had left them each with a grudging admiration for the other's abilities at detection.

"I guess we'll have to give you the benefit of the doubt, at least until a jury decides otherwise," he said, smiling as he sat down beside her. This was his version of a joke, she decided. "Just start at the beginning," he told her.

Obediently, Lucy went over the events of the afternoon as clearly as she could. When Horowitz asked why Franny had borrowed the camera, she hesitated before answering. She didn't want to incriminate Franny by saying Slack suspected her of stealing.

"I don't know why Franny wanted it," she lied. She knew from the drift of Horowitz's questions that Franny was the number-one suspect.

"Franny couldn't have had anything to do with this, any more than I did," she insisted.

"You've been real helpful, Mrs. Stone. Thank you. I'll let Officer Culpepper take you home now," said Horowitz, concluding the interview. "Have a nice day."

Lucy was furious when she climbed into Barney's cruiser. "What does he mean, have a nice day? I found a dead body, for God's sake. How am I supposed to have a nice day?"

"It's just one of those things people say. Doesn't mean anything. Now calm down, Lucy. All this excitement can't be good for the baby."

"I suppose you're right," admitted Lucy, finally clicking the belt into place. "Am I going to have to answer more questions? What about my car?"

"You're in no shape to drive. We'll figure something out."

"Okay, Barney. I don't mean to be unreasonable. I'm just upset. They think Franny did it, don't they?" she asked, turning to face him.

"Maybe the investigation will turn up somebody else, but right now she's the likeliest suspect."

"Because of her husband?"

"That's right. He had quite a knock on the head, too."

"I thought he fell down the stairs."

"That's what she said happened."

"It could have happened that way."

"Sure, but when the same thing happens twice you can't help being a little suspicious."

"Was there a trial when her husband died?"

"No. There was no physical evidence that she did it, and everybody felt sorry for her. He used to beat on her, you know. She was always going to the emergency room saying she fell down the stairs or accidentally bumped into a door. I questioned her myself, more than once. Things were different then. We all knew what was going on, but we couldn't do anything unless she pressed charges. She was too ashamed to admit the truth, I guess. Then when she called and said there'd been an accident and he'd fallen down the stairs, well, nobody pushed too hard. There was an investigation, but she stuck to her story and charges were never filed against her. Seemed like he got what was coming. Too bad there were no stairs this time."

Culpepper turned the cruiser smoothly into Lucy's driveway and braked.

"I can understand her striking back in self-defense," argued Lucy. "But I can't believe she would hit an old man, even someone as awful as Slack. She worked for him for years."

"And he took advantage of her for years. Kind of like that husband of hers, if you ask me. Something snapped then, and it probably happened again. If she gets a good lawyer, maybe she'll get off. You take it easy, now, Lucy."

Looking at the blank windows of the house, Lucy felt reluctant to leave the safety of the cruiser. She was suddenly afraid to be alone. Then the kitchen door opened, and Bill stood there, waiting for her. Reassured, she climbed out of the car and rushed into his arms. For the first time since she'd discovered Slack's body, she allowed herself to remember what she'd seen.

"Oh, Bill," she wailed, bursting into tears. "It was horrible."

"It's okay," he said, holding her close. "You're home."

Thirteen

Be sure to label all costumes with student's name.

"It's a simple system, crude but effective," explained Doc Ryder the next morning. "The brain doesn't get enough oxygen for one reason or another, so you black out and fall down. Once you're down, the brain gets plenty of oxygenated blood, thanks to gravity, and you revive. The thing to do is to avoid these sudden shocks. If you insist on discovering dead bodies, it'll probably happen again."

"Believe me, I'll do my best to avoid them," promised Lucy. "Is the baby okay?"

"Oh, sure," said the doctor, waving his stethoscope. "Nice strong heartbeat."

"That's a relief," said Lucy, sliding off the examining table. She had made the appointment at Bill's insistence, but in her heart she was grateful for his stubborn refusal to leave for work until she'd seen the doctor.

"He says there's nothing to worry about. We're both fine. Really," she told Bill. He'd been sitting in the waiting room, reading to Sara.

"I wish I wasn't working so far away," he complained. He'd been hired to oversee the repair of a two-hundred-year-old church in Gilead, about fifteen miles away. "I still think you ought to take it easy for a day or two."

"I really need some groceries. If you take me and

Sara over to the hardware store, I can pick up the car. Barney locked it up for me. He's got the keys at the police station."

"Okay," sighed Bill, working the spare key off his key ring. "I'll call around lunchtime, just to make sure everything's okay."

"What could happen at the IGA?"

"Something like what happened at Slack's," muttered Bill, starting the truck engine with a roar.

Bill waited in the truck while Lucy unlocked the Subaru, strapped Sara in her seat, and started the engine. It was only after she smiled and waved to him that he drove off.

Glancing over her shoulder at the hardware store, where a CLOSED sign hung in the door, Lucy gave a small shudder. She shifted into drive and went straight to the police station.

"Hi! Is Barney in?" she called to the pretty young dispatcher who was perched behind the counter.

"Sorry, Mrs. Stone. He had to go out, but he said to give you these if you came by." She held up the car keys.

"Thanks," said Lucy, taking them. "You don't happen to know where he is?"

"Sorry," said the dispatcher, shaking her perky blond ponytail. "Police business."

Disappointed, Lucy led Sara back to the car. She was once again buckling her in when she noticed the albums, still sitting in the cargo area, where she'd stowed them yesterday. She'd look at them as soon as she got home, she promised herself.

It was only a short drive to the IGA; sometimes Lucy thought she spent more time strapping and unstrapping Sara than she actually spent driving. Tempted as she was to skip the backbreaking procedure, she never did. It wasn't worth the risk.

Crossing the parking lot with Sara's little hand firmly in her own, Lucy was pleased to see Julia Ward Howe Tilley coming out of the store.

"Up to your old tricks, I see," said Miss Tilley, positively beaming at her. Miss Tilley had been the librarian at the Broadbrooks Free Library for many years. She had always encouraged Lucy's interest in crime and used to save the newest mysteries for her.

"I don't go looking for bodies," protested Lucy. "In fact, Doc Ryder has warned me to avoid them and I plan to follow his advice."

"Was it very gruesome, dear?" she inquired, smacking her lips.

"Rather." Lucy didn't want to think about it.

"I'm glad," declared Miss Tilley. "He deserved it."

"No one deserves that."

"Morrill did. He was an absolute Tartar, you know. Poor Kitty spent her life tiptoeing around him. Always afraid. That's no way to live."

"She told me Morrill would never let her retire," said Lucy. "I guess she can retire now."

"And in comfort. Morrill was quite wealthy. He never liked to spend money, he just squirreled it away. There's more than the store, you know. He had land and timber interests he inherited from his father. He never parted with anything."

"Who do you think killed him?" asked Lucy, ignoring Sara's impatient tugs on her arm.

"Any number of people would gladly have throttled the old goat. He had quarreled with almost everyone in town, even his own son. Even me, for that matter." The old woman seemed amazed at Slack's effrontery. "He tried to close the library, you know, when he was a selectman. To save the town money, he said. He was going to fire me and sell off the building, including the books. He was always penny wise and pound foolish." She clicked her tongue. "Look at that. Anne-marie's been shopping for the 'funeral baked meats.' "

"I guess so." Lucy was astonished to see Annemarie Slack leading a small procession of grocery carts across the parking lot to her Chevy Suburban. The IGA staff didn't include bag boys except on Saturdays, so Lucy was amused to see the bakery lady and Mort the butcher helping Annemarie with her bundles.

"Annemarie's doing everything herself," Miss Tilley went on. "Kitty told me she absolutely refused to hire a caterer."

"For some people cooking is a way of expressing love," mused Lucy. Thinking of the fish sticks and hamburgers she'd been serving lately, she added, "I prefer to express it in other ways."

"So I see." Miss Tilley was staring rather pointedly at Lucy's tummy.

Embarrassed, Lucy quickly asked, "Is Kitty very upset about losing Morrill?"

"It's hard to tell. You never really know what Kitty's thinking. My guess is that she's rather shocked. I stayed with her last night. She didn't cry, thank goodness, but she didn't seem interested in anything, either. She had the TV on, but I don't think she could tell you what she watched. She just sat there."

"Were Fred and Annemarie with her?"

"No. They were busy with the police and the under-taker. In fact, Fred called and asked me to stay with his mother because they couldn't. He's a good son."

"Mommy," whined Sara.

"Here, honey," said Lucy, digging in her purse for a coin. "You can ride the horsey." A small mechanical pony stood in front of the grocery, but Lucy always marched the children past it. Sara was thrilled with her treat and climbed right on.

Aware that she had only a few minutes before the

ride ran down, Lucy switched the subject of the conversation. She knew that Miss Tilley and Caroline Hutton were old friends.

"Now that there's been a murder, I hope the police don't forget about Caro." For a minute the words seemed to hang between them, and Lucy was afraid she had upset Miss Tilley.

"I'm hoping the opposite," the old librarian answered. She had obviously given the matter some thought. "They'll have to investigate both crimes to see if there's a link, won't they? This might be the beginning of a crime wave against senior citizens."

"Do you really think so?"

"No, but I think the police will have to consider it. Maybe they'll find some new information about Caro. I hope so."

"The worst thing is not knowing what happened to her," said Lucy. The horse was prancing more slowly now.

"I don't think Caro is dead. I think she's . . . what's that term?" Miss Tilley's face clouded with the effort of remembering, then brightened when she found the right words. "Missing in action." She smiled. "That's it. Missing in action."

"What do you mean?" began Lucy, as the horse ground to a halt and she went to help Sara get down. When she turned, Miss Tilley was gone.

One hour and a hundred and twenty-three dollars later, Lucy was on her way home. Sara, licking pink icing off her fingers, was in a cupcake-induced state of bliss.

Driving along Main Street, Lucy was soon past the hardware store. A block or so later the business district ended and the street was lined with the impressive mansions built in earlier centuries by sea captains and merchants. Lucy drove by the Slacks' ornate Victorian;

it seemed gloomier than ever. The overgrown fir trees that blocked out the sun couldn't entirely account for the atmosphere that seemed to surround the old mansion.

Fred and Annemarie's Federalist-style house stood nearly opposite, freshly painted gleaming white, the crushed-oyster-shell driveway sparkling in the sunlight. A new road had been cut alongside Fred's property, where plans for a new subdivision had been approved. The project never got off the ground; only the fresh blacktop and a single foundation stood as a monument to the recession that had stalled so much of the Northeast.

Lucy drove a few blocks farther before she passed the little bungalow where Franny lived with her mother on the outer fringe of the village. When Lucy saw several police cruisers parked in front, effectively barricading the house, her stomach lurched. Swallowing hard, she hoped Franny had a very good alibi.

Fourteen

No talking backstage.

Franny, however, had no alibi at all.

"You mean absolutely nobody can verify that you spent all yesterday afternoon at home?" Horowitz's soft voice betrayed no emotion and his eyes were pale blanks to Franny. If anything, he seemed tired. Investigating crimes must get rather depressing, she thought.

"I watched a little bit of TV. I looked through some magazines. I found an old Agatha Christie paperback and read it."

"You didn't get any phone calls?"

"No."

"Nobody dropped by?"

"No. Nobody would have expected us to be home. I'm always at work. And yesterday was Mom's day at the thrift shop."

Franny smiled weakly at her mother, who was huddled in a rocking chair in the corner of the living room. She was watching avidly and saving up all the details, but Franny was certain that this story wouldn't be served up to entertain the bridge club or the other energetic retirees who volunteered at Meals on Wheels.

There was certainly a lot to see. The little house had literally been invaded by police officers. When she had

opened the door, Horowitz had flashed a warrant and
sat Franny and her mother down in the living room.
He wanted to ask her some questions, he said, while
the house was searched. Franny had no idea what they
were looking for, but soon the house was filled with
policemen intent on exploring every nook and cranny.
Horowitz remained in the living room, along with a
second man whose job seemed to be operating a tape
recorder. A female state trooper, her rounded figure
looking slightly ridiculous in her mannish uniform,
stood nearby. Franny hoped she wasn't going to be sub-
jected to a body search and eyed the female officer
uneasily.

The problem was that Franny was having a hard time
believing in her own innocence. In fact, she had wished
more than once that Slack would drop dead, most recently on the day he fired her. And now that he was
dead, really dead, she was glad.

She knew it was wrong to feel this way. She went to
church every Sunday and believed in her heart that it
was wicked to rejoice in another's misfortune, but she
couldn't help it. He was a miserable, horrible old man,
he'd caused her a great deal of grief, and he'd finally
gotten exactly what he deserved. It just went to show
that there was some justice in the world.

Or would be if she could convince Horowitz that
she'd had nothing to do with Slack's sudden demise.
If only she didn't feel guilty. But there was, she'd discovered, this soft, rotten spot in her conscience, and
she knew Horowitz sensed it. He believed she'd killed
Slack, she knew it. Guilt-ridden as she was, she couldn't
hope to convince him that she was really innocent.

"Now, why didn't you go to work yesterday?" he
asked.

Franny was tempted to lie, to say that she'd been
sick, but decided it would be better to stick to the truth.

She had told Lucy she'd been fired, and for all she knew it was common knowledge by now.

"Mr. Slack fired me on Wednesday."

"Why was that? You'd worked in the store for a number of years, hadn't you? Why would he suddenly decide to fire you?"

"He said I was stealing."

"Why would he say that?" Horowitz's voice was smooth, seductive.

"There was a problem with shrinkage—money and merchandise."

"Really? How much?"

"It varied. Some days ten or twenty dollars. A total of a hundred and forty dollars."

"You say merchandise was also missing—what sort of merchandise was that?"

"Mostly batteries. Paint. Little stuff."

"Explosives?"

"No," answered Franny quickly, shocked. "At least I don't think so. I don't know for sure. The store stocks dynamite, but it's rarely called for. I hadn't checked it lately."

"Do you have any idea who was stealing, since it wasn't you?"

"No." Franny was reluctant to tell Horowitz about Ben. Complaining to Lucy was one thing, turning him in to the police was another. Across the room her mother opened her mouth to speak but apparently thought better of it and held her tongue.

"Did anyone work in the store besides you and Mr. Slack?" persisted Horowitz.

"Mr. Slack's grandson, Ben."

"He had access to the cash and the merchandise?"

"Yes."

"Wouldn't it be logical to suspect him? In fact, isn't that why you borrowed the camera?"

"Yes," agreed Franny, relieved that her suspicions were finally out in the open. She hadn't volunteered it; Horowitz had dragged it from her.

"We'll leave that for now," said Horowitz, and Franny breathed a huge sigh of relief. "Let's go back about fifteen years, to the accidental death of your husband, Darryl Morgan. Do you remember that?"

Franny lowered her head and began nervously smoothing her homemade wraparound skirt over her knees. Her mother pursed her lips and fixed her gaze on Franny.

"Of course I do," said Franny, staring hard at the irregular kettle-cloth weave.

"How long were you married?"

"Just over a year and a half."

"How did he die?"

"He fell down the cellar stairs and crushed his skull. He'd been drinking."

"Did he drink a lot?"

"You could say that."

"Was he abusive?"

Franny didn't answer, so Horowitz went on. "Records at the police station show a number of calls to the Morgan residence beginning in September 1976 and continuing through June 1978. The code was forty-one—domestic dispute. Do you recall these disputes?"

"I never called the police."

"The calls were placed by neighbors," explained Horowitz. "There's a pattern of increasing frequency, which ended abruptly with Morgan's death."

"I came home and found Darryl at the bottom of the stairs. He was dead."

"That's what you said at the time. The records show that the DA considered charging you with Morgan's death."

"I was never charged."

"No," agreed Horowitz. "But you were suspected."

"What does something that happened fifteen years ago have to do with this business here?" demanded Irma, no longer able to sit quietly by as Horowitz built a case against her daughter.

"It could indicate a pattern," answered Horowitz patiently. "A pattern of abusive relationships that end in violence."

"Don't be stupid. Franny had a good marriage. Darryl was a real catch." Irma had puffed out her chest and looked a bit like a broody hen, all flashing eyes and ruffled feathers.

"You didn't keep your husband's name. Why was that?" asked Horowitz, with his usual persistence.

"I wanted to forget him. I didn't even want his name. That's not a crime."

"That's right," proclaimed Irma. "You're barking up the wrong tree. What about them Satanists? Caro Hutton disappears, old Mr. Slack dies. It doesn't take a genius to see that boy Ben is involved. Him and his Devil-worshiping friends. You should leave Franny alone and arrest them before they take another victim!"

"I'm sorry, Mrs. Small. I can't ignore the evidence." He paused and turned to Franny. "I'm going to have to take you into custody. The charge is the murder of Morrill Slack."

"But what about Ben?" cried Franny.

"He couldn't have done it. He has an unbreakable alibi. At the time of Slack's death, Ben was in the custody of the Gilead police. Operating under the influence."

Horowitz nodded at the officer, who immediately slipped a pair of handcuffs around Franny's wrists and read the Miranda rights to her from a printed card. Franny was led out to one of the cruisers and quickly driven away in a procession complete with flashing lights, but no sirens. Irma Small watched from the window, a vague figure, her image blurred by the aluminum screen.

Fifteen

No undershirts or underpants to be worn under costume.

"There's nothing to do here. I'm bored."

Caro Hutton had no experience at parenting, so she took the complaint quite seriously. She looked up from her needlepoint and gazed directly into her young companion's clear blue eyes. She was glad she had chosen the name Lisa for her; somehow it suited her.

"There's no TV. There's hardly any toys. There's nobody to play with. I want to go home."

"I used to spend summers here when I was a little girl," said Caro. "I was never bored. I thought I was in heaven."

"What did you do?"

"Let me see if I can remember. It was a very long time ago."

Caro bent her head and took a stitch or two. Children nowadays watched too much television, she believed, and it robbed them of their imagination. When she was a child she had been surrounded by a large extended family, and she'd always had plenty of interesting things to do. When she began performing and teaching, time had always been at a premium. It was only after she retired and began watching television herself that she'd ever experienced the numbing effects of boredom. It was a terrible sensation and she sympathized with the little girl.

"First things first," said Caro. "Part of the problem is that you've got your shoes on." She indicated the pink and white Reeboks on Lisa's little feet.

"I always wear shoes," said Lisa, furrowing her brows together under a heavy fringe of bangs.

"I know, and that's the trouble. Shoes keep you from feeling with your feet, and discovering things. When you wear shoes you can step on a caterpillar and not even know it. Squish. No more caterpillar."

"Yuck." The little girl wrinkled her freckled nose.

"But when you're barefoot, you can feel that hairy caterpillar tickle your foot, just like this." Caro tickled Lisa's skinny ribs, covered only with a thin T-shirt on this hot and humid day, and was rewarded with a high-pitched little giggle.

"Then you stop, and look at the caterpillar. After you watch him for a while you might decide to pretend you're a caterpillar. You try to move just like he does, and see how the world looks when you're flat on your belly. After a while you might decide to keep the caterpillar, so you have to hunt for a jar to keep him in. You have to find a hammer and nail to make holes in the lid so he can breathe. Then you have to find food for him. Pretty soon, before you know it, the afternoon is gone and it's time for supper. But it all started with taking your shoes off."

Lisa sat right down on the cabin porch and yanked her shoes off, grabbing them by the heels and pulling. She grunted with the effort.

"It's easier if you untie them first," observed Caro.

The girl shrugged, pulled her socks off, stood up, and wiggled her toes.

"Now what?"

"Now you go exploring with your feet. Why don't you take a little walk around the cabin?"

Caro watched as the little girl skipped down the steps and began walking very carefully on her bare feet. She stopped and turned, looking up at Caro.

"What if a spider bites me?" she asked.

"Why would a little tiny spider bite a great giant of a girl like you? Any sensible spider would take one look at you and run for his life. Imagine how enormous you must look to a spider."

"Some spiders are poisonous."

"That's true, but it doesn't do the spider much good if he's squashed flat under your big foot. You don't need to be afraid of spiders. I'm sure they're much more afraid of you."

"Maybe," admitted Lisa, squatting down to turn over a rock.

Caro watched her movements as she investigated the roughly cleared area around the cabin. With her straight back, long neck, and slender limbs, the girl had the natural build of a dancer. She really ought to take lessons, thought Caro. Of course, it could all change with the onset of puberty. You could just never tell which girls would retain their graceful, lithe shapes and which would develop huge pendulous breasts and spreading hips that would put an end to their budding careers in dance.

Not that youth is always so wonderful. It must be dreadful to be small and powerless, dependent on the kindness, decency, and generosity of adults. No, childhood wasn't all fun and games. It certainly wasn't the innocent idyll free of responsibility that people liked to imagine.

This poor child had certainly endured her share of pain and uncertainty. Caro watched as Lisa bent down over a patch of wild berries.

"Can I eat these?" she called.

"Of course," laughed Caro. "They're strawberries. You had some this morning in your pancakes."

She smiled, watching as the little girl greedily popped berry after berry into her mouth. It was good to see Lisa enjoying herself. She'd been terribly tense and withdrawn the first few days at the cabin, and the nights had been absolutely dreadful. One nightmare seemed to follow another, and Caro had spent hours watching the little girl writhe and twist on her narrow cot. She had screamed and whimpered, and sometimes her cries were so loud that she woke herself up. Then she would sob hysterically as Caro tried to comfort her.

"Everything's all right, you're safe," she'd murmured, settling the girl beside her in her big bed. She had wiped her eyes and stroked her hair, and eventually the child had stopped crying and gone back to sleep. Caro herself would be too agitated to sleep, so she would sit up through the night, warding off the evil spirits that tormented Lisa. The nightmare-filled nights left Caro exhausted, however, and she was grateful that the bad dreams seemed to be coming less frequently.

"I didn't find any caterpillars," complained Lisa. "I'm bored."

"Bored already? I don't think you looked hard enough."

"There are absolutely no caterpillars anywhere around here," declared Lisa.

"We need to go on a caterpillar hunt. And since caterpillar hunts can be rather hot, it would be nice if our hunt took us someplace we could go for a swim. Can you swim?"

"Yes, I can," answered Lisa. "I passed Guppies and Goldfish and now I'm a Porpoise. Sharks is the only one better."

"That's wonderful," said Caro, honestly impressed. "Have you ever gone swimming in a waterfall?"

Lisa shook her head.

"Would you like to?"

"I can't. I don't have my swimsuit."

"That's no problem," chuckled Caro. "We're miles from anywhere. You won't need a swimsuit because there's nobody to see you. Now, follow me, and keep a sharp eye out for caterpillars."

Sixteen

No comic books.

"Mommy, what's this?" Sara held out her finger, to which a little green worm was clinging for dear life.

"It's an inchworm," exclaimed Lucy. "Isn't it cute?"

"No, it's icky," said Sara, frantically shaking it off. "How long do we have to stay here?"

"We just got here," said Lucy, looking around the baseball field for a place to sit. It was the Saturday morning Little League game, Bill's IGA Giants were playing the Yankee Real Estate Clippers, and Lucy was uncomfortably aware that Sara's sentiment echoed her own.

Toby's streak of no hits had turned the weekly ritual into an endurance trial for Lucy. She scanned the crowd of parents, determined to avoid Tim Rogers' overenthusiastic mother and her clique of friends. Lucy had made the mistake of sitting near her last week, only to discover that Tim was destined to be the next Wade Boggs. When Toby went up to bat for the third time, and struck out for the third time, Lucy knew death by firing squad would be kinder than Andrea Rogers' withering scorn. Even worse, since Bill was the coach, she'd had to listen to an extremely unflattering description of him after he'd benched Tim for arguing with the umpire.

Today, however, Lucy spied the friendly faces of Marge Culpepper, Barney's wife, and Pam Stillings, and went to sit with them. Marge had brought Caro's retriever George along, and had firmly fastened him to her folding chair with a sturdy leash. He was quite content, apparently chewing on a bone.

Lucy had barely sat down in her folding chair when Sara began complaining.

"Mom, there's nothing to do here," she whined.

"Don't you want to find out who's going to win?" shouted Pam enthusiastically. Pam invested everything she did with her boundless energy; she was always smiling.

"It's a close game," added Marge. "They're tied two to two, and it's the bottom of the fifth."

"Top of the sixth," corrected Pam.

"See, only one more inning," Lucy told Sara. "The game will be over real soon. Why don't you take this bubble stuff and see how many bubbles you can blow? Stay clear of the field, now."

Lucy watched as Sara ran off to join a pack of preschoolers who were playing on the grass, then turned to Pam.

"I'm here under protest myself. I'm not sure Little League is having a positive effect on my family."

"What do you mean?" Pam was incredulous.

"Oh, practices are always scheduled for suppertime, so all we ever eat anymore is hamburgers. Bill's coaching, and that's taking a lot of time. And Toby wants to quit the team, but Bill won't let him."

"Gee, Adam loves it," said Pam. "He lives, breathes, even sleeps baseball. He buys Big League Chew, he saves baseball cards, he sleeps with his favorite ball under his pillow. He wears his glove when he watches the Red Sox on TV. He's obsessed."

"So is Eddie," said Marge. "He's trained the dog to

bring back the ball and he spends hours practicing his pitching." Adam and Eddie were both on the Clippers, the team playing against Bill's."

"But they're both good players," said Lucy. "Toby can't seem to hit the ball."

"Eddie had trouble last year," said Marge. "It's something they have to grow into."

"Maybe it's just not his thing," added Pam. She was something of a self-styled expert on child psychology, having taught preschool before starting her family. "Ted wishes Adam would love reading and writing like he does. But there's no chance of that. He takes after me. Hasn't passed a spelling test yet this year. Ted can't understand what the problem is; he's just a naturally good speller and thinks Adam ought to be, too. I tell him we've got to help Adam discover the things he's good at and encourage him to do those things. There's no way Adam is going to be a newspaperman like his father." She laughed, tossing her short blond hair.

"What does Ted think about Franny getting arrested?" asked Lucy.

"Not much. He said it was one story he hated to write."

"Barney had to drive her up to Wilton," added Marge. "That's the nearest prison with a facility for women. He felt miserable."

"That's an awful place. I went there once, years ago, as a literacy volunteer. I was supposed to tutor one of the inmates so he could get a high school equivalency degree. I couldn't stand it. It smelled so bad, and the men all stared at me, even the guards. I only went once, I couldn't stomach going back," said Pam.

"That's where Franny is?" Lucy was horrified. A place that could quell even Pam's enthusiasm must be grim indeed.

"The women's part isn't so bad," said Marge. "At least that's what Barney says."

"I can't believe Franny killed Slack. And especially not with my video camera. She's too conscientious."

"Why did she have the camera, anyway?" asked Pam.

"She wanted to show that Ben had been stealing from the store. If you ask me, he's the most likely suspect."

"He drove into a tree, driving under the influence," reported Pam. "He had two friends with him."

"That's not all," added Marge. "Those boys had some sticks of dynamite they'd stolen from the store. God knows what they were planning to do with them."

"See?" exclaimed Lucy. "Maybe Slack caught the boys stealing the dynamite and they bashed his head in."

"The times don't work out," said Pam, shaking her head. "The boys were in the Gilead police station when Morrill was attacked."

"The most important rule in murders is to look at who benefits," said Lucy. "Who gets the money? His wife, and believe me, she had more reasons to kill him than Franny."

"Ted called yesterday to get information for the obit. He got the impression that nobody's exactly heartbroken, not even Kitty. But if she put up with him for fifty-odd years, it's unlikely . . ." Her voice was suddenly cut off by a gasp from the crowd. The three women turned just in time to see a high fly ball sail into the air.

"That's Toby," screamed Pam.

"Way to go!" shouted Lucy, but her heart sank as she spotted Eddie Culpepper, the pitcher, already in place, waiting for the ball to plop neatly into his glove. It was Toby's first hit and he was going to be an easy out.

Just then George, having chewed himself free of the leash, bounded onto the field eagerly, ready to play with his new buddy. He jumped up to give Eddie a friendly lick and knocked him off his feet before he could catch the ball. Toby made it to second while Eddie fought off the affectionate dog and scrambled to reclaim the ball. He finally managed a weak throw to third, but Rickie Goodman fumbled. Toby was safely home by the time the ball finally reached catcher Adam Stillings. Toby, much to his amazement, had made the winning run.

His jubilant teammates thronged about him, congratulating him and giving him high fives. Bill joined the celebration, sweeping Toby up in a big hug before resuming his role as coach.

"Okay, you guys. Line up to shake hands with the other team. And be good sports or we'll start the next practice with wind sprints," he warned, giving Lucy a private smile over the boys' heads.

"See, Little League can be fun," said Pam, beginning to gather up her things. "Don't forget the service tomorrow. It's at two o'clock, and everybody's invited to Fred and Annemarie's afterward. You won't want to miss it. Ted says it's going to be the funeral of the century."

Seventeen

Older girls—black mascara, blue eye shadow.

Lucy spent Sunday morning in an agony of indecision. What does one wear to the funeral of the century, especially if one is pregnant and has a limited wardrobe to choose from? Lucy finally eliminated the denim jumper, deciding it was too casual. That left a silky gray polyester dress with rather frivolous puffed sleeves.

Expecting a baby didn't mean she wanted to dress like one, she thought, staring at her reflection in the dressing table mirror. Oh well, she consoled herself, at least it didn't have an arrow pointing to her midsection proclaiming BABY in large letters.

That was about all she could say for herself, she decided. She had never been so dissatisfied with her appearance. Her face was puffy and splotched and her hair, usually a neat, shining cap, was getting harder and harder to manage. No matter how she tried, she seemed unable to control her appetite, and she hated to think how much she'd gained. She looked like a blob.

Turning from the mirror, she noticed the albums stacked neatly on the blanket chest. With one thing and another, she hadn't had a chance to look through them. Perching on the edge of her bed, she carefully turned the brittle pages filled with newspaper announcements, programs for dance recitals, and cast photographs.

A yellowed newspaper photo of five-year-old Caro as an angel in a dancing school production of *Hansel and Gretel* made her smile. Other clippings indicated she'd attended dancing classes in Boston throughout her childhood, right up until her graduation from the Brookline Country Day School. She hadn't gone to college after graduation, but instead went to New York, where she performed with the Joffrey Ballet and studied with Martha Graham. Eventually she also performed with the Graham company.

The latter pages of the album were filled with original mimeographed programs for the annual student performances at Winchester College. Scattered among the memorabilia Lucy found wedding invitations and birth announcements from Caro's students, as well as newspaper clippings announcing their various triumphs.

One year the students had pooled their funds and bought Caro a pair of diamond earrings. The card they gave her, which pictured a Degas sketch of three dancers, was carefully preserved. Inside someone had written, "Those beautiful arabesques on points, / How they give us a pain in our joints! / Even though you constantly pull us apart, / We have only an abundance of love in our hearts."

Lucy chuckled, gently closed the book, and sat holding it in her lap. She felt just a little bit like a voyeur; she hadn't expected the albums to be quite so revealing. From what she knew about Caro she would never have expected her to be so sentimental.

Lucy had a memory book herself. It was filled with souvenirs from her early childhood and high school years. But once she'd started college she'd stopped adding to it. Now it was in the bottom of a trunk shoved way in the back of a closet. She'd become so busy living her life that she hadn't had any time to record it for posterity, except for snapshots and videos.

Caro, on the other hand, had devoted a good deal of time and care to this collection, and she kept it near at hand in the coffee table drawer. Maybe someday I'll spend my days looking at old photos of the kids, thought Lucy, standing up and smoothing her skirt. Maybe not, she thought, thinking of her mother, who had joined the outing club at her retirement community and was so busy that she recently forgot to send Bill a birthday card.

Glancing at the clock, Lucy realized she was in danger of being late for the funeral. She quickly slipped a black blazer over the dress and decided it seemed to improve matters. She couldn't button it, of course, but even left open it added a touch of sophistication. Her black pumps, tight when she bought them last fall before she became pregnant, were hopeless. She had no choice but to make do with a pair of black Birkenstocks and tights.

"Lucy," said Sue, opening her front door, "you can't possibly wear those Birkenstocks." It was only June, but Sue already had a golden tan and looked terrific in a black linen coat dress.

"I'm pregnant," she snapped. "My feet are swollen. I want to be comfortable and I don't have anything else that fits except my Reeboks."

"Oh, well," said Sue. "Let's go. Maybe no one will notice."

It was only a short walk from Sue's house to the white-steepled clapboard community church. A steady stream of people were making their way up the steps, and the pews were almost full when Sue and Lucy arrived. That meant they were seated at the back and didn't have to turn around and crane their necks to see who else was there, as so many people in the front were doing.

Since hardly anyone had fond memories of Morrill Slack, or anything at all nice to say about him, the family had wisely asked Dr. Churchill to limit the service to a simple reading from *The Book of Common Prayer.* Lucy found the words oddly appropriate.

"In the morning it is green, and groweth up; but in the evening it is cut down, dried up, and withered," intoned the minister. Lucy couldn't imagine Morrill Slack as a fresh, limber youth, but he had certainly labored and sorrowed and shriveled, and now he was gone. And, as the book noted, he had heaped up riches and he would not know who would gather them. Or how they would be spent.

In the front pew, Lucy observed, the Slack family were models of decorum. Fred, uncharacteristically somber in a dark suit, sat between his mother and his wife. With his broad shoulders and solid frame, he was a reassuring presence. Ben, on the other hand, was clearly uncomfortable in a navy blazer that was a shade too small for him, and fidgeted restlessly in his seat, earning a warning stare from his mother. Kitty didn't notice; she seemed to be in a world of her own.

Dr. Churchill augmented the services with several old hymns, supposedly favorites of Morrill's. Lucy enjoyed the thunderous chords of "A Mighty Fortress Is Our God" and the somewhat gentler strains of "Faith of Our Fathers." The service concluded with "Onward, Christian Soldiers," and the tune was still ringing in her ears as, duty done, she joined the procession of mourners marching down the street to Fred and Annemarie's house for the glass of sweet sherry and slice of pound cake customary after a Tinker's Cove funeral service. She would skip the sherry.

"I'm so sorry," murmured Lucy, taking Fred's hand.

"Well, we have the comfort of knowing he didn't suffer," said Fred, passing her along to Annemarie.

"And he lived a very full life," added Annemarie, taking her hand and passing her on to her mother-in-law, Kitty.

"And a very long life," nodded Kitty. "Lucy, thank you for coming. I do hope you will stay and have something to eat and drink."

"It's an open bar," whispered Sue, pointing to a table set up at the back of the hall, under the stairs. It was manned by a white-jacketed bartender.

"I'm not supposed to," said Lucy, patting her tummy.

"A little glass of white wine couldn't possibly do any harm," coaxed Sue.

"All right," agreed Lucy, succumbing to temptation. "A small chablis," she told the bartender, who proffered a generously filled wineglass.

The two women sipped their wine and strolled across the hall to the archway leading into the dining room, where they supposed the pound cake would be. There they stopped, amazed.

"I've seen this sort of thing in magazines," began Lucy.

"But not in Tinker's Cove!" concluded Sue.

Every surface in the room was covered with lavish displays of food. Shrimp, spread on a bed of ice, spilled from a crystal cornucopia set on the sideboard. Chafing dishes filled with scallops wrapped in bacon, Swedish meatballs, and Chinese chicken wings were set alongside. There was a collection of cheeses, surrounded by thinly sliced breads and assorted crackers.

"Look at the centerpiece," whispered Sue, giving her a nudge. An entire poached salmon dominated the mahogany table, completely covered with cucumber-slice scales and coated with glistening gelatin. A black olive

filled the creature's eye, and a strip of pimento outlined his mouth.

"I wonder who the caterer was?" said Sue. "Someone
from Portland?"

"I think Annemarie did it herself. I saw her at the
IGA with carts and carts of groceries. It must have cost
a fortune," said Lucy.

Deviled eggs, cold meats of every description, including a whole ham and a roast turkey, were also set out,
as well as bowls of dip and generous piles of crudités.
Entire lettuces, fans of Chinese pea pods, and artfully
curled scallions completed the display.

"Are they mourning the old guy's death, or celebrating it?" asked Lucy, under her breath.

"A little bit of both," said Sue, grinning wickedly.
"It's a black-and-white cake."

A small drop-leaf table stood by the doorway leading
into the library, and the sweets had been placed there.
In addition to the checkerboard cake, which magically
combined devil's food and yellow cake in a pattern of
squares, there were platters of cream puffs and éclairs,
and heaping plates of cookies. Pyramids of whole fruits,
including pineapples and bananas, created a backdrop
against which slices of kiwi and mounds of berries were
piled.

"Grab a plate, Lucy," urged Sue. "You're holding up
the line."

It was only later, when she'd found a seat in the living
room and was nibbling at the plate of food she didn't
really want, that Lucy had a chance to look around.
She had never been in Fred and Annemarie's house
before and she was frankly curious.

"This place looks like a furniture store," said Sue.
"That's Colefax and Fowler chintz on the windows, in
case you didn't know."

"I know," said Lucy. "And you're sitting on a

Braunschwig et Fils tapestry chair, in case *you* didn't know."

Sue jumped up. "You're right. And this rug? I think it's silk." She tapped the gorgeous Oriental with her black patent-leather sandal.

Everything in the expensive and tastefully furnished rooms appeared brand new, and the effect was oddly impersonal. Lucy thought of her own house, where a mix of flea market finds and antiques was usually overlaid with scattered Barbie dolls. Or Barney's house, where his huge recliner and TV dominated the living room. In Pam Stillings' house, newspapers and magazines cluttered the horizontal surfaces, and the walls were papered with the children's artwork. Even Sue, who decorated her house as carefully as she dressed herself, displayed whatever she was currently collecting. Recently, the teddy bears and Saint Nicks had disappeared, Lucy noticed, and had been replaced by a growing assortment of cookie jars and silly salt and pepper shakers.

"Do you think I could get a peek at the upstairs if I ask to use the bathroom?" asked Sue, echoing Lucy's own thoughts.

"Bring me back a report," Lucy whispered. She was content to stay in the chair, allowing her strained digestive processes to work and indulging in a little people-watching. As her gaze flitted from face to face, she wondered if Morrill Slack's killer was among the crowd filling the house. According to Miss Tilley, there were plenty of people in Tinker's Cove who had a score to settle with Morrill.

Although there was no lack of suspects, Lucy found her gaze returning again and again to Annemarie. What makes her tick, wondered Lucy as she watched Annemarie move from guest to guest. Annemarie plumped up a pillow and tucked it behind old Mrs.

Humphrey, she made a little plate of sweets for Adele Delaporte to save her the trouble of getting up when her arthritis was so bad, and she gently teased select-man Hancock Smith about his entirely mythical sex appeal, pleasing him no end. Annemarie seemed to strike the right chord with everyone. Today, however, the dazzling smile was strained. Probably because of her son, Ben, thought Lucy. The boy must be facing some sort of charges for the incident in Gilead. Come to think of it, although Ben had sat with his family at the service, he seemed to have made himself scarce immediately afterward—he was nowhere to be seen at the reception.

"Lucy, can I get you something?" asked Fred, hovering over her.

"Oh, no. I've eaten far too much. Everything was so delicious."

"Annemarie did it all," he said proudly. "She's a terrific cook, just like her mother. A real Italian mama. Loves to feed people." He sat down in the chair Sue had vacated. "You know, Lucy, I'm awfully sorry you had to be the one who discovered my father. It must have been a dreadful shock, especially in your condition."

"It was," admitted Lucy. "But there haven't been any ill effects. I'm really very sorry about your father," she added politely.

"Well, it was dreadful to lose him so suddenly," sighed Fred. "I hope Mom has some time to really enjoy life." He looked across the room at his mother, newly fashionable in a navy blue Chanel-style suit and salon hairdo, and smiled encouragingly at her. There was real love in the gesture, thought Lucy.

"She hasn't had an easy time," continued Fred. "Dad wasn't an easy man to get along with. Believe me, I know." He seemed about to enlarge on this theme when he caught himself. "I guess I'd better get back to work keeping those glasses filled, Lucy. Thanks for coming."

Fred has no sooner gotten up than Tatiana slipped into his chair. The ballerina was as chic as ever in a simple black sheath that emphasized her slender shape, but she looked tired and fidgeted nervously with her fingers.

"Tatiana," Lucy greeted her. "It was sure lucky for me that you canceled that rehearsal. I never could have made it."

"That's right. That's when you found the body!" How awful for you!"

"It was." The image of Slack's battered head surfaced in her consciousness, but Lucy refused to dwell on it. "Will there be a rehearsal on Tuesday?"

"I've decided to carry on," said the dance teacher, smoothing back her glossy black hair. "Rehearsals Tuesday and Thursday, show on Friday. That's what Caro would want. Besides, it isn't fair to the kids to keep putting it off. I'm hoping she'll turn up this week. She never misses the show, you know. I can't imagine having it without her."

"Have you had any news of her?"

"Yes and no. I call the police every day and Barney says there have been reports from all over. One man insists he saw aliens abduct her from a highway rest area. Somebody else saw her at Graceland. She was spotted at the Macy's in White Plains, New York, and at an ice cream stand in North Conway."

"Graceland?"

Tatiana shrugged. "It makes about as much sense as the others. Barney's wonderful, though. He keeps a list of every sighting and follows up when he has a free moment. He says something will turn up. I keep hoping she went off on a cruise or something and forgot to let anyone know."

"Maybe." Lucy smiled encouragingly. Across the room she noticed Miss Tilley among the group of chatty old women gathered around Slack's widow. "You know," she said, "Miss Tilley told me she thinks Caro is missing in action. What do you think she meant?"

"Like a spy mission? Going undercover?" Tatiana was doubtful.

"I'm not sure what she meant," admitted Lucy. "Maybe that Caro is off on some business of her own. Barney told me the police don't think any crime was involved."

"I know. That ought to make me feel better, but it doesn't. It all seems so out of character."

"What do you mean?"

"She was dependable, she didn't break commitments."

"Maybe this was more important."

"More important than my show?" Tatiana was incredulous.

"An emergency or something. Who did she care about the most?"

"Her students," answered Tatiana with no hesitation. "She never married or had children. Her students were her family."

Lucy leaned forward. "Can you keep a secret?"

Tatiana nodded.

"I took some albums from Caro's house." Lucy felt her face growing warm. "I didn't steal them. I borrowed them and I'm going to return them. But before I do, would you like to look at them with me?"

"You mean, look for a clue?" Tatiana's eyes were bright. "I'd love to. Today?"

"I can't." Lucy thought guiltily of Bill, who was home watching the kids. "Tomorrow afternoon?"

"At the studio? I'm free until three."

"Good." Lucy looked around the room. The drinks

and refreshments had definitely had an effect on the mourners. Conversation was no longer hushed, voices had risen, and bursts of laughter were heard. "This is turning into a terrific party."

"Especially for a funeral."

"Old Morrill must be furious, wherever he is."

"Perhaps his present companion is keeping him busy," said Tatiana, smiling wryly.

"And who might that be?" said Lucy, mimicking the Church Lady on *Saturday Night Live*.

Tatiana laughed, and together they chorused, "Satan?"

Eighteen

Parent, take child to bathroom before putting on costume.

Somewhat ashamed of herself, Lucy glanced around to see if anyone had observed their indiscreet behavior, and noticed Sue beckoning her from the bottom of the stairs.

"I guess it's time to go," she told Tatiana as she struggled to rise from the comfortable chair.

"Try sliding forward and getting your feet under you," advised the ballerina. "Find your center of gravity and work with it."

"That's much easier," said Lucy. "Thanks. I'll see you tomorrow."

Tucking her fanny under her and straightening her spine, she crossed the room. Much to her surprise, she discovered walking this way was a lot more comfortable than the waddle she'd slipped into.

"You certainly took your time," said Sue. "Let's get out of here."

"What are you in such a hurry for?" asked Lucy, looking about for Fred or Annemarie. "We can't leave without saying goodbye."

"Forget it, Lucy. Let's just go, okay?"

Sue hustled her outside to the sidewalk, where Lucy stopped and demanded, "Now, what's the matter?"

"You'll never believe what happened. I'm so embarrassed. I'll never be able to face him again."

"Who? Why? What happened?"

Sue took a deep breath and began talking while they walked.

"I had no problem at all getting upstairs. The door to the powder room under the stairs was shut and I looked distressed and the bartender told me there was another bathroom upstairs. So up I went, with official permission. There wasn't much to see, though, since all the doors were closed except for the bathroom. I do that, too, if I don't have time to make the bed, or when the kids' rooms get really bad. I decided I might as well use the bathroom since I was up there, so in I went.

"It wasn't anything special. No Jacuzzi or anything. Pretty wallpaper, though. Unusual. Kind of an abstract flower design. Almost impressionistic. Shades of pink and coral and green."

"What color were the towels?"

"Coral, but that's beside the point," insisted Sue, waving her hands. "So I'm sitting there when I hear voices from the next room," recounted Sue to an eager Lucy. As she spoke, it was almost as if she were back in the bathroom, perched on the environmentally correct low-flow toilet.

"Why didn't you tell me?" demanded Annemarie. "I had to hear it from Hancock Smith. That bug-eyed old lecher was practically drooling all over me. He's going on and on about what a wonderful legacy dear Morrill left for future generations. He said the historical society's getting everything—the house, the furniture, and plenty of money to maintain it. They're going to make the house into a museum, as if anybody'd want to look at all that ugly old stuff!"

"Lower your voice," warned Fred. "We've got a houseful of people. The historical society doesn't get a thing until Mom dies. She gets everything."

"What about us?"

"You didn't really think he'd leave us anything, did you?"

"I was hoping," admitted Annemarie. "Especially since he was so fond of Ben. A nice inheritance would sure come in handy right now."

"Wills can be changed, you know," said Fred, slipping his arms around her and nuzzling the back of her neck. "Maybe I can convince Ma to write a will of her own."

"That's a good idea," said Annemarie, turning to face him and draping her arms over his shoulders. "Is it legal?"

"I dunno. I'll ask Phil. He said he'd be here tonight."

"Phil's just defending Ben, right?" she said, pulling away. "You're not still thinking of having him help Franny, are you?"

"Why not? He said he's happy to do a favor for an old fraternity brother, and he's got other business here anyway."

"How can you be so dumb?" Annemarie shook her head. "You think you're helping, but you're only making things worse."

"Look," said Fred, grabbing her by the wrist. "I'm doing the best I can to get us out of this mess."

"Let me go," she snarled. "We've got company. I've gotta go downstairs.

* * *

"That's when Fred opened the bathroom door and saw me," said Sue.

"He saw you?" repeated Lucy.

"I forgot to latch the door," admitted Sue. "He caught me hiking up my panty hose."

"Was he embarrassed?"

"He sure was, he was beet red. And so was I. I can't believe he saw me in my Underalls." The two women stopped in front of Sue's house. "Do you want to come in for some coffee or something?"

"No, thanks. I should go home. Bill's babysitting."

"Lucy, you can't babysit for your own kids. He's fathering them, parenting them. It's good for kids to spend time with their fathers."

"You know, you're right," said Lucy, climbing into the Subaru and starting the engine.

Why, she wondered as she drove home, did she always feel so guilty whenever she left the kids? And why did Fred hire a lawyer to defend the person accused of killing his father? And what was Caro doing at Graceland?

Nineteen

No radios or tape players at rehearsal.

Throughout Tinker's Cove Sunday dinner was over and children were taking advantage of the last hours of weekend freedom as dusk settled in. Boys of a certain age formed small packs and prowled the town on bicycles, hunting for something to do. These long evenings gave them plenty of time to get into mischief.

"What the devil are those boys up to?" muttered Barney Culpepper. He was talking to himself as he made a routine patrol around the elementary school. Sunday evening, he knew, was prime time for preadolescent vandals. Barney wondered what that little group was up to at the far end of the parking lot, where the principal and other school officials parked their cars in neatly marked spaces. He turned off his headlights and proceeded very slowly and quietly toward the group.

What Barney saw, as he got closer and his vision became clearer, astonished him. Four boys, all sons of upstanding Tinker's Cove families, were busy painting a message for the principal on the gymnasium wall.

"Stop where you are, don't move, this is the police," he announced over the speaker, at the same time flicking on the cruiser's powerful lights. Startled by the sudden bright light and the amplified voice of authority, the boys froze. Barney hauled his considerable bulk out of the car and firmly grabbed two of the miscreants by their collars, but the other two hightailed it across the parking lot and escaped into the woods. Barney started to pursue them, but stopped, realizing it was hopeless.

"Can't catch me fat man!" heckled one of the escapees.

"Mebbe," growled Barney, "but I know who are you, Tim Rogers."

He turned and waved his flashlight at the two captives. "Into the cruiser," he ordered.

"Just once," complained Eddie Culpepper to Rickie Goldman, "just once I wish I could get away with something. It's awful having a cop for a father."

By Monday morning the wheels of justice were in full grind and four sets of parents had been invited to discussions with the principal at the elementary school: the Culpeppers, the Rogerses, the Goldmans, and the Stillingses. Soon after, Pam called her friend Lucy to vent her frustration.

"I'm so embarrassed," she confessed. "This is the sort of thing that happens to other people, not me."

"Think how Barney must feel. Catching his own kid."

"He looked pretty grim. We all did. Those boys weren't brought up to vandalize public property. I can't believe Adam would do a thing like that."

"Are you sure he did? How do they know it was Adam? Barney only caught Eddie and Rickie."

"The principal took one look at the wall and knew Adam was involved. Ted tells me the F word is always spelled with a 'u'."

"How was it spelled on the wall?" asked Lucy.

"F-O-C-K," answered Pam.

"Isn't that better? At least it wasn't an obscenity," reasoned Lucy.

"I guess the meaning was clear enough. Anyway, Adam admitted the whole thing. He said it was Tim Rogers' idea and he dared the rest of them to do it."

"Doesn't surprise me. Bill says he'd gladly trade him for a 'player to be named later.' Any player," said Lucy. "Don't feel so bad. The only reason Toby wasn't there is that we live too far out of town for him to bicycle in. There's not enough for kids to do around here—that's why they get into trouble."

"I know it. Barney said those boys who where in that car crash—you know, Ben Slack and his friends?—Barney said they were going to set off sticks of dynamite out in some field just for the hell of it. They could have blown themselves to kingdom come!"

"Maybe getting caught now will teach Adam a lesson. It's too bad nobody caught Ben Slack before he got into so much trouble."

"Adam and the others have to clean off the wall and repaint it. That'll keep them busy for a while. This summer I'm signing Adam up for swimming lessons, sailing lessons, and tennis lessons. Plus he's going to be tutored in spelling."

"Sounds expensive," said Lucy.

"It'll be worth it if it keeps him out of jail," said Pam.

"That reminds me. I'd better get a move on. I'm going over to Wilton this morning to see Franny."

"At the jail? Oh, Lucy, you're a saint."

"No, I'm not. I just feel guilty about all that Austrian ravioli in my freezer. Whenever I needed a hand, Franny was always the first to come. Now she's in trouble, and the least I can do is visit."

"I'm sending her a card. Wild horses couldn't drag me to that place."

"Thanks for the encouragement," said Lucy sarcastically, hanging up the receiver.

Once she was on the road to Wilton, after depositing Sara at Kiddie Kollege, Lucy began to wonder if going to the prison was such a good idea. She hadn't told Bill about her plans for the day; she knew he wouldn't approve. In fact, she wasn't sure if she would tell him tonight. She could just imagine his reaction. If he had his way, she would spend her entire life at home cooking and cleaning with occasional trips to the grocery store for good behavior. Sometimes he would tease her by saying the best way to handle a woman was to keep her barefoot in the winter and pregnant in the summer. It was supposed to be a joke, but it came awfully close to reality.

Set high on a hill over the little town of Wilton, the brick prison overshadowed everything around it. A complex of buildings, including the Superior Court and offices for county agencies such as the agricultural extension service and the health department, was situated at the bottom of the hill. A large parking lot separated it from the prison building, which was surrounded by a chain link fence topped with rows of barbed wire.

Lucy parked the Subaru and climbed out, then on second thought she struggled back in and locked all the doors. After all, she wouldn't want to help some desperate character escape. There were no trees shading the parking lot, so Lucy was grateful for the gray, overcast sky. It was hot and humid and she was panting slightly when she reached the fence surrounding the prison. A sign indicated the way to the women's facility, so Lucy followed the walkway that ran alongside the fence.

She was uncomfortably aware of a group of male inmates standing idly inside the fence, smoking, and felt
their eyes following her as she walked along.

"That one's got a bun in the oven," remarked one
inmate, just loud enough for her to hear. Lucy ignored
him and kept her eyes straight ahead, but she heard
the snickers of the others. He raised his voice and
called after her: "Hey, little mama, you like doing the
wild thing? Wanna do it with me?"

The other inmates found this very amusing, and he
was rewarded with a chorus of laughter. Another pris-
oner whistled and yelled out to her: "Don't listen to
him. I'll show you a better time!"

Lucy was mortified as hoots of laughter followed this
remark, but she refused to turn her head or quicken
her pace. Her face felt very warm, however, and her
hair was damp with perspiration. She heard a guard
order the men to be quiet, and she made straight for
the safety of the entrance just ahead, beyond the
fenced corner of the yard. A lone figure stood in the
corner, dressed in the regulation navy blue jumpsuit.
He, too, was smoking a cigarette, and he had several
days' growth of beard. His eyes glittered dangerously
and his gaze caught hers as she passed, separated from
her by the chain link fence.

"I could make you scream," he said flatly, his voice
gruff and his eyes hypnotically holding hers.

Lucy quickly shifted her gaze past him to the door
of the women's wing of the prison and hurried toward
it. A large, motherly matron opened the door when
she rang, welcoming her with a big smile. "Don't mind
them, honey. They get kinda funny, being cooped up."

"I guess they would," said Lucy, relieved that a thick
brick wall now protected her from the men. "I'm here
to see Franny Small. I called earlier and they said it
would be all right."

"It sure is," the matron told her. "Sign here, give me your purse, and walk through that metal detector." After checking Lucy's bag the woman returned it to her and unlocked a gate made of heavy wire mesh. "Go on in. Franny'll be down in a minute."

Lucy found herself in a rather bare reception room. Chairs and sofas upholstered in sturdy vinyl lined the walls; the color scheme was faded mustard and avocado. The walls were covered with a thick coat of cream-colored high-gloss paint; a few amateurish landscapes, their tones oddly flat, hung on the walls. The windows were covered with heavy wire mesh, and a second doorway was also blocked with a gate. It was here that Franny suddenly appeared, accompanied by a second matron.

"Lucy, it's wonderful to see you. Thank you so much for coming," she exclaimed, polite as ever, when the gate was opened for her.

"Oh, Franny," she said, unable to conceal her dismay when the gate was slammed shut and locked. Grasping both of Franny's hands she asked, "How are you?"

"It's not so bad, honest. See? I can even wear my own clothes. Everyone's real nice. The people who work here, I mean. I haven't met anybody else. They keep me separate from the other prisoners because I haven't been tried yet. I'm still officially not guilty." Franny sat down on one of the Naugahyde couches and neatly crossed her ankles. She might have been at an afternoon tea party.

"I'm glad you're not in with the criminals," said Lucy.

"Not yet, anyway," said Franny. "There's only a handful of women here. Very few women commit crimes. And when they do, they usually hurt a relative. Least that's what Verna says. She's my favorite matron."

"They hurt their relatives?"

"Husbands, generally. In self-defense. Verna says one lady here drowned her kids—all three of them. One was a baby, the oldest was four."

"Why did she do such a terrible thing? Was she crazy?"

"Kind of, I guess," admitted Franny. "She said it was the only way she could think of to keep them safe from their father. I never talked to her myself. I just know what they tell me."

"Have you had many visitors?" asked Lucky, eager to change the subject.

"Mom, of course. She's pretty upset. You can imagine. And Reverend Churchill, from the church. He told me not to worry because I'm in the Lord's hands. And Fred called and said he got me a lawyer and I'll probably be out on bail tomorrow after the arraignment."

"That's good news."

" 'Course, there's still the trial." Franny was philosophical.

"Oh, Franny, you'll get off. No jury could convict you. You're innocent!"

"I think I am. I don't remember killing him. But I wanted to, lots of times. In a way, that's the same thing."

"No, it's not." Lucy was definite on that point.

"Maybe. I've been thinking a lot lately. That's really all you can do in a place like this. It's like Reverend Churchill told me. ' "The Lord works in a mysterious way / His wonders to perform." ' We're all part of a big plan, and as it unfolds we each get what we deserve. It all works out in the end."

"I'm sure it will," agreed Lucy. "But I don't see why you have to be in jail now."

"I don't mind. I should be in jail. I've done terrible things."

"We've all done things we shouldn't have," began Lucy.

"I killed my husband."

"No," Lucy said. "Barney said . . ."

"Barney said everybody thought I killed Darryl but they couldn't prove it."

"He said Darryl got what he deserved," corrected Lucy. "Barney said everybody knew he was abusing you, but they didn't know how to stop it. You kept insisting your injuries were from accidents."

Franny turned away from Lucy and stared at the wall; tears were welling up in her eyes and she brushed them away with her hands.

"All I wanted was for Darryl to stop hitting me. I used to beg him to tell me what made him so mad so I'd know not to do it. He made lists for me. Pages and pages. 'Don't cry in front of me, speak to me in a respectful tone of voice, don't talk on the phone for more than three minutes.' I studied the lists, I tried to remember, but I always forgot something and then he'd have to punish me. It was all my fault."

"How was it your fault? He was hitting *you.*"

"He had to, because I wouldn't pay attention. 'If you won't pay attention,' he'd say, 'then I'll have to *make* you.' He'd slap me and I'd try so hard to listen but I couldn't. I was so scared all I wanted to do was get away."

Lucy got up from her chair and sat down on the couch beside Franny. She put her arms around her and hugged her close, as if she were comforting one of her children.

"When I banged up the car I knew I was in big trouble. I wasn't usually allowed to drive, but my leg got hurt."

"He broke your leg?"

"No, it was just bruised, but I couldn't walk very well.

I was wearing one of those neck collars, too, and I couldn't turn around to see when I backed up. I hit something and broke the taillight. I knew he'd be real mad."

"Couldn't you go to your mother's. Or stay with a friend?"

"I knew Mom would send me back to Darryl. She'd say my place was with my husband. I didn't have any friends, really. Nobody who'd want to get involved. So I sat there in the car praying for a way out and it came to me. I saw each step just as clear as could be.

"I stopped at the liquor store and bought a bottle of whiskey. I left it on the kitchen table, along with a note that said I'd be back at six. I knew that would make him mad—I was supposed to have supper on the table exactly at five-thirty. I knew he'd start drinking.

"Then, just to make sure he'd go down in the cellar, I left the dryer going. It had a real loud buzzer that went off when the clothes were dry, so you'd know it was time to take them out. It was real annoying, and I was sure he'd want to stop it.

"I worked out the times so he'd be drinking for a good while when the buzzer went off. And just to make sure he'd fall down the stairs I loosened the railing. Those cellar stairs were awful rickety, anyway. They were an accident just waiting to happen, and I made sure it did."

Lucy dropped her arm from around Franny's shoulders and moved over a few inches on the sofa, putting a little distance between them. This was a side of Franny she'd never seen before.

"So he was dead when you found him?"

"No. I guess he was so drunk that he just rolled down the stairs. He was coming around when I found him."

"What did you do?" Lucy had to know.

"I went back upstairs and got out the vacuum. That

was one of the things on the list. 'House must be vacuumed thoroughly every day. Or else.' I hadn't done it yet.

"At first, when I turned it off, you know, to unplug it and take it into another room, I heard him yelling. Shouting at me. Real mad. Ordering me to call for help. I told him I'd call when I got done vacuuming. Pretty soon he started asking for help. Promising he'd never hit me again. I didn't believe him. I'd heard that before. Then he was begging me. His voice got weaker. By the time I finished vacuuming the bedroom I couldn't hear him anymore. That's when I called the ambulance. Just like I said I would."

"Oh, my God." Lucy was stunned. "How could you ignore him?"

"When I look back at it, it's as if somebody else did it. I felt as if I was following instructions or something. I was sure they'd put me in jail, but nothing happened."

"You didn't tell anyone?"

"I wanted to, but I couldn't. After Darryl's funeral I went to live with Mom and got the job in the hardware store. I began to feel better. The time I spent with Darryl was like a nightmare. I almost believed it happened to somebody else, not me. Now I know that was an illusion. You can't get away with killing someone. Poor Mr. Slack's become the instrument by which I'll be punished."

It occurred to Lucy that Franny's view of the universe had become rather egocentric. Maybe jail did that to a person. Lucy knew she wouldn't want to be locked up with nothing but her thoughts.

"Did you kill Mr. Slack, Franny?" The unthinkable now seemed possible.

"No."

"You're sure?"

"I'm sure."

"That means there's a murderer out there. If you take the blame for Slack's death, his real killer might never be found. That wouldn't be right, would it?"

"I guess not."

"I think you need to talk this over with somebody professional, like a therapist." Lucy took Franny's hand in hers. "Have you met your lawyer yet?"

"No. He's coming this afternoon. His name is Philip Roderick. He's an old college friend of Fred Slack's."

A loud bell rang, startling the two women. Lucy flinched as the baby gave her a hard kick, uncomfortably close to her bladder.

"That means it's lunchtime," explained Franny. "I gotta go."

Lucy watched as the matron opened the gate for Franny and locked it carefully behind her.

"Franny," Lucy called to her. "Let this lawyer help you, okay?"

Franny nodded and turned to go. Then it was Lucy's turn to go through the other gate and the metal detector once again. The door swung open easily, it didn't even clang behind her, but Lucy still felt an incredible sense of lightness when she stepped outside. A languid puff of wind ruffled her hair, she took a deep breath of clean air, and she suddenly understood what prison was all about. She was free to go; Franny wasn't

Twenty

Toe students, be sure to stretch out before rehearsing.

Lucy couldn't get away from the prison fast enough. Safely back in her Subaru, she wanted to press the gas pedal to the floor and fly along the country roads as fast as the silver car would go.

Instead, she kept an eye on the speedometer and let up on the gas whenever the needle approached fifty. She switched the radio to a rock station, turned up the volume, and pounded her hands on the steering wheel in time to the beat.

What would she do, she asked herself, if she were trapped in a marriage like Franny's? Could she actually kill someone, even to save her own life? Looking into her heart, Lucy wasn't sure how far she would go to defend herself, but she knew without a doubt that she would use every last shred of strength she possessed to protect her kids.

Repelled as she was by Franny's story, Lucy wasn't about to judge her. The way she saw it, Franny had acted in self-defense when she killed her husband, and she didn't believe Franny could have killed Slack.

If only Ben didn't have an alibi, he would be the prime suspect. From what she'd seen, Slack's death had been the result of a violent confrontation. It hadn't been premeditated or planned; it had all the signs of a clash of tempers that got out of hand.

If old Slack had viewed the tape and saw the boy stealing, he would certainly have confronted him. From what the medics said, it hadn't taken much of a blow to kill him. Ben was young and strong, and he could have just overreacted to his grandfather's accusations.

That would explain the argument between Fred and Annemarie that Sue had overheard, too. As parents they wanted to protect their son, but Fred didn't want to see Franny punished unfairly.

Lucy couldn't understand why the police were so sure they had a case against Franny. She decided to talk to Barney as soon as she could.

Convinced she had neatly solved Slack's murder, Lucy turned to the tantalizing question of Caro's disappearance. She turned into the parking area in front of Tatiana's studio, grabbed the albums off the passenger seat, and hurried inside.

"Hi, Lucy," said Tatiana, who was standing with one foot hooked over the barre in what looked to Lucy to be an impossible position. The dancer didn't turn to face her but made eye contact in one of the floor-to-ceiling mirrors that lined the studio. "I was just about to have some lunch—want to join me?"

"Thanks," said Lucy gratefully. "I forgot to eat. These are the albums."

"Let's go upstairs to my apartment. We'll be more comfortable there."

Inside Tatiana's immaculate little apartment, Lucy pulled a chair up to the low counter that separated the kitchen from the living room. Tatiana busied herself pulling containers of food out of the refrigerator and produced a lunch of rice cakes, fruit salad, cottage cheese, and sparkling water.

"How did you get these albums, anyway?" asked Tatiana, pulling them toward her.

"My daughter discovered them when I was helping Kitty Slack close up Caro's house. I probably shouldn't have taken them," admitted Lucy, reddening slightly.

"What exactly are we looking for?"

"I'm not sure. You know her better than anyone. I thought you might find some sort of clue."

"These must be family," said Tatiana. The first page of the album featured studio photographs of an attractive couple. From their age and clothing Lucy thought they must be Grandma and Grandpa. The next page included a photograph of a substantial house. "Sylvan Lane" read the spidery handwriting underneath it.

Tatiana leafed through several pages before she came to a snapshot of a young woman proudly holding a very plump baby.

"This is Caro," exclaimed Tatiana, pointing to the caption. It read, "Dear Caroline—Her First Visit."

"There's a picture exactly like that of me in my mother's album," said Lucy.

"My mother has one of me, too," said Tatiana, laughing. "Sometimes I think all families have the same photo albums."

"All happy families, anyway," said Lucy, pushing her plate away and bending closer to study a series of photos taken at a summer place, a log cabin somewhere in the woods.

"Look at those swimsuits!" she said, pointing to a photo of a group of smiling children wearing old-fashioned black jersey bathing outfits. A shot of a waterfall looked vaguely familiar, but Lucy's attention was caught by a photograph of Caro as a little girl with bobbed hair, clutching a huge beach ball. In another picture she was dressed in a ridiculous starched and ruffled dress, standing with one hand at her waist and her elbow jauntily cocked.

"You can see she had a mind of her own, even when she was very young," observed Tatiana.

Turning the page, the two women stared at a formal portrait of a handsome man in a military uniform. His picture took up an entire page. It was followed by several snaps of him and a group of his teammates in jersey swimsuits with a "Y" on the chest.

"A Yale man," said Lucy, and Tatiana nodded.

In the last photograph he leaned casually against a vine-covered wall, seemingly without a care in the world, holding a tennis racket.

"What happened to him?" asked Lucy.

"He died in the war."

"She never married?"

"No. She turned to dance. 'Dance is my husband,' " recited Tatiana dramatically, " 'You students are my children.' It sounds kinda corny, but she really meant it."

"Besides you," asked Lucy, "who were the students she was closest to?"

Tatiana stood up and went to the table that stood behind her sofa. She picked up a framed photograph and showed it to Lucy.

"This was taken at her retirement dinner. Here's Jennifer Whitman, Bonnie Freed, Maria Bondi, Ludmila Oberanskaya. Maybe you recognize them, they're all successful dancers. This is Louise Comden. She could do incredible fouetté turns, but she married a lawyer or something. Janet Waters got pregnant and left school. She's a librarian now. Sally Liberty writes for *Dance* magazine. That's me."

"Have you spoken to them? Do they know she's missing?"

"I didn't think of that," exclaimed Tatiana. "I can

get their numbers from the alumnae office. I'll call them tonight."

"If nothing else, maybe you can get them to chip in and hire a real investigator," muttered Lucy, going back through the book. She stopped at the picture of the waterfall. It looked so familiar. She propped the book on its edge and leaned back in her chair to study it. A corner of a folded piece of paper slipped out from behind the snapshot.

"What's that?"

"It's a map," said Lucy, smoothing out the brittle paper. "It looks like something out of an A. A. Milne book." The crayon drawing included a cabin, winding trails, a carefully marked Snake's House, a creek, and a waterfall labeled Crystal Falls. "Our Summer Heaven" was written in large letters across the top.

"Caro must have drawn this."

"Did she ever talk about her childhood?" asked Lucy.

"No. She really didn't talk about herself much. This stuff is fascinating. Do you mind if I keep these books for a few days?" Tatiana glanced at the clock. "I'd like to take my time and go through them."

"Why should I mind? You have more right to them than I do," said Lucy. "It's late. I better get going."

"I've got a class in a few minutes. I'll see you tomorrow at the rehearsal."

"Maybe you'll have some news," said Lucy, picking up her bag.

"I hope so," said Tatiana. "She's been gone for too long. I'm really worried about her."

Twenty-one

The use of the auditorium is a privilege which can be withdrawn by the school administration. Leave the facilities in the same condition you found them.

On Tuesday, Lucy decided she hated mornings. She'd forgotten to set the alarm, so everybody got off to a late start. The family no longer sat down to breakfast together—these days everybody grabbed their own. Bill fried himself a couple of eggs, Toby ate a bowl of cold leftover spaghetti, Elizabeth refused to eat anything but peach yogurt for breakfast, and Sara always had a bowl of Cheerios. Lucy sipped at a cup of decaf and wrote notes.

"Dear Mrs. Wilson," she scribbled on a piece of notebook paper. "Toby should not take the bus home today, as he is going to a friend's house after school."

"I need a note, too, Mom," reminded Elizabeth. "The ballet rehearsal is right after school."

Lucy opened Toby's notebook to tear out another piece of paper and discovered an overdue book notice.

"What's this, Toby? This book was due in March."

"I think I lost it."

"You better find it. It says here they won't promote you unless it's returned."

"Honest, Mom. I've looked everywhere." He believed it, too, thought Lucy, studying his earnest expression.

"Oh, well, we'll look for it later. You guys better hurry or you'll miss the bus."

The two older kids clattered off, and Bill sat down at the table opposite Lucy.

"Don't forget," said Lucy, pouring a cup of coffee for him. "It's Tuesday. Little League tonight."

"Mmmph," he nodded, his mouth full. A trickle of egg yolk dribbled down his chin and caught in his beard.

Lucy turned to Sara, only to discover she was attempting to blow milk bubbles.

"Why did I ever get married?" muttered Lucy, thinking of Tatiana's exquisitely neat apartment.

"You wouldn't have it any other way and you know it," said Bill, dabbing his chin with a napkin. "Besides, we need you. You're the only one who can keep the schedule straight."

"Today's Franny's arraignment."

"Are you going?"

"I think I should," said Lucy. "Just to give Franny a little moral support." Her tone was defensive, but Bill didn't seem to notice.

"There's a new video store just opened up over in Wilton. Why don't' you take a look at the camcorders? Barney says we won't have ours back for a long time."

"I know." Lucy sighed. "We can't afford one right now."

"Maybe our insurance will cover it. I saw Fred Slack yesterday and he said something about it."

"That sounds too good to be true."

"Why? We pay a hefty premium every year and we've never filed a claim. Might as well try. What's Sara going to do while you're in court?"

"Kiddie Kollege, then she's going to Jenn's house."

"Well, I better get a move on," said Bill, draining his cup.

He bent down and gave Lucy a quick kiss. His beard tickled, and Lucy smiled.

"You're a good man, Bill Stone," she said, slipping her hand around his neck and pulling his face toward hers.

"Stop that kissing," shrieked Sara. "You'll get germs."

Lucy laughed. "I said not to kiss *dogs* because you'll get germs. It's okay to kiss Daddy."

"Oh." Sara hopped down from her chair and ran to present her cheek for a kiss. Bill bent down and gave her a quick peck, grabbed his lunch, and was out the door.

When she walked into the courtroom an hour later, Lucy didn't know what to expect. She looked around for familiar faces, but the only people she recognized were Ted Stillings and Franny's mother. Lucy would have preferred to sit by Ted, who was covering the case for the *Pennysaver*, but felt she really ought to sit with Irma. She looked so lonely, sitting there all by herself, clutching her tan vinyl purse.

"How's it going?" asked Lucy, slipping in beside her.

"Lucy Stone, bless you," said Irma, clasping Lucy's hand and squeezing it. "They haven't started yet, they're still doing some sort of roll call. That man"— she indicated the court clerk, seated at a desk just below the judge's bench—"calls the cases and the lawyers tell him if they're ready. That's Franny's lawyer over there."

Lucy followed Irma's finger and stared at Philip Roderick. He was sitting back comfortably in one of the armchairs provided for the lawyers, his long legs crossed at the knee and a thick briefcase resting beside him. He looked different from the other lawyers, who were joking among themselves. His suit, black with a faint gray stripe, was better cut. His shirt was whiter. He was almost obsessively well groomed, Lucy observed. His olive skin was flawless, his thick black hair was brushed smoothly back, and his nails were manicured. A gold Rolex, his only jewelry apart from a heavy wedding ring, flashed at his wrist. Philip Roderick exuded confidence; Lucy was glad he was defending her friend and not prosecuting her.

"All rise," announced the bailiff. "Court is now in session, Judge Joyce Ryerson presiding."

Seeing the judge, a fiftyish woman with neatly coiffed gray hair, Lucy felt like celebrating. She nudged Irma with her elbow and smiled encouragingly.

"The State of Maine versus Frances Mary Small," called the bailiff.

A door, almost concealed by the matching paneling, opened, and Franny appeared in handcuffs, accompanied by a uniformed matron. The officer showed Franny where to sit and then stood behind her. Franny looked very tiny and frightened, and Lucy's heart went out to her.

"How does the defendant plead?" asked the clerk.

"Not guilty," announced Roderick in ringing tones.

"So noted," replied the clerk. "Trial is set for September twenty-ninth at ten A.M."

"My client requests release on her own recognizance, pending trial," said Roderick. "She has lived in this community for virtually all her life. She has deep ties here, and her mother also lives in Tinker's Cove."

"The prosecution objects," said Holmes, the assistant DA. In contrast to Roderick he looked rather shabby in a rumpled seersucker suit. "The defendant has a history of violence, and we believe the public would best be served if she remains in custody."

He gave the clerk a thick file folder, which was passed along to the judge. The judge began leafing through the folder while Holmes continued his argument.

"The state is also requesting a complete psychiatric examination of the defendant, in light of the extreme violence of the crime with which she is charged. This was an attack upon a frail and elderly gentleman which resulted in his death."

The judge looked up from the folder and glanced at Roderick.

"Your Honor, if the court wishes, my client is willing to post bail. However, Frances Mary Small is not guilty, as I will prove beyond any reasonable doubt. The case against her is little more than a collection of hearsay evidence and coincidence. There is simply not enough evidence against her to justify holding her without bail, much less subjecting her to invasive psychiatric tests."

Roderick delivered his statement smoothly, with great conviction. Lucy was impressed.

"Your Honor," drawled Holmes. "The state respectfully disagrees with my learned colleague. We allege the defendant has shown herself on two occasions to be capable of violent and destructive behavior. We believe the public interest, and indeed the defendant's own interest, are best served by holding her in the state facility for the criminally insane."

The judge thoughtfully chewed her lip for a moment and then came to a decision. "Agreed," she said, and turned to face Franny. "Your trial is scheduled for September twenty-ninth. Do you understand?"

Franny nodded.

"Speak up for the record. Say yes or no," instructed the judge.

"Yes," whispered Franny.

"Until then, you will remain in custody, in the state hospital, where you will undergo psychiatric tests. Do you understand?"

"Yes," repeated Franny. Her response was barely audible.

"Next case," said the judge, banging the gavel.

"Just a moment," said Roderick, "praying the court's indulgence. I must object." His voice and facial expression remained calm and unruffled, but Lucy noticed her was spasmodically clenching and unclenching his left hand as he spoke. "I respectfully beg the court to reconsider this decision. My client is willing to post bail at a considerable personal sacrifice. There is no court record of past violence and she represents no threat to her community."

The judge tapped her polished red nails impatiently, her eyes flashed, and she appeared to be quite angry. "Request denied," she snapped. "I would like to remind the learned counsel for the defense that this court takes its responsibility to the public very seriously. I should not need to remind you that the defendant is charged with a violent crime, a crime that appears to be the result of an emotional outburst. I am not prepared to risk a recurrence. Twice is enough. That is all. Next case."

"Your Honor," insisted Roderick. "Once again, begging the court's indulgence, I believe the court's decision is quite wrongfully based on hearsay evidence concerning an incident that occurred fifteen years ago. I must remind the court that Ms. Small has never been charged with the murder of Darryl Morgan, and unless she is so charged, that evidence may not properly be considered by the court."

"I must warn the learned counsel for the defense that this court's indulgence has been tested beyond its usual . . ." Here words seemed to fail the judge. "Oh, whatever. I'm warning you," she said, glaring at Roderick. "Don't try this fancy stuff in my courtroom, Counselor, or you'll be up on contempt charges." She banged the gavel once again, and Roderick went back to his seat. He replaced a folder in his briefcase, rose, and made his way to the exit. Lucy jumped up and followed him, catching up to him in the lobby.

"Mr. Roderick," she called. "Could I speak to you for a minute? I'm Franny's friend, Lucy Stone. Isn't there anything you can do to get her out? That judge seems to have decided she's guilty without even trying her."

Roderick turned and smiled at her. His eyes crinkled nicely at the corners. "I noticed that, too. Her Honor could use a refresher course in the rights of the accused. That's to be expected in a rural area like this. Don't worry about your friend. I'll just have to try another tack." He looked up, acknowledging the presence of Irma and Ted Stillings, who had his notebook open and his pen ready.

"Do you have any comment about what happened this morning?" asked Ted.

"Nothing you can print," answered Roderick quickly. Then he reconsidered and said, "Just this: Franny Small is innocent and I won't give up until she is free and all charges against her have been dropped."

"What's your next move?" asked Ted.

"I'd prefer not to comment just now," said Roderick. "I have another case coming up and I need to consult with my clients."

"Off the record, then," said Ted, walking alongside.

Lucy smiled and shook her head. "The news hound in action," she said, turning to Irma. She was horrified to see her face crumple as she burst into tears.

"Please don't cry," said Lucy, producing a tissue. But the older woman was not about to be easily comforted. She began sobbing loudly.

"Come on," said Lucy, wrapping an arm about her heaving shoulders and steering her toward the door.

The lobby was crowded with a new wave of people, including quite a few teenagers. Juvenile court must be about to go into session, thought Lucy. Her hunch was confirmed when she spotted Fred and Annemarie standing anxiously by while Roderick consulted earnestly with Ben.

It was too bad no spectators were permitted in juvenile court, thought Lucy as she led Irma outside to a park bench. She'd never liked Franny's mother, and she resented being saddled with her.

"We'll just sit here for a minute," said Lucy, "while you collect yourself."

Any hopes Lucy might have had of escape ended when Irma clutched her hands and began sobbing harder than ever.

"Franny's in good hands," began Lucy. "She's got a good lawyer, and, well, try to look on the bright side. Maybe she'll get the help she needs in the state hospital."

"What do you mean?" Irma's tears ceased abruptly and she dabbed at her eyes with a tissue. "Franny doesn't need any help. She's just fine."

"She's not fine," contradicted Lucy. "She feels horribly guilty about killing Darryl."

"She didn't kill Darryl. He fell down the stairs."

"With a little help from Franny. She couldn't take any more abuse from him."

"Where did you hear all these lies?" demanded Irma. "Franny had a good marriage. Darryl was a real catch. Of course, I used to worry that she didn't have quite what it takes to keep a man like him. He was a lot of man, you know, and Franny's not much to look at. She was never popular. I was surprised when he married her, I would have thought he'd want someone more womanly."

Lucy's mouth fell open and she stared at Irma in disbelief. It was clear she'd worked out her own interpretation of Franny's marriage.

"You knew something was wrong," said Lucy, determined to break through Irma's denial of the truth. "Didn't you wonder about all those accidents? What did you think when you saw her bruises?"

"Franny's always been clumsy," snapped Irma. Her eyes were round and dark, like tiny, hard berries. "And besides, I don't know what I could have done. What went on in their home was between them. It was private."

"You could have asked her for the truth and supported her," Lucy said hotly.

"I'm sure I don't know what you mean, Lucy Stone. Franny's lived with me ever since Darryl died and I've never begrudged her a thing. Not even when she had no job and had to depend on me for everything. Couldn't even pay the little bit for room and board that I asked."

"Of course," said Lucy, realizing unconditional love was an unfamiliar concept to Irma. Poor Franny. Her life had certainly not been easy. No wonder she didn't seem to mind jail. The matrons Lucy saw had been warm and friendly, tolerant of human failings.

"I just don't know how I'm going to hold up my head in town, Lucy," said Irma, dabbing at her eyes with a tissue. "Especially now that they're putting Franny in a mental hospital."

"If I were you, I'd worry a little more about Franny and a lot less about what other people think," said Lucy, rising. "Can you drive yourself home?"

"Yes, I'll be all right." Irma sniffed. "Don't worry about me."

"I won't," said Lucy under her breath as she marched off to find her car.

Twenty-two

To insure a smooth rehearsal, please arrange a babysitter for your small children who are not in the show.

Lucy's first impulse after leaving Irma was to drive straight home. Then she realized it was past one o'clock and Sara had already gone to Jenn's house, so she decided instead to stop at McDonald's for a quick lunch. Remembering her doctor's appointment the next day, she virtuously chose a salad.

She felt somewhat better after lunch and decided to stop at the video store to price camcorders. While they cost less than she expected, purchasing one would definitely strain the family budget. Disappointed, she headed the Subaru toward Tinker's Cove. Usually she enjoyed the drive along the winding country road still dotted with old farmsteads, but today the lowering clouds and humid weather made her feel even more depressed. She needed to cheer herself up.

On impulse she stopped at several antique stores along the way, looking for an old-fashioned wicker bassinet for the baby. She didn't find one, but she did find two little plaster plaques, probably from the fifties, picturing ballerinas in various poses. Spruced up with fresh pink ribbons, they would be just the thing to give the girls as mementos of the big show.

She tucked the package out of sight in her big purse,

entered the now-familiar auditorium, and slipped into the seat next to Karen, Jenn's mom.

"Thanks," she said. "I owe you a big one."

"Don't be silly, Lucy. Jenn and Sara are such good friends it's easier to have Sara over than to listen to Jenn whine all afternoon."

"I'm still grateful," said Lucy.

"How did it go? Is Franny out?"

"No. They sent her for psychiatric tests at the state hospital. Her lawyer really fought for her, but the judge wouldn't have any of it. The judge was a woman, too. I thought she'd be more sympathetic."

"You know what they say—never work for a woman boss," said Karen.

"Or have one for a mother," said Lucy, thinking of Irma.

"What do you mean?"

"Oh, nothing," said Lucy, as the music began. "Look, they're starting."

A horde of small ballerinas thundered on stage, dressed in multicolored practice leotards, and began jumping about exuberantly.

"That isn't Sara's leotard," said Lucy, spotting her youngest in an unfamiliar outfit.

"My mom sent a package of clothes for the girls. She lives in North Conway and gets them real cheap at the outlets there. That one didn't fit Jenn, so we gave it to Sara. I hope you don't mind."

"Are you kidding? How much do I owe you?"

"Forget it. Mom gets them on clearance for practically nothing. She lives to shop." Hearing Tatiana's voice, she fell silent.

"No, no, no!" cried Tatiana. "Stop the music. Girls, you've forgotten everything I've taught you. Remember, you run on tippy toes, and take tiny little steps. And when you jump, you float to the ground like little feathers. Now, back to your places and we'll start from the beginning."

The rehearsal proceeded, but it was very rough. The students seemed to have lost their focus, and Tatiana frequently interrupted to correct them. With so many stops and starts, the show lost momentum. Lucy found herself yawning, except, of course, when Sara and Elizabeth were on stage.

As she watched them perform she thought how sweet their soft little bodies were, clad only in tights, leotards, and ballet slippers. Their bodies belong only to them, she thought, and she vowed to make sure they knew it. She was determined they should never have to suffer the way Franny did. It was up to her to make sure they valued themselves, that they believed no one had the right to hurt them.

By the time the music crested to signal the grand finale, Tatiana's nerves were clearly frayed. She stood to one side of the stage, tapping her foot, as the students trooped onstage to practice their final curtsies.

"Stop, stop the music," she called. "Everyone, look where you're standing. You're not leaving any room for the babies. Now, take a deep breath and step back."

The dancers, busy chatting among themselves, ignored her.

"Ladies," she roared, stamping her foot. Her black eyes flashed, indicating the famous temper was coming to a boil.

"Uh-oh," warned Karen, nudging Lucy with her elbow.

The auditorium was suddenly quiet. Everyone, even the mothers, stopped talking.

"Take a deep breath and step back," repeated Tatiana, almost whispering. The dancers obeyed. "Start the music. We will continue," she said.

The mothers all let out a collective sigh of relief. Tears and hysteria had been avoided.

Now there was room for the littlest dancers, the preschoolers, to tiptoe on stage to complete the tableau. Finally the music stopped, and the curtain closed, with all the dancers behind it.

Tatiana stepped forward to give her final instructions to the mothers. She leaned forward, clutching her clipboard and squinting against the spotlights.

"Dress rehearsal will begin at three-thirty sharp on Thursday. All the instructions are on the pink sheet. I hope you'll all cooperate. *Please* don't bring children who aren't in the show to the dress rehearsal.

"Today's rehearsal was not up to standard, but I expected that. We'll have all the kinks worked out by Friday." She crossed her fingers and held them up. "Now, open the curtain," she instructed, turning to face the dancers and consulting the clipboard.

"Mindy Carter, I hope you will have your hair in a bun on Thursday. Caitlin and Catherine Brown, you have to get rid of those bangs for the dress rehearsal. Use gel. Jennifer Volpe, pink tights means theatrical pink, not fuchsia. No jewelry of any sort—that includes earrings, Michelle Pinkus."

Karen nodded as Tatiana went down the list. "The girls call that the black list," she told Lucy. "It's, like, so embarrassing," she said, mimicking her oldest daughter. She rolled her eyes and went off to retrieve Jenn.

Lucy followed her backstage to look for Sara and Elizabeth. Shepherding them out of the auditorium, she paused to talk with Tatiana.

"How did the phone calls go? Any news?"

Tatiana shook her head.

"I guess it wasn't such a good idea after all."

"I wouldn't say that. I picked up some interesting gossip. Jennifer and Ludmila aren't speaking to each other. Something about a man." Tatiana nodded know-ingly. "And Louise is in jail!" Her eyebrows shot up. "Janet says it's something to do with a custody case. She's divorcing her husband. And Sally, she's the one who writes for *Dance* magazine? She's going to put something in her column about Caro and she told me to get on the local TV news. I called WPZ this morning and they're sending a crew over. In fact," she said, nar-rowing her eyes and peering past the stage lights into the auditorium, "I think that's them now."

Lucy turned and recognized the attractive newscaster who presented the local news every night. She was fol-lowed by a large man burdened with numerous bags and cases.

"She looks much smaller than she does on TV," said Lucy.

"And younger," said Tatiana. "Hi! I'm over here!" she called, waving to catch their attention.

"Can we stay and watch?" asked Elizabeth.

"Sorry, it's getting late."

"Please?"

"We don't have time. Besides, you can see it all on TV tonight."

When she pushed open the door to leave the build-ing a sudden gust of wind caught it, and she struggled to hang on to the heavy door so it wouldn't swing back and hit one of the children.

"Hurry to the car, girls," she said. "It looks like we're in for a storm." The oppressive stillness of the early afternoon was gone and the sky was filled with ominous dark clouds. The leaves on the trees were blown bottom side up, a sure indication that rain was on the way.

"Now, where is Toby?" she asked, once the girls were safely buckled in and she'd started the car. "I told him to be here at four-thirty, and it's past that." The school parking lot was emptying out rapidly, and there was no sign of her son.

Lucy drove around back, taking a swing past the ball field, and then headed for the park. Huge raindrops began pattering down on the windshield, and she thought he might have taken refuge in the bandstand. As she circled the park the rain began falling in heavy sheets, and even with the wipers going full speed she could just barely see it was deserted. She finally spied him on the front porch of Country Cousins, along with a handful of other boys. They were seated on the long deacon's bench, eating the penny candy the store was famous for.

Lucy pulled up, honking, and Toby hopped in the car. "This isn't the high school auditorium," she snapped.

"No, Mom. It's a store," he said.

"Don't be smart with me. I told you to meet me at the school," she fumed. "You've got to start being more responsible."

"Sorry. I forgot. Do you think they'll have practice tonight?"

"Probably. Little League is like the postal service. Neither rain nor snow . . ." She was interrupted by a clap of thunder.

"You're not supposed to stand out in the open during a thunderstorm," said Toby.

"No, you're not," she agreed, as a jagged fork of lightning flashed in the sky.

When Bill dashed into the house an hour later, his beard and eyelashes glistening with raindrops, Lucy greeted him with a big kiss and a smile.

"What are you so happy about?" he asked. "I had to call off practice."

"I thought you would," she said, giving the gravy a stir before raising the spoon to her lips to taste it.

"Hey, is that gravy?"

"It is. We're having your favorite supper: meat loaf and gravy, mashed potatoes, sugar snap peas from the garden, and salad, of course, with our own lettuce and radishes. For dessert, there's chocolate pudding with whipped cream. Better get out your fork."

"Wow, Lucy. How'd you do it?"

"Do not question the wonders of modern food technology. Just enjoy. Would you prefer ze Bud or ze Rolling Rock for ze cocktail?"

"Don't care."

He watched, grinning, as she popped the tab with a flourish and poured the beer into a pub mug for him.

Dinner didn't take long to eat, even allowing for the fact they were sitting in the dining room instead of the kitchen and using forks instead of fingers. Lucy assigned Toby to do the dishes and, conscious that his stock was not very high with his mother, he mounted only a weak protest before heading into the kitchen.

Lucy and Bill and the girls went into the family room to watch the news.

"We saw that lady," exclaimed Sara when the newscaster appeared seated alongside a male colleague.

"Turning to you, Janet," he said, "I understand you have a special plea from a local teacher."

"That's right, Jack." The camera closed in on Janet. "Tinker's Cove dance teacher Tatiana O'Brien appealed today for help in finding her missing friend and mentor, retired dance professor Caroline Hutton. I spoke with Tatiana today in the auditorium of the Cove Regional High School, where she was conducting a rehearsal for an upcoming performance."

"That's Tatiana! There she is," squealed Sara, her voice shrill with excitement.

They all watched intently as Tatiana held up a framed photograph of Caro.

"I'm asking anyone who may have seen this woman to contact the police immediately."

"How long has she been missing?" asked Janet, waving a microphone in front of Tatiana.

"There's been no sign of her for almost three weeks. I'm very concerned."

"Why exactly are you so concerned?" Janet adopted a serious expression; she was determined to show she could conduct an in-depth interview. WPZ was fine for now, but she had big plans for the future.

"Because this is so out of character. Caroline Hutton is a responsible, caring person. If she was planning a trip, she would have told her friends and neighbors. She lived alone, she has no family, so it's up to us to find her and bring her home safely."

Tatiana's face faded from the screen, replaced by Jack and Janet at the news desk.

"Janet, what do the police say?"

"Well, Jack, local police conducted an extensive search but found no trace of the vanished woman. I spoke today with Tinker's Cove Police Chief Oswald Crowley."

"He doesn't look very happy to be on TV," observed Lucy when the chief's scowling face appeared.

"Chief Crowley, have there been any new developments in the Caroline Hutton case?"

"No." Crowley was a man of few words. There were beads of sweat on his forehead; he was obviously uncomfortable about being on TV.

"Are you following any new leads?"

"One or two," said Crowley, "but it's too soon to comment."

"If one of our viewers recognizes Caroline Hutton, what should they do?"

"They should call the department, on our nonemergency business line. That number is 861-1234."

The number appeared on the screen in white letters, which remained after Crowley's image disappeared, replaced by the photograph of Caro.

"Once again," came Janet's voice-over. "If you have seen this woman, please call 861-1234."

"Thanks for that report, Janet," said Jack. "It's quite a mystery, isn't it?"

"It sure is, Jack. And after these words from our sponsors, our Channel Five weatherman, Ed Santini, will explain another mystery, tomorrow's weather."

After the newscast, Lucy helped Toby look for the missing book and found it under his bed. She supervised baths for the girls, read them their favorite Angelina book, and tucked them in bed. Toby was allowed to stay up an hour later, and when Lucy peeked in on him he was sorting through his baseball cards.

The house seemed unusually quiet to Lucy, and she could hear the rain drumming on the roof when she returned to the family room. It had originally been a sun porch, but Bill had made it into a year-round room by installing insulation and thermal glass windows. Instead of turning on the TV, she pulled out the old basket in which she kept family photographs. She always meant to put the best ones in an album but somehow never got around to it. She was looking for a particular envelope of photos, and it wasn't long before she found it.

She had snapped an entire roll of film one day last summer when she and Bill took the kids on a picnic.

One of Bill's customers had told him about a beautiful waterfall hidden deep in the woods.

As she flipped through the photos, Lucy remembered how Bill had taken a day off between jobs, and she had packed a lunch of fried chicken, tomato sandwiches, hard-boiled eggs, lemonade, and brownies. It had been a real adventure as they followed the unfamiliar directions Bill had scribbled down on an envelope. They were explorers in a fragile craft seeking the eighth wonder of the world. At least, that's what she had told the kids as they pressed on, leaves and branches brushing against the Subaru.

They heard the falls before they saw them, a torrent of ice-cold water rushing along a downhill streambed littered with slippery black boulders. It was not one single waterfall but many, and the rushing water had carved out pools deep enough to swim in. One pool glowed a beautiful luminous green, catching and concentrating the sunshine in its depth. They had never seen anything like it.

It had been a special day for the whole family. Bill and the kids swam, Lucy dangled her feet in the frigid water, and they made short work of the huge picnic. It was quite late in the afternoon before they packed up their things; they all hated to leave the magical place.

"What are you doing?" asked Bill when he found her on the couch. He'd finished an estimate for a possible job and was looking for company.

"Taking a trip down memory lane," said Lucy. "Remember the day we went to the waterfall? What was it called?"

Bill settled beside her, draping an arm around her shoulders, and took the photo.

"Crystal Falls."

"Near Bridgton, right?"

"Yeah. It's a good drive from here." Bill took the

pictures from her and looked through them. "The kids have grown a lot, haven't they?"

"Especially Toby."

Bill got up and switched on the TV. "The Sox are supposed to play tonight."

"They probably got rained out."

"The game's in New York. They'll be back in Boston tomorrow, and Fred Slack said he'd give me his tickets. I'd love to take Toby. He's never been to Fenway Park."

"Tomorrow? It's sort of short notice."

"He has season tickets and he can't go. They're box seats, right behind first base. We could leave in the afternoon, catch the game, and sleep over at my sister's house. If we got an early start in the morning we could even be back before school starts. What do you think?"

"It's fine with me. I didn't know you were such good friends with Fred."

"I didn't either. I stopped by his office to ask about the camera."

"I checked prices. They're still about a thousand dollars. We can't afford one now."

"Fred says there's no problem. He said to go ahead and get one and he'll push the claim right through."

"What about the deductible?"

"Unh?"

"We have a five-hundred-dollar deductible on our policy. It doesn't pay until we pay the first five hundred."

"No problem. He said the deductible is waived. Special circumstances."

"No way. I never heard of an insurance company paying a claim without asking a lot of questions."

"I'm gonna get the camera tomorrow morning, okay? That way I can tape the game and the rehearsal, too. I'll use plastic but Fred said I should have the money real quick."

"It's okay with me, but I bet we'll get stuck with the bill," predicted Lucy gloomily.

"Damn." Bill reached for the remote and started switching through the channels. "It's raining in New York. Game's over."

"That's too bad," said Lucy, laying her head on his shoulder. "What could you do instead?" She reached up and stroked his beard, gently pulling his face toward hers. She kissed him lightly on the lips, and was gratified when he responded with a long, lingering kiss.

"I have a few ideas," he said, and flicked off the TV.

Twenty-three

Pale pink tights (no shiny tights).

The thunderstorm had cleared the air, and Wednesday dawned clear and bright but chilly. Lucy made Toby and Elizabeth wear their jackets to school, but saw they made a point of taking them off as soon as they got out of the house. She had better luck with Sara, who was little enough to enjoy being fussed over as Lucy zipped up her pink windbreaker. Lucy dropped her off at Kiddie Kollege, and then went straight to the post office. She wanted to mail a "thinking of you" card to Franny before she went to her appointment with Doc Ryder.

Even Franny's grim situation couldn't dampen her spirits this morning. Last night she'd been reassured that Bill still desired her, even after twelve years of marriage and three children, and in the middle of her current pregnancy. She felt remarkably light on her feet as she skipped up the post office steps.

"You look mighty cheerful this morning," said Barney, greeting her with a big smile.

"I am and I have to admit I feel a little guilty about it, what with Franny locked up in that awful place. I wish I could do more than send her a card."

"I think that's prob'ly all you can do, Lucy. Visitors are pretty much limited to relatives and attorneys, and they're strictly regulated. I'm sure she appreciates knowing folks are thinking about her."

"We can do more than that, Barney. How come there wasn't more of an investigation? Why is Horowitz so eager to pin this on Franny?"

"Lucy, I've been through that file myself about a hundred times. Do you think I want to see her spend the rest of her life in jail?" Barney took off his police cap, ran his hands through his salt-and-pepper butch-cut hair, and replaced it. "Trouble is, sometimes cops are more interested in making the conviction than finding out the truth."

"What do you mean?"

"Horowitz has got one hell of a case against Franny. It's straight out of a criminal-science textbook, complete with means, motive, and opportunity." Barney ticked them off. "Means—the video camera was in her possession and it's covered with her fingerprints. Motive—Slack fired her and she wanted to get back at him. A classic case of revenge. Opportunity—who knew the old guy's routine better than Franny?"

"What about his wife? Maybe she was sick and tired of him after fifty years."

"She was having lunch with Miss Tilley."

"I wouldn't put it past Miss Tilley to stretch the truth for a friend. She had her differences with Slack."

"Lucy, we're talking about two elderly ladies who happen to be very civic-minded," protested Barney.

"What about Ben? I just have this gut feeling that he did it. Even good boys can get in trouble," she said, wishing too late that she could swallow her words. Barney must be sensitive about Eddie's brush with the law.

"Don't I know it," agreed Barney ruefully. "I've gone over it and over it. Unless the Gilead police can't tell time, he was in their custody from ten o'clock on."

"Time of death?"

"Between twelve-thirty and two P.M."

"Okay, what about Fred? It's no secret he didn't get along with is father."

"Fred was showing houses to some clients, and Annemarie had an appointment with her therapist from twelve-thirty to one-thirty and went straight to a one-thirty meeting of the Junior Women's Club. The other members say she arrived a few minutes late."

"Oh," said Lucy, momentarily distracted by the news that Annemarie was in therapy. "What about fingerprints? Did you check the camera for fingerprints?"

"We did," said Barney. "And you know what? Practically everybody in this town left their prints on it at one time or another. What do you do? Lend it out to anybody who asks?"

"Pretty much," admitted Lucy.

"Well, like I said, the thing was covered with prints. But one person's prints definitely weren't on it. You know whose?"

"Ben's."

"Right."

"I'm still not convinced." Lucy had a sudden inspiration. "What about the tape? The one that was in the camera?"

"Gone."

"Then if you find the tape, you'll find the killer. Did Franny have the tape?"

"They didn't find it when they searched her house, but she coulda got rid of it."

"Darn. There must be some way we can prove Franny's innocent."

"I sure as hell don't know how," said Barney, looking extremely glum.

"We'll think of something," she said, hoping she

sounded more optimistic than she felt. "Hey, what's this I hear about Caro turning up in Graceland?"

"We've been getting reports from all over. You wouldn't believe the crazies that call when a story makes the TV news. And you know what? I think she really was spotted in North Conway."

"North Conway?"

"Yeah. A New Hampshire state trooper says he's pretty sure he talked to her at an ice cream stand. Passed the time of day with this nice old woman and didn't think anything of it till he got back to the barracks and saw her photo on a bulletin board. Doesn't even remember what kind of car she was driving. He did say she had a little girl with her. She claimed it was her grandchild."

"Caro isn't a grandmother," said Lucy.

"Not that we know of. Well, I better get back to work before the chief misses me."

Lucy got in line at the stamp window. There were several people ahead of her, but she didn't mind. There was no sense in hurrying to her appointment just to sit in the doctor's waiting room. Besides, she couldn't help overhearing the conversation selectman Hancock Smith was having with Winchester College president Gerald Asquith. The two men had met in front of the numbered boxes.

"Can hardly believe it myself," she heard Smith proclaim. "He left his entire fortune to the historical society, house included. All told, it could come to nearly a million dollars," he told Asquith, who looked slightly sick at the thought. It was no secret that the college had been flirting with financial disaster for some time.

"The house is a gem," continued Smith. "Virtually untouched. A fine example of Victorian architecture, with the original furniture. What a treasure!

"Of course," he said, thoughtfully scratching his

chin, "Mrs. Slack has a life tenancy, but she's pretty old. I don't imagine it will be too long before the society takes possession." Smith paused; a rather unpleasant thought had obviously occurred to him. He lowered his voice. "I just hope she doesn't take it into her head to modernize the place or something. You can never tell with these old ladies."

"That's for sure," agreed Asquith, visibly brightening. "Take my aunt, for instance. Her husband died confident that he'd left his considerable fortune to the National Rifle Association. Somehow she undid the will and the money went to the Ethical Culture Society instead."

"Really?" Smith was clearly unsettled. "How could that be legal?"

"I don't know." Asquith shrugged, but something in his tone told Lucy that he was planning on finding out.

"Next," said the postal clerk. Lucy was embarrassed to realize she was holding up the line and quickly stepped up to the window.

"Lucy, this will never do." Lucy was standing on the scale in Doc Ryder's examining room, and the doctor was sliding the weights across the bar. "You've gained nine pounds in four weeks. That's more than two pounds a week. That's double what you should gain," he scolded, beginning his usual harangue.

Lucy, however, didn't hear him. Her thoughts were miles away as she climbed onto the examining table.

North Conway, she thought to herself as the doctor lifted her shirt and palpated her abdomen. There was a dance outlet in North Conway; Karen had mentioned it. Maybe Caro was stocking up on leotards and tights. It was a link of sorts, anyway.

Lucy hardly noticed when the doctor applied the

cold stethoscope to her tummy. Barney had said Caro was with a child, a little girl. A student? A child of a student? That was more likely, thought Lucy. But why?

Mechanically placing her feet in the stirrups, she remembered the photographs of laughing children in Caro's album, and the childish map. Snake's House. Crystal Falls. Of course, she realized, sitting bolt upright.

"Whoa!" exclaimed a surprised Doc Ryder. "If you wouldn't mind lying down, I'll be finished in a minute."

"Sorry," said Lucy, reclining on the table. Crystal Falls. No wonder the photographs seemed so familiar. Wasn't Crystal Falls the place where they'd had the picnic last summer?

"You haven't heard a word I've said, have you?" demanded the doctor, offering his hand so she could hop off the table.

"What?" asked Lucy.

"Everything's fine. See you in four weeks."

"Okay." Lucy nodded.

"Four weeks, four pounds. Got that?"

"Right. Four weeks, four pounds. See ya."

Hurrying out of his office, Lucy glanced at her watch. It was only ten-thirty; Sara would be at Kiddie Kollege until noon. She had plenty of time; she'd just stop by at Sue's house. There was something she wanted to ask her.

Twenty-four

Male relatives are NOT *allowed in the dressing room.*

"Lucy, what's the matter?" exclaimed Sue, opening the door for her. "You look upset."

"I'm fine," said Lucy. Passing the hall mirror, she noticed her hair was sticking out wildly all over her head. "I've been thinking," she said, rummaging in her bag for a comb and smoothing it back in place. "I think I know where Caro is."

"Really?" Sue's face lit up in excitement. "Where?"

"It's really just a hunch."

"Tell me all about it. I just made a lemon pound cake. Want some?"

"Sure." Lucy sat down at the kitchen table and glanced around while she collected her thoughts. Sue had recently redone the kitchen, abandoning the country look for a slicker fifties effect. Now the floor was covered with black and white vinyl tile, and custom-made shelves displayed her collections of cookie jars and humorous salt and pepper shakers.

Sue put the cake in the middle of the red Formica table and poured two cups of herb tea. Lucy waited for her to sit down and slice the cake before beginning.

"I think Caro's at her family's old summer place. It's way off the road in the woods near Bridgton, close to Crystal Falls."

"How did you come to this conclusion?" asked Sue, taking a bite of cake.

"Lots of little things kind of fell into place. I had a chance to look at her family album and there were pictures of the cabin and the falls. Barney said she was actually seen in North Conway, and that's not far from there. It seems right somehow."

"Who saw her?"

"A state trooper. And she had a little kid with her."

"It doesn't make sense to me," argued Sue. "Why would she make such a secret about going to her summer place?"

"That's what I wanted to ask you about," said Lucy. She took a sip of tea. "Tatiana told me one of Caro's old students is in jail because of a divorce. Maybe she's refusing to give up her child and she's asked Caro to hide the kid. Do you know anything about that sort of thing? Does it come up at the women's center?"

"What's her name?" asked Sue sharply.

"I think it's Ludmila . . . no. Louise."

"Louise!" exclaimed Sue. "Where have you been, Lucy? Don't you read the papers?"

"All I seem to read anymore is this book on painless childbirth. I can't seem to get through it."

"I hate science fiction, too," quipped Sue, leaving the kitchen and returning with a pile of *People* magazines. "There was a story in here pretty recently," she muttered, checking the tables of contents. "Here it is. 'Sexual Slavery in D.C.' All about the Philip Roderick case. It's been in the news for weeks."

"Philip Roderick? That's the name of Franny's lawyer."

"Fred's old college buddy is Philip Roderick?" Sue was incredulous. "If it's the same Philip Roderick, he's a beast."

"I met him," said Lucy. "He's charming."

"Well, read this." Sue shoved the magazine across the table. "See how charming you think he is."

Lucy helped herself to another piece of cake and took the magazine.

" 'Normally unflappable residents of the nation's capital, jaded as they are by the antics of congressmen and senators, reeled last week as details of a bizarre case of sexual slavery and child abuse unfolded in probate court,' " read Lucy.

" 'Pleading for a divorce, Louise Roderick charged that her husband, prominent lawyer Philip Roderick, had abused her and forced her to become a sexual slave.

" ' "I trained as a ballet dancer, so I was used to discipline. I never questioned the things my husband asked me to do; I guess I wanted to be dominated," confessed Louise Roderick, explaining why she went along with her husband's demands for kinky sex, which included bondage and whippings.

" 'Louise Roderick's tolerance ended, however, when she discovered Philip Roderick was having sex with their daughter, Melissa, then five years old. "I found bloodstains in her underwear, and when I questioned her she became very withdrawn. She used to have lunch with Philip every Saturday, and afterward he'd take her to a movie. I didn't realize that they stopped at his office in between."

" 'This realization prompted Louise Roderick to seek counseling, and soon after she demanded a separation. Melissa, now seven, lives with her mother, and her therapist reports she has made "great progress toward recovery."

" 'Family Court Judge Willard Hayes, however, was not impressed with Louise Roderick's claims and awarded custody of the child to Philip Roderick. In his decision he cited Louise Roderick's mental instability, and her inability to support the child. Louise Roderick has been collecting welfare since the separation, having refused her wealthy husband's offer of a generous allowance and child support.

" 'Welfare officials are reportedly looking into whether Louise Roderick is legally entitled to collect payments, now that it has been revealed that she refused support from her husband.'

"Oh, my God," said Lucy, slicing another piece of cake. "He had sex with a five-year-old?"

"His own child." Sue nodded. "Is it the same guy?"

Lucy studied the picture alongside the article. "It's him. But maybe he didn't do it. The judge didn't believe the wife's story."

Sue gave a snort of disgust. "It's classic. They never do. They always side with the man, especially if he's rich and prominent."

"So you believe the wife?"

"Lucy, imagine how much courage it took for her to speak out. She's gone to jail rather than let the child go with the father. She wouldn't do that if he were Mr. Rogers."

"This must be the 'other business' Fred said Phil had in the area," mused Lucy. "He must suspect Caro's hiding the child."

"He probably does. He's no dummy. You mustn't breathe a word about this cabin. Do many people know about it?"

"I don't think so. I've never heard anybody mention it. Miss Tilley didn't say anything about it, and I think she would have if she knew Caro was in the habit of going there. Barney didn't say anything, so I don't think the police checked it. When we looked at the albums, Tatiana didn't recognize it or anything. It's kind of odd when you think about it, that she never invited anybody there."

"I don't know. There are times I'd like to have a private retreat. Someplace I could go where nobody could find me."

"A place where you could take a bath without anyone knocking on the bathroom door."

"Or find the scissors exactly where you left them," said Sue, shutting a drawer. "I was going to cut that article out for you, but I can't find the damn scissors."

"Never mind. I can tear it. I want to show it to Tatiana and Miss Tilley. Barney, too. If they know what's going on they'll pipe down about looking for Caro."

"Don't tell Barney," warned Sue.

"Why not?"

"Lucy! Caro's breaking the law, and he's a cop. He'd have to arrest her and give the little girl to Roderick. He's got legal custody."

"This stinks," said Lucy. Until now, she'd always believed the law was on her side.

"Yeah," agreed Sue. "Want to split the last piece of cake?"

Twenty-five

This performance is dedicated to Caroline Hutton—dancer, mentor, friend.

Finding Tatiana's studio empty, Lucy climbed up the stairs to her apartment. The door was ajar, so she called out a hello and went in.

Tatiana was kneeling on the floor in front of her stereo, surrounded by a clutter of tapes and papers.

"I'm just making sure the music is perfect for the show," she said, looking up. "I don't want any glitches."

"I can't believe it's this Friday," said Lucy. "It's pretty exciting, isn't it?"

"Nerve-racking's more like it. I only wish Caro was going to see it . . . but we had to go ahead and schedule it," said Tatiana.

"Everything will be fine," said Lucy. "I've got something to show you. Look at this." She retrieved the magazine page from her bag and held it out. "Is this the Louise you told me about?"

"I can't believe this," said Tatiana, slowly sinking onto the sofa as she read the article. When she finished, she looked up at Lucy. "All I can think of is how she adored him, she couldn't wait to get married. I remember her carrying around *Bride's* magazine for months. It was a gorgeous wedding. Incredible flowers, something like six bridesmaids. I never saw her look so beautiful. This is horrible. Poor Louise."

She folded the paper and stroked it with her fingers.

"I used to wonder how she did it. She'd dance until her feet bled. She could do things I could never hope to do. Thirty-six fouetté turns in a row; she could hold an arabesque en pointe forever. I envied her so much. We all did.

"Then one day I found her throwing up in the bathroom right after she ate lunch. I was concerned, and I asked her if she was sick. She said she was fine, she just had to watch her weight. I was disgusted. I'd never heard of such a thing."

"Were she and Caro very close?"

"Oh, yes. I used to be jealous of that, too. Then I realized Caro knew she had problems and was trying to help her."

"You know she's in jail now? She wouldn't let him have the child."

"The child!" exclaimed Tatiana. "That's what this is all about. I bet she asked Caro to hide her."

"That's what I think, too," said Lucy. "At the cabin. The one on the map. Near North Conway."

"It all fits together, doesn't it? That's where Barney said she was spotted."

"We can't tell anybody," cautioned Lucy. "It has to stay a secret. Roderick's right here in town."

"He is?"

"He's supposed to be defending Ben Slack and Franny. Doing a favor for Fred."

"Of course. They went to the same university," said Tatiana. "They used to come to mixers at Winchester together."

"Don't tell anybody about the cabin," warned Lucy. "Roderick mustn't find them."

"You're right, Lucy. I won't say a word."

"I'm getting kind of nervous about those albums," said Lucy. "I feel responsible for them. I think I'd better return them."

"Okay," agreed Tatiana. "I'm done with them. They're in the bedroom."

She went to get them, but returned empty-handed. "It's the oddest thing," she said in a puzzled tone. "I know they were on my bed. I was looking at them this morning."

"What do you mean?"

"They're not there. They're gone."

"Are you sure?" Lucy went to look for herself. "Did you check under the bed? Maybe they fell."

The women went through the bedroom, and the living room, too, but they didn't find the albums.

"They've been stolen," concluded Lucy. "Is anything else missing?"

Tatiana shook her head.

"Roderick must have slipped in while you were teaching."

"Roderick? Here?"

"Who else?"

"I had two classes of babies this morning. I can't take my eyes off them for a minute. Anybody could have come in. I never bothered to lock the door." She shuddered. "I hate the thought of him in my apartment, touching my things. What if I'd come upstairs?"

"It's lucky you didn't. Lucy suddenly felt sick. "Damn. He's got the map."

"It was just a kid's drawing."

"It was pretty detailed. It gave the name of the town, and the state highway number. All he has to do is compare it to a geological survey map. Lots of places around here sell them. To hikers."

"We've got to warn Caro. Do you think she's got a phone?"

Lucy dialed 411, and learned there was no listing for Caroline Hutton in Bridgton.

"What about the police?"

"They'd have to give the child to Roderick. He's got legal custody."

"Then we'll have to go ourselves," decided Tatiana. "I'll cancel my afternoon classes. Come on."

Lucy hesitated.

"Well, what's the matter?" demanded Tatiana. "They could be in danger. We don't have any time to waste."

"You're right," agreed Lucy, surprised at her reaction. There was a time when she would have dashed off without a thought. Now, she found herself ticking off a checklist of responsibilities. Bill and Toby were going to the ball game, Sue wouldn't mind taking the girls for the afternoon. She was free to go. Still, she felt reluctant.

It must be the baby, she decided, patting her tummy. All those mothering hormones were making her cautious and conservative.

"Come on, kiddo," she said, addressing the baby. "It's about time you learned there's more to life than eating and sleeping."

Twenty-six

Pink slippers, strings tucked in.

"Is this right? Is this fifth position?"

Seated in a creaky old rocker on the cabin porch, Caro looked up from her needlepoint. Lisa, in her swimsuit and ballet slippers, had neatly put her feet in a close approximation to fifth position and was struggling to straighten her body and keep her balance.

"Almost," said Caro encouragingly. "You've almost got it."

She smiled, watching the little girl's intense concentration as she tried to bring her swaying hips under control; then she returned to her needlework. If she was honest with herself, she had to admit she really enjoyed teaching the little girl she'd come to think of as Lisa. Where she had once been merciless with her college students, now she could relax and watch a young dancer develop. Immature muscles could not be forced into the proper positions, they had to be gently stretched, and coaxed to turn out.

Caro would have been the first to say she'd had an extraordinarily rewarding life, but there had been no room for marriage or motherhood. In her day a woman had to choose; it was unthinkable to have both a career and a family.

How long had it been? Almost three weeks since

she'd left home and driven to the tourist information center at the Maine border. As instructed, she'd left her own car at home and used a secondhand car bought for cash through the want ads. Once she was at the information center, she'd looked for a woman in a lobster hat and followed her to the section of the parking lot reserved for campers. Caro brought her car alongside a twenty-two-foot Winnebago and in seconds the transfer was made. Lisa was buckled into the front seat, a duffel bag was thrown into the back, and Caro became an instant grandmother.

Watching Lisa practice the five positions, Caro nodded approvingly. The dark smudges under Lisa's eyes were gone, and her cheeks were now tan and plump. Her little body had also rounded out, thanks to Caro's old-fashioned notions about feeding children. In her day boys and girls ate nursery food, dishes rich in milk and carbohydrates, so Caro cooked pancakes, macaroni and cheese, rice pudding, and tuna wiggle for Lisa. And carrots, lots of carrots.

Lisa wasn't used to these kinds of meals but she ate heartily. Caro was surprised at how much this pleased her. Somehow she'd never pictured herself in the role of grandmother bountiful. She blushed to think how she used to castigate her students if they gained an extra pound or two.

Most dramatic of all, Caro thought, was the change that had occurred in Lisa herself. The anxious hunched-forward slump and the scuttling run were gone. Nowadays she threw her shoulders back when she ran. Best of all, her nightmares had stopped and the little girl slept deeply and peacefully through the night.

Caro didn't know how long they could hope to stay undiscovered in the woods. At best, the unheated cabin was a summertime solution.

For the time being, however, things were working out. Caro believed their time together had done Lisa no harm, and she hoped it had done some good. As for herself, she was wholeheartedly enjoying the present, taking each day as it came. She refused to worry. Tomorrow, she thought to herself, would take care of itself.

Twenty-seven

Students are responsible for their belongings.

"Damn."

Philip Roderick stared at the brittle and faded crayon drawing in his hand, crumpled it in disgust, and tossed it away.

The trail he'd been following had petered out—it was a road to nowhere. He was alone in the woods in his black Saab, surrounded by relentless green forest.

He got the topographical map and a compass out of the glove compartment and climbed easily out of the car. He'd been driving for hours, and it felt good to stretch his long legs and muscular frame. He unfolded the map, spread it out on the hood of the car, and studied it.

A cloud of gnats buzzed around his head, and he waved them away, annoyed. He didn't like the woods. The outdoors was dirty and uncomfortable; it was certainly no place for Melissa. He couldn't wait to take his precious girl back to civilization. The car was filled with lavish presents for her—Madame Alexander dolls, party dresses, and a huge stuffed teddy bear.

It was suddenly clear where he'd gone wrong, he realized, checking the compass. Restarting the car, he retraced his route and soon found another trail that showed signs of recent use. When he realized he was approaching a cabin, he braked and reached for his binoculars.

Propping his elbows on the steering wheel to steady the glasses, he raised them to his eyes. He scanned the clearing, the cabin, the porch. When he caught a glimpse of the old woman at the door, his attention was riveted.

His hands tightened on the binoculars, and his body tensed. Anger burned through him. She was poisonous. He hated her. The old witch. She'd wrecked his marriage. Always there, always meddling. She'd fastened herself on Louise. It was the one tie he'd been unable to break. She'd turned Louise against him.

Even now, after the trial and the publicity, he still loved Louise. He'd always loved her, from the first moment he saw her. It was the way she moved, the way she tossed her shiny golden hair, the way she lowered her eyes when she spoke. He'd never wanted anyone so much before. It was more than an obsession—it had been an overwhelming physical need, like an addiction. He'd had to have her.

He'd courted her carefully, knowing he couldn't bear rejection. He'd showered her with notes and flowers. He'd taken her to the most expensive restaurants and the plays it was impossible to get tickets for. When she was with him, he enjoyed knowing her safety depended on him. He'd phoned her constantly, craving the sound of her voice when she said his name. He thought his heart would break when he finally heard her answer the minister, "I will." She was finally his.

She was everything to him, so he hadn't understood her need for other friends. "Why do you want to go out with your girlfriends when you could be with me?" he'd ask. "Let's have lunch at that new French restaurant downtown. I've heard it's great."

Her lashes would flutter, her lips would form a little

half smile, and she'd obediently call the girls and say her plans had changed. Gradually, the friends disappeared from her life; even her mother and sister rarely called. Only the old hag was left, sticking her nose in where it wasn't wanted.

A man has a right to a peaceful home, he'd told Louise. Especially a man who works hard and provides extremely well for his family. He required a more private lifestyle in which he could indulge his desires. After all, the demands of his extremely sensual nature were best met in secret.

He believed in the old saying that a man's home was his castle. In his home, he was the absolute lord and master. That was how it had been in his father's house. When he was a boy, he remembered, his own father had been quick to order him to take down his pants so he could apply the belt. "Spare the rod and spoil the child," or "This hurts me more than it hurts you," his father used to say as his lips twitched in a little smile.

Of course, he now knew the old man had been having his little joke when he said that. Whipping his son hadn't hurt him at all, it had given him enormous satisfaction. Just as he himself derived tremendous pleasure from punishing his wife. The dread in her eyes as he bound her, letting his fingers linger over her skin, and her cries of pain when he lashed her gave him a sense of power and control like no other.

At first, when Louise told him she wanted a divorce, he hadn't believed it. She was as much a part of him as his arm or his leg. He'd felt as if he were being drawn and quartered when she said she was leaving him. "Those whom God hath joined together let no man put asunder." That's what the wedding service said, and that's what he believed. He wouldn't let her leave, and he certainly wouldn't let her take Melissa.

Melissa. He'd adored her from the first moment he saw her, red and wrinkled in the doctor's hands. "Is she all right? Is everything there?" he'd anxiously asked.

A few months later when he was bathing her, he'd been unable to resist the temptation of slipping his smallest finger inside her. He just wanted to make sure she was complete, he rationalized. Her eyes had widened in surprise, and then she'd smiled and chortled. She liked it, he decided, there was nothing wrong with it. She was his, after all, just like her mother. She belonged to him. And now he was going to get her back.

Caro stood in the cabin doorway, looking out. The woods were quiet and still, the air was filled with golden light. Inside, the plain pine walls shone like honey, and bits of mineral in the fieldstone chimney sparkled. Blood-red wild roses, stuffed in a quart jar and set on the table, glowed like jewels in the sunlight. Caro could even see a line of fragile bubbles caught between the water and the glass wall of the jar.

She took a deep breath of the sweet, woodsy air and thought how lucky she was. The old place was full of memories that comforted and warmed her, like the old sweater she pulled around her shoulders on chilly afternoons.

Hearing the gentle hum of an approaching car, she looked up and saw Philip Roderick's black sedan pull into the clearing. Fighting the urge to flee, she forced herself to stand and face him.

At least the little girl she called Lisa was out of the way for the moment, she thought thankfully. The child was playing in the woods, out of sight of the cabin. Caro hoped she would remember the instructions she had repeated so often.

Over and over she had told the little girl, "If someone comes to the cabin you must run and hide until they leave and it's safe to come out."

Caro concentrated on taking steady, regular breaths and willed her heart to stop beating so frantically. She clasped her hands together and straightened her back, watching as Roderick mounted the steps and crossed the porch.

She remembered things Louise had told her about Philip, shameful secrets she could barely speak out loud. How causing pain gave him pleasure, how he loved power and thrived on fear. No matter what happened, she told herself, she mustn't let him think she was afraid.

"Philip," she said, in what she hoped was a conversational tone. "What a surprise."

"Where is she? Where's my daughter?" he demanded, looming over her.

"I don't know what you're talking about," she answered, taking a step backward but looking up at him with steady eyes. Feeling her hands tremble, she shoved them in her pockets.

He was taller than she remembered, and stronger. Physically, she was no match for him. Without any weapon, with no way of calling for help, she was extremely vulnerable. She would have to rely on her wits to defend herself and the child.

"Why don't you come in and talk to me?" she said. "You must be thirsty after your long drive."

Her only hope was to convince him she was alone in the cabin. Fortunately, she was neat and tidy by nature and all traces of the child were tucked away.

"Take a seat," she suggested, casually going to the refrigerator.

"Okay," he said, smiling easily and pulling a chair out from under the table.

Maybe it would work, she thought, reaching for the pitcher of lemonade and pasting a smile on her face. Maybe she could win him over.

"We haven't gotten along very well in the past, have we?" she said. "I can understand why you think I'm hiding Melissa. But I'm not. In fact, I'd like to help you find her." She poured a glass of lemonade and set it on the table.

"Really? I'm surprised," said Roderick.

"Absolutely. Stability is everything for children, and I know you'll provide a good home for her."

"You're good," said Roderick, with a calculating nod. "But you're not good enough." He held up a small pink sock. "It was on the chair."

"Where did that come from?" she exclaimed. She even managed a little laugh.

She had underestimated Philip Roderick, she realized with a sinking heart. She hadn't fooled him, and now she was firmly in his grip. Struggling against him, she tried to think of a way to free herself. She couldn't bear to think what would happen to the child if Roderick found her.

"Stand still," he commanded, and she found herself obeying. Panting from fear and exertion, she watched as he took a length of sturdy cord from his pocket. Bits of self-defense films ran through her mind. A knee to the groin, a quick thrust of the hand, two fingers extended, to his eyes. But even as she remembered the movements she knew she couldn't perform them. She was overpowered in every way, she realized. She was old and tired. Her best hope was to avoid angering him.

"Put out your hands," he ordered. Humiliated, she did, even though they were shaking. "Don't be afraid," he said softly. "I don't want to hurt you. I only want my daughter. Where is she?"

"I don't know what you're talking about," she answered, trying to sound convincing.

"Cut the crap," he growled, grabbing the upper part of her arm and dragging her to the doorway. "You're violating a court order, you know. I've got custody of Melissa. You're breaking the law. Tell me. Now. Where is she?" He tightened his grip on her arm.

"I don't know," insisted Caro, blinking back tears that stung her eyes. She hoped with all her heart that the little girl would stay safely in the woods, far from the cabin.

"You're not fooling me. I know she's here with you," he said, grabbing her arms by her bound wrists and twisting them painfully. "Call her."

Caro gritted her teeth against the pain. "Let go of me," she said. She hated the way her voice sounded— weak and pitiful.

He glared at her, eyes narrowed in disgust, and raised his hand. She turned her head just as his fist crashed into her jaw.

Moaning, she collapsed against the doorjamb and slid to the floor. Her ear roared, the raw skin on her jaw burned, she felt as if the top of her head would explode. She gently explored her mouth with her swollen tongue and tasted blood. Cowering against the doorjamb, she hardly dared to look at him. She was terrified he would hit her again.

"Do it now," he ordered. "Call her."

When she remained stubbornly silent he hauled her to her feet.

"Bitch, bitch, bitch," he muttered, shaking her by the shoulders. Her vision blurred, but she saw his mouth, spitting the words out at her through his teeth. She tried to turn away.

She suddenly felt herself flying across the room, so quickly that she didn't have time to react and break her fall. She fell like a rag doll. She felt blows, kicks jarred her spine, her hips, and she curled into a fetal position. It was dark, and everything was slipping away.

Twenty-eight

Lost and found—at studio.

His rage spent, Philip Roderick went out and stood on the porch.

"Melissa," he called softly, letting his tongue slip over the syllables. "Melissa, come to Daddy."

Hearing no reply, he scanned the woods surrounding the cabin. He smiled to himself. The little minx. They had played this game before. Hide and seek. He loped down the steps and began searching.

He was sure she hadn't gone very far but was hiding nearby, waiting for him to find her. He listened for a soft giggle or a caught breath; he looked for a scrap of bright clothing or a wisp of blond hair. He heard birds. He saw leaves. He'd had enough of the game.

"Melissa!" he called sharply, resting his hands on his hips. "The game's over. It's time to go home."

The birds fell silent, the woods were still. There was no sign of his daughter. He heard the thumping strains of rock music from a car radio and caught a sudden flash of light, a reflection from a windshield or chrome bumper. Someone was coming, he realized, thinking guiltily of the old woman in the cabin. Time for a strategic retreat.

* * *

"That must be it," said Lucy, pointing to a clearing just ahead.

"This was easier than I expected," said Tatiana, glancing at her watch. "We made good time."

"It was lucky those directions were still in the glove compartment. Being a pack rat has its advantages."

"I wouldn't go that far," said Tatiana, casting a disapproving glance at the litter of toys, books, and gum wrappers that filled the Subaru.

As soon as Lucy braked, Tatiana threw open the car door and leaped out, calling Caro's name as she ran to the cabin.

Lucy followed slowly behind her, stiff and tired from the drive. All that was forgotten, however, when she heard Tatiana's shriek. Heart pounding, she ran to the cabin doorway. She clutched the rough wooden frame for support when she saw Tatiana bending over Caro's prone body.

"Is she alive?"

Tatiana answered with a wordless wail.

"Don't move her," cautioned Lucy, trying to remember the first aid course she'd taken soon after Toby's birth. Faced with the responsibility of caring for such a fragile young life, she'd wanted to learn all she could. She grabbed a blanket off one of the beds and gently tucked it around the old woman, assessing her condition as she worked. "She's in shock. We have to get her to a hospital. I'm sure she's got some broken bones, probably internal bleeding, plus the cuts and bruises we can see."

Tatiana wasn't listening. She was cradling Caro's head in her arms, sobbing softly over her

"You'll have to pull yourself together," snapped Lucy. "I can't take care of the two of you. Help me get this mattress off the cot so we can slip it under her."

* * *

From her hiding place in the woods, Lisa watched everything. She saw her father arrive in his car and go into the cabin. A while later she saw him come out. She heard him calling her. He wanted to play hide and seek. She curled herself up into a little ball and wished she could disappear. She didn't like that game.

When she heard the engine of her father's car start, she looked up and saw him drive away. A few minutes later another car came into the clearing and two women got out and went into the cabin.

She wanted to stop hiding and see what was happening inside, but she remembered what Caro had told her. So she stayed in the little hollow at the base of the big pine tree and tried not to move. Her khaki shorts and green T-shirt were good camouflage. She would be discovered only if a searcher stumbled upon her; she was as invisible as a little brown fawn.

"I'll get the car," gasped Lucy. She was out of breath from the exertion of getting the old woman onto the mattress, but she hurried across the clearing. She knew every minute counted.

As she pulled the car up to the porch and flipped down the seat back to make room for Caro, she looked about the clearing anxiously. Where was the child? What if she was hiding in the woods? They couldn't leave her there. A child couldn't survive alone in the forest.

Back in the cabin, Lucy and Tatiana took opposite sides of the mattress and lifted Caro as gently as they could. Panting and struggling with even her small weight, they carefully carried her out to the car. Tatiana climbed in back beside her, crooning words of comfort and stroking her hand.

Once the old woman was settled, Lucy knew she had to find the child. She felt desperately torn; anxious to get Caro the help she needed but unwilling to abandon the little girl.

"Melissa," she called. If the child was in the woods, she was probably terrified. She tried to make her voice warm and friendly, even though she felt frantic. "Melissa, I'm your friend. We have to get Caro to the hospital. You can't stay alone in the woods. Please come out."

The little girl heard Lucy's voice, she heard her say that Caro needed to go to the hospital. She remembered Caro warning her about that. "Someone might try to fool you, they might say I was hurt. They might offer you candy. Don't believe them. Hide. Remember, your friends know what to call you."

Tears trickled down her cheeks. She was scared, and she wrapped her arms tightly around her knees.

"Melissa," called Lucy. Suddenly inspired, she reached into her pocket and pulled out a roll of mints. "I have some candy for you."

There was no answer. Lucy walked around the clearing, scanning the woods, looking for any sign of a child. Maybe she wasn't there after all. What if Roderick had found her and taken her away with him? Maybe she was wasting valuable time that could mean the difference between life and death for Caro.

She decided to give it one more try. "Melissa," she called. "Melissa, Meleese, Meleesa," she sang, remembering how Sara and Elizabeth had special nicknames for their friends. "Melissa, Melessa, Meleesa."

Lucy was astonished when a little girl's head popped out of the bushes directly in front of her. Her blue eyes were round with fear, and her skin was so pale the freckles on her nose stood out sharply.

"It's all right," said Lucy. "I won't hurt you."

"I know," said the child.

Stunned, Lucy thought how close she'd come to leaving the little girl, and hugged her close. Glancing around uneasily, she thought how dark and threatening the woods seemed.

"Hurry," she said, taking Lisa by the hand and running to the car. "Let's go home."

Twenty-nine

A first aid kit is available backstage.

Lucy drove along the rough dirt road as quickly as she dared, gripping the steering wheel with trembling hands and trying to avoid the worst of the ruts and potholes.

Caro appeared to be unconscious, but after one particularly bone-jolting stretch Tatiana saw her eyelids flutter, and she gently stroked the old woman's forehead.

"You're going to be all right," she told her.

Looking down at the little girl who was sitting so quietly beside her, Lucy tried to think of something reassuring to say.

"We're almost there," she said. "There's a store up ahead. We'll call the ambulance from there."

The trees thinned a bit as they drew closer to the main road, and soon Lucy made out the weathered siding of Bickle's Country Store. HOT COFFEE, BAIT, FOOD read the faded signs beside the door.

"I need help," yelled Lucy, running up to the counter. A grizzled old character in overalls nodded sympathetically as she explained, "I've got a badly injured woman in my car. I need to call the rescue squad."

Reaching under the counter he pulled out a phone

and shoved it toward her. A label with emergency numbers had been pasted on the receiver, and Lucy dialed as fast as she could. Her hands were still shaking; she wondered when they'd stop.

"They'll be here real quick," said the storekeeper. "Those EMTs is real smart. Sewed up my leg real good last winter." He hitched up his pant leg and displayed an impressive scar for Lucy's benefit.

She nodded her approval. "I'd better get back to the car and see how my friend's doing. Thanks for the phone."

She strained her ears, hoping to hear the faint wail of the ambulance siren as she crossed the gravel parking area, but she didn't hear anything. She peeked into the car at Caro's still form, her breathing growing ever more shallow, and prayed the rescue squad wouldn't be much longer. She was afraid time was running out for Caro.

Minutes later the ambulance arrived, spitting up gravel as it spun into the parking area, followed by a police cruiser. The sirens were promptly silenced, but the vehicles' red and blue lights continued to flash, and bursts of static noise from their radios filled the air. The uniformed EMTs immediately began tending to Caro, and the police officer approached Lucy.

"I need some information," he said, taking out a black leather notebook. He was wearing dark sunglasses and Lucy could see herself reflected in them as she gave him Caro's name and address, and her own. When he asked what had happened, Lucy remembered Sue's warning that the police would have to return Lisa to her father. She knew she had to answer carefully.

"My friend and I went to visit Caro at her cabin. This is how we found her."

"Any idea who attacked her? Did she have any enemies?"

Lucy shook her head. "Not that I know of."

"Who's this?" asked the officer, glancing at Lisa.

"My daughter," answered Lucy quickly, surprised that she could tell such a bold lie so easily. She put a protective hand on Lisa's shoulder and drew her close.

The officer made a notation in his pad, thanked her, and conferred with the EMTs. They had efficiently transferred Caro to a stretcher, applied an oxygen mask, and started an IV, and they were ready to whisk her away.

Tatiana, who had been hovering nearby, asked if she could accompany Caro to the hospital.

"No reason why you can't," one of the EMTs told her sympathetically. "But she'll be going straight into surgery. You might end up waiting for hours. Why don't you go home and call later?"

Tatiana seemed unsure what to do. She turned to Lucy.

"You can't do anything at the hospital."

"Okay." Tatiana nodded. "Take good care of her."

"That's guaranteed," said the EMT.

They watched as the ambulance sped off, siren blaring and lights flashing. Lucy glanced at the officer; he was leaning against his cruiser filling out a report.

"Can we go?" she called.

He gave a wave, which she took for permission, and they all climbed back in the Subaru. Lucy rested her head on the steering wheel and let her arms fall into her lap.

"I don't know if I can drive," she said. "I'm so tired."

"I know," agreed Tatiana. "It's like a bad dream, but I can't wake up."

"We need sugar or something."

"I'll get sodas from the store," offered Tatiana.

She watched as Tatiana went into the store. The ballerina wasn't graceful today, she was moving woodenly, reminding Lucy of shell-shocked refugees on TV news clips. Lucy turned to Lisa, who was sitting beside her.

"Don't worry," she said, starting the engine. "I'll take care of you." It was a promise.

The rest of the day was a blur to Lucy. They returned to Tinker's Cove, and she dropped off Tatiana. Then she drove to Sue's to retrieve the girls.

"Lucy, what happened? You look ill. Do you want some tea?"

"No. I want to go home. I'll call you okay?"

Back in the car, an exhausted Lucy thought this was surely the longest day in her life.

Sara and Elizabeth were full of energy, however, and thrilled to learn that Lisa would be staying with them for a few days. No explanation seemed necessary, so Lucy didn't give one. The girls were used to having their family expand when their friends slept over, or when Lucy babysat.

Bill, however, might not be satisfied with such a casual explanation. Lucy was trying to think up a plausible story when she pulled off Red Top Road into her own driveway. She was surprised when she saw Bill and Toby ready to leave in the pickup; she'd completely forgotten they were going to the Red Sox game tonight.

"I got the camcorder," said Bill, holding up a vinyl case for her to see. He was grinning broadly.

"Great." She couldn't help smiling, too. He looked so happy.

"Fred said he'll be by tomorrow with the check."

"Okay. Have a good time," she called, waving goodbye.

It wasn't until she'd ushered the girls into the house that she realized she would be alone with them for the night and they might all be in some danger. Philip

Roderick hadn't hesitated to beat up Caro; he was a violent man. What could she do if he tried to take Melissa, alias Lisa? She hadn't noticed anyone following them, the few times she'd thought to check her rearview mirror. That didn't mean anything, she realized—he could get her name and address from the Bridgton police. Lucy shivered, and shot the bolt on the kitchen door.

Thirty

Thank you to the volunteers who make the show run so smoothly.

Shortly after Lucy and Bill had moved into the old farmhouse in Tinker's Cove, they had gone to the Broadbrooks Free Library and applied for library cards. Lucy had been thrilled when Miss Tilley told her their house had probably been a station on the Underground Railroad.

"After all," the librarian told her, "the original builder, Simon Lothrop, was an abolitionist of the first order. He originally lived on Center Street, but he sold that house in 1851 and built your house, where he lived until he died in 1894. It's always been rumored that he found the house in town too risky, so he moved out to Red Top Road, where the fugitive slaves wouldn't be observed." Miss Tilley leaned closer. "Are there any secret passages? Tunnels? Hidden rooms?"

"Not that I know of," said Lucy. But that evening they had searched the whole house, top to bottom. Bill took measurements, they knocked on walls and pried up floorboards, but they couldn't find any trace of a hiding place.

"Maybe they meant the root cellar," said Lucy, grimacing. She'd had to go down there once to turn off the water when a pipe burst, and she hadn't enjoyed the experience. It was dirty and spidery, accessible only through a trapdoor in a small closet off the pantry, tucked under the kitchen stairs.

"Those old-timers were pretty thrifty," concluded Bill. "If there was a hidden chamber, it was probably converted into a usable room when the war was over."

"I'm disappointed," Lucy told him. "It would have been neat."

"I'd be more disappointed if she'd said he was a pirate, or a miser, instead of an abolitionist. Then there might've been a hoard of gold coins," speculated Bill.

"Or love letters. Or a diary," Lucy added wistfully.

Tonight, when she heard a light tap and opened the kitchen door to admit three women, Lucy couldn't help thinking that the house was finally living up to its reputation as a shelter for fugitives.

"Lucy, this is Paula, from the shelter." Sue introduced a slight, wiry woman with tightly curled hair.

"Hi," said Lucy. "Glad to meet you," she added when Paula stretched out her hand. Lucy wasn't used to shaking hands.

She turned and gave Tatiana a quick hug. "Any news from the hospital?"

"I spoke to the doctor. He said it was a real good sign that she made it through surgery. She's got lots of broken bones, a bruised kidney, some brain damage. She's in a coma."

"She'll come through it, she's a fighter," said Lucy, trying to sound confident. She wrapped her arm around Tatiana's shoulders and led her to the table. "I thought we'd meet here," she said. "There's coffee, and the kids are watching TV in the family room."

"Fine with me," agreed Sue, pulling out a chair. "Paula, why don't you tell Lucy what you told us in the car?"

"Okay. I called a few people I know. At the shelter

we're very careful to stay on the right side of the law. It's taken years but now we have a good working relationship with the police and the DA and we don't want to jeopardize it. But I do have contacts with some people who are part of an underground network, and your friend Caro was working with them. My contact was pretty upset when I told her what had happened. They want to get Melissa into a safe house as soon as possible. Until then, it's up to us to protect her."

"I'm having second thoughts, especially since Bill's away tonight," said Lucy, resting her hands on her tummy. "What if Roderick followed me home? I wish I could call Barney."

"You can't do that, Lucy," said Sue. "Barney's a cop and he'd have to hand her over to Roderick. Remember, he's got legal custody."

"Why is Roderick free?" demanded Tatiana. "Why haven't they arrested him for attacking Caro? Lucy, what did you tell the policeman this afternoon?"

"I told him that **we** didn't see Caro's attacker, and I said Lisa was my daughter. Was that the right thing to do?" she asked, turning to Paula.

"I would have done exactly what you did," said Paula. "But you could be charged with obstructing justice. Maybe even conspiracy, or kidnapping."

"I had no idea," said Lucy, turning pale. "I was only trying to protect Lisa."

"You didn't actually see Roderick, did you?" asked Paula.

Lucy shook her head.

"Of course it was him," insisted Tatiana. "Who else could it have been?"

"The police can't arrest him without evidence. Only Caro can identify him, and she's unconscious. He's still holding all the cards, believe me."

"It's not fair," complained Tatiana.

"That's why women like Louise Roderick have to break the law to protect their children," said Paula. "Studies show women are at a real disadvantage in court."

"So what are we gonna do?" demanded Sue. "Lucy's scared, and she ought to be. She could be in real danger out here all alone. Maybe Lisa'd be safer at my house in town."

"It would be very risky to move her," added Paula.

"Thanks for the offer," said Lucy. "I think she should stay here. She's gone through an awful lot for a little girl. I feel like I'm the one reliable person in her life right now. I want to keep her."

"Then I'll stay here with you tonight," said Sue.

"Thanks," said Lucy, smiling at her friend.

"That's the best plan," agreed Paula. "The network will be coming for her tomorrow. Just hang in there till then."

"How will I know who they are?" asked Lucy. "Is there a secret password or something?

"Actually, there is," said Paula, slightly embarrassed. "You'll get a phone call inviting you to a Tupperware party."

"You've gotta be kidding," muttered Sue, rolling her eyes.

"As God is my witness," said Paula. "Tupperware. They'll give you a time and place, and you bring the kid. They might come here, in which case they'll thank you for hostessing the party and tell you what prizes you can win."

"I don't really have to have a Tupperware party, do I?" asked Lucy warily.

"No," said Paula, smiling for the first time that evening. "It's just a cover. You're not going to win any prizes either. Oh, there's one other thing. Keep calling her Lisa. It's important. She has identification as Lisa Williams. Don't use the other."

"Okay," said Lucy as an explosion of youthful voices erupted in the family room.

"Sounds like bedtime is overdue," said Tatiana. "We'd better get going."

"Be sure you lock up tonight. Don't take any chances," urged Paula, squeezing Lucy's hand.

"I'll be careful," she promised, locking the door behind them and turning to face Sue.

"What are you looking so glum for, Lucy? I'm surprised you're not more excited. This is a real adventure!" Sue's eyes were sparkling.

"Well, since you're so thrilled to be spending the night in mortal danger, I guess you won't mind taking the first shift," said Lucy, yawning, as she loaded the coffee mugs into the dishwasher. "I'm going to bed as soon as I get the kids settled. Wake me at two!"

Thirty-one

All ensemble dancers' names appear in alphabetical order.

Although Lucy was bone-tired and couldn't wait to get to bed, she couldn't fall asleep. Her body refused to relax, and she found herself replaying the day's events over and over in her mind. She panicked every time she remembered how close she'd come to leaving the woods without Lisa.

The little girl had joined easily in Sara and Elizabeth's bedtime routine. Now, teeth brushed, face and hands washed, she was tucked in the trundle bed in the girls' room.

Lucy couldn't understand how any sane authority could return the child to her father. He seemed nice enough, she admitted to herself—she'd actually liked him when she met him at the courthouse. But now she knew his polished appearance and suave manners concealed a sadistic character.

Why do men do these things, she wondered.

She thought of Franny, so terrified of her husband that she believed the only way to escape was to kill him. And poor Kitty Slack, treated like a servant for years by a man who certainly abused her mentally, if not physically.

They do it because they can get away with it, she decided, punching her pillow and turning on the light.

Women had to fight back, Lucy decided. Giving in just made it worse. They had to demand fair treatment or they'd never get it. And as soon as Lisa was in the safe house, she promised herself, she was going to do whatever she could to help Franny. The way to start, of course, was by finding out who really killed Slack.

She picked up a pad and pencil and began making a list of possible motives. First, of course, was money. Who would benefit? She thought of Hancock Smith, bragging to Gerald Asquith in the post office. Just how far would he go for the historical society, she wondered.

Revenge? Plenty of people, Miss Tilley included, had reason to hate Morrill Slack. Who knew what grudges and resentments seethed inside the breasts of these proper New Englanders, buttoned-down under layers of oxford cloth and virgin wool?

Family? From what she'd learned from Kitty, she suspected there were plenty of motives there. She knew he was a horrible husband. What kind of father had he been? Strict? Demanding?" Authoritarian? She was willing to bet Fred had felt the back of a hairbrush or the sting of a belt more than once.

Slowly, Lucy drew a circle and wrote Kitty's and Morrill's names inside it. Fred and Annemarie went inside another circle, along with Ben.

Lucy looked at the two circles, then she crossed out Ben's name. She rewrote it, placing it inside a small circle of its own, between the other two.

That was interesting, she thought, yawning. She began ticking off alibis, calculating hours and minutes. Next thing she knew, Sue was shaking her.

"Wake up, Lucy. It's almost three."

"Three? You were supposed to wake me at two."

"You were so tired I wanted to let you sleep, but I couldn't do it. I found myself nodding off. Sorry."

"That's okay," said Lucy, getting up. "Climb in before the bed gets cold."

She stumbled into the bathroom and splashed cold water on her face. Yawning furiously, she staggered downstairs to the kitchen and reached for the coffee tin with the plastic scoop inside. Desperate times called for desperate measures, she rationalized, amused at the pun.

While she waited for the pot to finish brewing, she walked through the house checking the doors and windows. All was secure, at least for the moment.

Lucy sat at the kitchen table, sipping her coffee and staring at the door. She'd made Bill replace the solid door that was originally there, choosing one with a window so she could watch the children playing in the yard. Now that seemed a dubious advantage. It would be so easy for someone like Roderick to smash the glass, reach in, and unlock the door. She froze in her chair, visualizing a black-gloved hand turning the knob.

What would she do then? She had no weapon; they were probably the only people in America who didn't own a gun. They didn't even have a dog. Probably a mistake, she decided, getting up to pop a tape in the portable stereo that stood on the kitchen counter.

A flurry of kicks inside reminded her that physical confrontation was out of the question. Besides, now that she thought about it, she didn't think Roderick would resort to physical violence again. Paula had said he held all the cards, and Lucy was sure he'd use them.

Most probably he'd show up clutching a fistful of legal papers, accompanied by an officer of the law. There were plenty of ways a man could get his way, and most of them were perfectly legal.

* * *

Later, standing in the dining room, Lucy watched the sun rise. Alerted by the birds, who began singing when the sky was still dark, she went to the east-facing windows.

She waited patiently as the black sky became gray, then white, and gradually took on a rosy glow. A few small clouds caught the sun's first rays and glowed luminously, fading only when the sun itself climbed above the mountains. The colors promptly disappeared, a veil of clouds settled in, and another gray day began.

Lucy jumped, startled by the phone, and hurried to answer before the rings woke everybody up.

"Hello," she said, afraid Roderick would answer.

Hearing Bill's familiar voice—"It's me"—she relaxed. "What's up?" she said.

"I've got trouble. The muffler kinda fell off the truck last night. I can't drive it this way, so I'm taking it to a mechanic first thing. Hopefully, I'll be on the road by ten, home by noon."

"That's too bad."

"Is everything okay?" asked Bill, hearing the disappointment in her voice.

"Sure," she answered quickly. "How was the game?"

"Great. I'll tell you all about it when I get home. Love ya."

Lucy replaced the receiver. Somehow she'd thought that if she made it through the night, everything would be all right in the morning when Bill came home. Now she knew how Custer felt when he learned the reinforcements weren't coming.

"Mom, am I going to school or what?" demanded Elizabeth. "Why didn't you wake me up?" It's late."

"Is it? I didn't realize." Lucy bit her lip. Elizabeth

could make the bus if she hurried, but she didn't like the idea of sending her out alone to wait at the bus stop. "On second thought, you might as well take the day off."

"Are you sure?" Elizabeth clearly thought her mother had lost her mind.

"I'm sure. Why rush? School's almost over anyway. You can help me make breakfast, okay?"

The three little girls looked so cute sitting at the table eating their pancakes that Lucy wished Bill hadn't taken the new camcorder last night. She got out the instant camera instead.

Peering through the viewfinder, she focused first on Sara. Impishly, the four-year-old stuck out her tongue, shoved her thumbs in her ears, and waggled her fingers. Lucy took the picture.

The camera buzzed and produced the exposed film. Lucy set it on the table and they all watched as Sara's picture magically appeared.

Inspired, Elizabeth cupped her hands under her chin, pulled down the skin under her eyes, and stuck out *her* tongue. Lucy snapped the photo, then focused the camera on Lisa.

In contrast to her own rowdy girls, Lisa seemed very quiet and withdrawn. She watched their antics as they mugged for the camera, a wistful expression on her face, but didn't join in. When she realized Lucy was going to take her picture, she became self-conscious. Her round, soft features stiffened and took on a wary, adult expression.

"Okay, girls," said Lucy, lowering the camera. "You've got to get dressed and make your beds. Then you can show Lisa your Barbie collection."

Shooing them out of the kitchen, she decided they'd

have to play indoors today. She wasn't about to let them out of the house until Lisa was safely on her way. Checking the clock, she wondered when Sue would wake up. She didn't like being alone, and kept peering anxiously out the window.

Lucy had just finished tidying the kitchen when Sue clattered down the cramped back staircase.

"These things are dangerous," exclaimed Sue, regaining her balance.

"You get used to them. They're part of the antique charm."

"How are you holding up?" asked Sue, making a bee-line for the coffeepot.

"I'm a nervous wreck," answered Lucy. "I guess I'm not cut out for this sort of thing."

"Any word from our friends at Tupperware?"

"Not even a burp," quipped Lucy.

"Well, you haven't lost your sense of humor."

"Mommy," interrupted Sara, tugging at Lucy's sleeve. "Can you put this outfit on Barbie for me? It's too tight."

"Sure," said Lucy, adjusting the doll's costume. "You know," she continued, speaking over Sara's head to Sue, "when Barbie came to our house she had nothing but the evening gown she was wearing. I think her date jilted her and left her at the ball. We took her in out of the kindness of our hearts and she's done very well for herself. Now she has a town house, a Ferrari, tons of clothes, and lots of friends. I should be so lucky."

"It's an inspiring story," agreed Sue, wrapping her hands around her coffee mug. "Let's go into the family room and indulge in some mindless depravity."

"I can't imagine what you have in mind."

"Daytime TV, of course."

Thirty-two

All choreography—Tatiana O'Brien.

While Sue turned on the TV and flipped through the channels, Lucy paced from window to window scanning the yard.

"When will Bill be home?" asked Sue, settling down with Regis and Kathie Lee.

"Around noon, if everything goes all right. He has to get the muffler on the truck fixed."

"Noon sounds kind of optimistic. I think we're on our own. Have you got a plan or anything?"

"Not really," admitted Lucy. "I'm hoping the network gets here before Roderick does. If he's got all the legal papers and everything, I guess I'll have to let him take Lisa. What else can I do?"

"We could hide her. An old house like this ought to have some hidey-holes."

"Well," said Lucy slowly. "There is one, but I wouldn't want to have to use it."

"Maybe he won't come," said Sue, crossing her fingers.

Lucy sipped her coffee and tried to care as an unbelievably beautiful supermodel explained how anyone could improve their appearance by practicing yoga and eating nothing but fruit. Then two hotel chambermaids competed to see who was the fastest bed maker, something the live studio audience seemed to find hilarious. Lucy was glad for the distraction when the girls trooped into the room toting a couple of plastic tubs filled with dolls, and a bright pink wardrobe case.

"Now, who's this?" asked Sue, picking up a little doll.

"That's Skipper," explained Elizabeth. "She's Barbie's younger sister."

"I like Skipper," said Lucy. "Barbie makes me feel so inadequate."

"I know what you mean," said Sue, skeptically taking Barbie's measure. "She's quite a woman. How does she keep her figure?"

"I don't think she ever eats. She's an anorexic with breast implants," said Lucy.

"That would explain it," chuckled Sue. "Does she have lots of boyfriends?"

"Lots and lots," said Elizabeth. "They're all named Ken. I like this Ken best. He never loses his head."

"That's important in a man," said Sue, studying the headless figure Sara showed her.

"Who's this?" asked Lisa, fingering a black-haired male figure doll dressed in a gray suit.

"That's Mr. Heart. He's married to Mrs. Heart and they have twin babies," said Elizabeth.

"Gus and Granola," said Sara, rummaging in the bin and retrieving two small baby dolls dressed in matching pink and blue gingham playsuits.

"Granola is not a name," Elizabeth informed her. "They're really named Andrea and Andrew."

"Granola is too a name," insisted Sara, bolstering her point by appealing to a higher authority. "Isn't it, Mom?"

"Why not? I used to have an imaginary friend called Routine," remembered Lucy. "Mom was very big on structure," she told Sue.

"Routine's not a name either," said Elizabeth.

"It sounds like a name. I think you can name dolls whatever you want. What do you think, Lisa?"

Lisa was huddled over the Heart family dolls. She'd placed the twins in a toy stroller and propped Mrs. Heart behind it. Mr. Heart stood by himself some distance away.

Suddenly, she scooped up Mr. Heart and carried him out of the room. A moment later she returned without him.

"Where's Mr. Heart?" asked Lucy.

"Away on business," she answered, serenely picking up one of the tiny dolls. "I think Granola's a good name." She kissed the little figure and tucked it in the stroller.

There was little to do except wait, and the morning passed slowly. Although Lucy checked the phone frequently to make sure it was working, there was no call from the network. She wandered from window to window, constantly on guard in case Roderick should appear. She helped Sue keep the girls amused by playing an endless game of Monopoly and several hands of Old Maid. She was certain the tension and boredom would drive her mad, and she was absurdly relieved when it was finally time to make lunch.

They had just finished eating their peanut butter sandwiches when they heard the familiar crunch of gravel that meant a car had pulled into the driveway. Lucy rushed to the window hoping to see Bill's red pickup. Instead, she saw a shiny black Saab.

"It's him," she hissed. "Quick. You've got to hide in the root cellar." Lucy rushed into the pantry and yanked open the closet door. "Down there!"

"There?" said Sue, hesitating before descending into the dark, musty hole.

"Make a game of it," said Lucy, thrusting a flashlight into her hand. "Down you go, girls." She picked them up under their armpits and lowered them one by one to Sue. She slammed the trapdoor shut and replaced the piece of linoleum that concealed it. Then she closed the closet door and went out to the kitchen.

Quickly glancing around, she noticed the lunch plates still on the table. She scooped them into the garbage and covered them with a crumpled piece of paper towel. Then, taking a deep breath to steady her nerves, she opened the door. Roderick was just stepping onto the porch.

"Mrs. Stone," he began politely. "I believe we met at the courthouse."

"I remember," said Lucy. "You're Franny's lawyer. How's the case going?"

"No new developments, I'm afraid," he said, furrowing his brow in a concerned expression. "Everything's on hold until the psychiatric exam is completed. Actually, I've come to ask your help on a different matter." He shifted from foot to foot, adopting a pleading expression Lucy had seen on certain dogs. "It's kind of a long story. Do you mind if I come in?"

"I'm sorry," said Lucy. "My husband doesn't allow me to let men into the house when he's not home."

"Very wise of him, I'm sure. But you have nothing to fear from me." His manner was deferential, his smile was reassuring, and his eyes crinkled at the corners.

What an actor, thought Lucy, bracing the door with her foot. "I don't think I can help you."

"I'm sure you can," he said, adopting a slightly more aggressive tone. "I think you might have my daughter. She was staying with Caroline Hutton. When I heard what happened yesterday, on the radio, I was horrified. I checked with the police. They told me you found her." As he spoke his eyes darted around the room behind her, then locked onto hers. "Was my daughter at the cabin? Did you find her?"

"No," said Lucy, staring right back at him. "Only Caro. If I hadn't seen her with my own eyes I wouldn't have believed one human being could hurt another like that."

"Horrible, I agree," he said, adopting a concerned expression. Then his eyes lit on something. He shouldered his way into the room, flinging the door wide open and shoving past her. He crossed the room in two or three strides and seized the photographs she'd left lying on the counter.

"It's time to stop playing games," he said, narrowing his eyes. "This is Melissa. Where is she?"

"I don't know," insisted Lucy, praying that Sue could keep the girls quiet in the root cellar.

"These pictures were taken in this room." Roderick's eyes blazed. He tapped the photos against his fingernails.

"She was here," admitted Lucy. "But she's not here now. I think you'd better leave before I call the police." She reached for the phone.

"I don't believe you," he said, grabbing her wrist. "Let's look and see if she's here."

"That hurts! Let go of me," she cried as he pulled her into the dining room. "See? There's no one here. I'm all alone."

Grabbing her upper arm, he dragged her into the hall and stood her against the wall. Lucy felt his body pressing against hers as he looked through the doorway into the living room and the family room beyond. He glanced at the stairway, glared at her, daring her to move, and dashed upstairs.

Nauseous and out of breath, Lucy clung to the newel post for support. She heard his heavy footsteps as he crashed through the rooms over her head, knocking over the furniture as he searched for his daughter. He was angry, and she was afraid he would turn his fury on her when he returned. The knob on the newel post was loose in her hands. Maybe she could knock him out with it.

Hearing him on the stairs, she raised her head and waited warily, fingering the solid wood knob, ready if he attacked her. He stopped a few steps from the bottom, where he towered above her.

"You know where she is," he said, leaning over her. Even if she summoned up the courage to knock him on the head with the knob, she realized, she couldn't reach him unless he came down the last few stairs.

He grabbed her shoulders with both hands and squeezed. His breath was hot on her face and she stepped backward, trying to shake out of his grasp.

"You can't get away from me," he said, his lips twisting into an unpleasant grin. He leaped down the last few steps easily and stood in front of her. "I can do whatever I want with you."

Taking his hand off her shoulder, he chucked her on the chin. Then he slowly lowered it and fondled her breast. Lucy stared at the wallpaper. His hand moved lower, across her belly, and he reached between her legs. She bit her lip and stood very still.

He moved his hand back and forth. "Do you like that?" he asked.

Lucy froze, trying to send her mind somewhere else, pretending that this wasn't happening.

"Say you like it," he said, squeezing her shoulders with his other hand.

"I like it," said Lucy, humiliated.

"How do you like this?" he asked, suddenly grabbing her upper arms and slamming her against the solid pine front door.

Stunned and shaken, Lucy wrapped her arms protectively across her chest and rubbed her bruised arms. Instinct told her to run, but she didn't have the strength. A warm flood poured down her legs, and her cheeks burned with shame.

"Where's my little girl? Better tell me now," he advised, rubbing his thumbs against his fingers. "I won't ask again."

"I don't know." Lucy could only whisper as she felt his hands tightening on her neck. She was fighting to breathe, her heart was pumping in her chest, and her head rang. She was growing dizzy, her body reflexively gulping for the air he was denying her. She wrapped her hands around his wrists and tried to pull them away, she kicked at his legs.

"You're like all the others," he said, tightening his hands and shaking her. Lucy felt the almost irresistible pull of unconsciousness, but her body still fought for breath. She heard his voice, as if from a distance. "Liar. Bitch. Whore."

"Stop it, Philip. Let her go."

The voice was cool and authoritarian. Miraculously, his hands loosened and Lucy slid to the floor, retching and gagging.

Annemarie stood in the doorway, wearing a pink cardigan embroidered with a picket fence, flowers, and bunnies with fluffy angora tails. She was holding a .22.

"The police are on the way—I called from my car phone. Get out now," she said, waving the gun. "I'll say I didn't get a clear view of the assailant."

"Efficient as always, Annemarie," said Roderick, adding a patronizing little chuckle. His tone was casual, but his hands were clenched. "I think you may have forgotten something. I'm running this show. You do what I say, cutie-pie, or you'll be looking at the inside of a jail cell for a real long time."

"I don't care."

"What?"

"I'm going to tell the police the truth. I can't live like this anymore. It's getting so I can't stand to look in the mirror."

On the floor, Lucy groaned and stirred. Roderick glanced at her.

"Do what you want," he said, dismissing Annemarie. "I want to find my daughter, and the bitch knows where she is." He started toward Lucy.

"No." Annemarie waved the gun. "Leave her alone."

"Or what? You'll shoot?" Roderick was sarcastic.

"Yeah, I'll shoot. Don't make me. Just leave. You don't have much time."

"That's right. And she knows where Melissa is."

He bent over Lucy and began shaking her. Lucy's eyelids fluttered, and he slapped her face.

"That's enough," warned Annemarie.

"I'm getting sick of you," growled Roderick, turning and advancing toward her. "Give me that gun."

Annemarie's face turned white, and she took a few steps backward, bumping into one of the kitchen chairs. It fell with a loud clatter. Roderick laughed and grabbed for the gun. Annemarie bit her lip and squeezed the trigger.

Thirty-three

Sound courtesy of Down East Music.

"Fred, my husband, asked me to stop by at Lucy Stone's and drop off an insurance check, since I was going out that way anyway. When I pulled into the driveway I saw Philip Roderick's car, and when I got up on the porch I heard a crash. I looked through the window and saw Philip attacking Lucy. I ran back to the car, called the police, and took my little twenty-two out of the glove compartment. Fred gave it to me because I'm out alone at night quite a bit, at business meetings. I warned Philip to stop, he turned on me, and I fired. Is he dead?"

"The medics say the wound isn't life-threatening," answered Detective Sergeant Horowitz. He was sitting opposite her at Lucy's kitchen table. Lucy was strapped to a stretcher, ready to be taken to the hospital.

"Good. I think one murder is enough for anyone."

Horowitz raised an eyebrow. "Are you telling me that you've killed somebody else?"

"I killed my father-in-law, Morrill Slack."

"Ready to go, Mrs. Stone?" asked the EMT. "Your friend Mrs. Finch says she'll stay with the kids."

Lucy shook her head no, frantically. Her throat was so sore she couldn't speak.

"Let her stay a minute," advised Culpepper. "I'm sure she wants to hear what Annemarie's got to say."

Lucy nodded her head gratefully, listening avidly as Annemarie began her confession.

"My father-in-law called and told me to come by the store because he had something to show me. He did that pretty often, called up and demanded an appearance. I had a twelve-thirty appointment with Dr. Fox and was always out by one-twenty, so I thought if I went on my way to the club meeting it would be a good excuse not to stay too long."

Lucy nodded, remembering the timetable she'd worked out earlier.

"As soon as I got there he grabbed my arm and pulled me into the office, demanding I look at this video. It was just the replay on the camera, black and white and about an inch square, but I could see Ben in the store, reaching into the cash register. He was obviously stealing.

"I told Morrill we'd pay it back, however much it was, and thought that was the end of it. I started to go, and he blocked the door.

"Paying it back wouldn't be enough, he told me. He was going to go to the police, turn Ben in. I begged him not to. 'Can't we keep this in the family?' I asked. 'We don't have to air our dirty laundry in public.'

"He just laughed at me. Said I probably knew plenty about dirty laundry, since I was just a filthy dago. That's what he called me. I said my family was just as proud of our heritage as he was of his.

"He said then I'd understand how it was part of his heritage to obey the law, even if it meant embarrassing me.

"I said I thought he was more interested in embarrassing me than obeying the law, and we ought to be thinking about Ben.

"He said it would teach Ben a lesson. I said it could ruin his life and there was a better way to handle it. Then I picked up the camera and started to remove the tape. He tried to grab it back. We struggled and I yanked the thing out of his hands and smashed it on his head.

"That's exactly how it happened. I didn't mean to kill him. Things just escalated.

"I was horrified. All I wanted to do was get away from there. I took the tape, stuffed it in my bag, and went out onto the sidewalk. Nobody was around. I could see myself in the plate glass window—I looked all right—and it was still only about twenty to two, so I went to the meeting. I decided to pretend it hadn't happened.

"It wasn't much of a strategy, but it seemed to work. When I got home there was a message that Ben had been arrested in Gilead and I had to go bail him out. Next thing I knew Franny was arrested, and I was off the hook.

"Fred had an old fraternity brother, Philip Roderick, who'd become a successful criminal lawyer, and he asked him to defend Ben. I thought that was enough, but Fred felt bad for Franny and asked Phil to defend her, too. I knew he was getting divorced from his wife but I didn't know the rest until I ran into Tatiana this morning. She told me how he'd beaten up Caro and abused his wife and daughter. It made me sick.

"I began thinking. I'd sort of been on hold, waiting for this all to end. Then I realized it would never end, because I was lying and I'd have to keep lying and I was teaching my son to lie. I couldn't pretend I hadn't killed Morrill and let Franny suffer for it. I had to admit the truth and take the consequences, and so does Ben."

Lucy thought of the little diagram she'd drawn last night. One circle with Morrill and Kitty, one circle with

Fred and Annemarie, and the third circle with Ben inside. She tapped Barney's hand, eager to try to tell him about it, but he misunderstood.

"Take her away, boys," he said. "And Lucy, do what the doctor says, okay?"

The yard was filled with emergency vehicles, reminding Lucy of the disasters Toby used to stage on the floor of his room, pulling out every toy car and truck he owned. Sue was keeping the girls clear of all the activity, supervising as they played on the swing set. They didn't seem any the worse for the time they spent in the cellar, and Sue gave a little wave as they slid Lucy into the ambulance.

The ambulance had just gotten under way when it suddenly stopped; the driver braked as Bill's red pickup turned into the driveway, brakes squealing.

"What's going on?" he shouted, throwing open the door and jumping down. "Who's hurt?"

"Your missus had a little trouble, but she's all right," the driver told him. "Doc Ryder wants to check her out."

"I'm coming," decided Bill. "I'll follow you."

Returning to the truck, he put an arm around Toby's shoulders and gave him a squeeze.

"You've gotta be the man of the house till I get back, okay?"

"Sure, Dad," said Toby, surveying the assorted vehicles with the rapt gaze of a true believer. "Why'd you make me go to that crummy baseball game, anyway? We shoulda stayed home. Look what we almost missed!"

Thirty-four

No seating until doors open at 7:00 P.M.

Even though Lucy had stayed in the hospital only overnight—"for observation," as Doc Ryder put it—she was treated to a hero's welcome when she returned.

"Mom's home!" shouted Toby as soon as the car pulled into the driveway, and Sara and Elizabeth came running. They danced around her, waving handmade welcome-home signs, as Bill helped her out of the car and escorted her to the house. A smiling Sue met them at the door and instructed Lucy to go straight to the family room couch.

"What did Doc Ryder say?" she asked Bill in a low voice. "Is everything all right?"

"The baby's fine," he assured her. "They did a sonogram. Lucy will be okay, too. Lots of bruises, a real sore throat, and a broken coccyx."

"Coccyx?"

"Tailbone. Very painful," explained Bill.

Lucy nodded emphatically, and sat down very carefully.

"Kids, get your mom some pillows," instructed Sue, and Lucy smiled gratefully.

"You can't talk, can you?"

Lucy shook her head.

"You poor thing," cooed Sue. "Do you want a cold drink?"

Lucy nodded enthusiastically and made a writing motion with her hand. Bill sent Toby to hunt for a pad and pencil for her and sat down beside her. The girls tucked pillows around her and perched at her feet.

"I missed you," confided Sara, with a little pout.

"It was absolutely awful while you were gone," began Elizabeth, and Lucy prepared to hear a long list of complaints.

"Toby said he should be in charge because he was the oldest, but I told him I should. I'm the oldest girl, so I had to be in charge. The mommy runs the house and mommies are always girls. And we had to have scrambled eggs for supper because that's all Daddy knows how to cook." Elizabeth rolled her eyes dramatically.

Taking the pad from Toby, Lucy wrote something and handed it to Elizabeth, who read aloud, "Which was worse: eggs or cellar?"

"The eggs definitely. They were burned."

Lucy cast a questioning glance at Sue, who had returned with a tray of cold drinks for everyone.

"It wasn't so bad, honest," said Sue, setting the tray on the coffee table and handing the glasses around. "The worst part was hearing noises—especially the gunshot—and not knowing what was going on."

"Spiders?" wrote Lucy.

"We were a little concerned at first, especially Sara," recounted Sue. "But Lisa straightened us out. She said we were much bigger than any spiders and they were probably afraid of us. After that we sang 'Itsy Bitsy Spider' in very soft voices and tickled each other and it was okay. We came out when we heard the sirens."

"Lisa?" wrote Lucy.

"She's in foster care. Her father's no threat now,

he'll be in the hospital for quite a while, and then he'll be tried for attacking you and Caro. After all that's happened, Louise will eventually get custody of Lisa-Melissa."

Lucy smiled her approval. "Caro?" she wrote.

"Tatiana called this morning," reported Sue. "She said there have been some hopeful developments and the doctors are encouraged, whatever that means."

Lucy shrugged and took a sip of her juice. She looked around the sunny room filled with people she loved and scribbled furiously on her pad. "I'm so happy to be home," she wrote, and held it up for everyone to see. "Everything looks so nice," she added, and pointed to Sue. "Thank you," she mouthed.

"It was nothing," insisted Sue, with a dismissive gesture. "The kids really pitched in."

"You gave me some scare," confessed Bill. "When I got home the yard was full of police cars." He swallowed hard and took her hand. "I don't want to have to go through anything like that again. Ever."

"Me either," squeaked Lucy. Her voice sounded so funny that after a shocked moment, everybody laughed.

"I can't get over it," said Sue, shaking her head. "Annemarie killed Morrill Slack. I hate to think of all the energy I wasted being jealous. Now I just feel sorry for her. Imagine how guilty she must have felt to poach that salmon."

Lucy started to laugh, yelped instead, and took another sip of her juice.

"Fred's the one I feel bad for," observed Bill. "He's a good guy. He felt responsible; he couldn't let anybody down. He had to protect Annemarie, but he couldn't abandon Franny, so he hired a lawyer for her. He even gave me the Red Sox tickets—I think he was trying to make up for you finding Slack's body. I found the check for the camera on the table," he said, handing it to Lucy.

She pointed to the name on the check, Yankee Village Insurance Agency.

"So?" Bill didn't understand.

"Claims are usually paid by the insurance company, not the agency," explained Sue. "In other words, Fred's paying for the camera himself."

"The insurance didn't cover it?"

Lucy shook her head.

"I don't want to take Fred's money. He's got enough trouble right now. What do you think, Lucy? Shall I tear it up?"

"No way," mouthed Lucy, slipping the check into her pocket.

"I'll never understand women," said Bill. "A guy doesn't stand a chance."

Lucy's and Sue's eyes met, and this time Lucy joined in the laughter, even though it hurt.

Thirty-five

Show begins at 7:30 P.M. Sharp.

Finally, after months of preparations, the big show was about to begin. The high school auditorium was packed; everyone in Tinker's Cove seemed to be there. Hardworking fathers, uncomfortable in their Sunday best, tugged self-consciously at their ties and stretched their necks. Brothers and sisters fidgeted restlessly in their seats. Grandparents, veterans at these affairs, chatted quietly and idly fanned themselves with their programs. And almost every mother, decked out in heels and makeup, had a bouquet of flowers or a prettily wrapped gift for her favorite ballerina.

Backstage, Lucy led Sara and Elizabeth to the dressing room. Staking out a spot in the crowded room, where every inch seemed occupied by tiny dancers in various stages of undress, Lucy helped the girls into their costumes.

"I can't believe there's no curtain or anything," complained a newly modest Elizabeth. "How do they expect us to change with everybody watching?"

"Nobody's watching. Just be quick," urged Lucy, helping her step into the tutu. Her voice was still a hoarse whisper.

"You look beautiful," she said, stepping back to admire her daughters.

"The other girls are wearing lipstick," Elizabeth informed her.

"I know," said Lucy, unzipping her makeup bag. "The pink sheet says to use lipstick and rouge." She was just adding a final touch of blush when Karen Baker asked if the girls would pose for a snapshot. Linking arms, the girls smiled prettily.

"Off you go," said Karen, replacing the camera in its case.

"Break a leg!" said Lucy, giving them a wave for luck.

"How are you feeling?" asked Karen. "You've had a lot of excitement lately."

"I'm okay, we're all okay. It was horrible, though. I'm still having nightmares about it."

"How are the kids doing?" Karen took her arm, and the two women walked slowly down the hall to the auditorium. On the way, they passed Tatiana, splendid in harem pants and bolero jacket. She always performed in the show and this year she was dancing the part of the Arabian from the *Nutcracker.* She had painted eyeliner out to her ears, attached fantastic false eyelashes, and added a sprinkling of glitter. The effect was extremely dramatic, and some of the youngest dancers couldn't resist hugging her.

Catching her eye over the heads of the children clustered around her, Lucy gave her a thumbs-up sign. Tatiana winked back.

"The kids are fine," said Lucy. "I think they liked all the excitement. Toby says he wished he'd been home to videotape it. Then he could have sent it in to *Eyewitness Video.*"

"Somehow that doesn't surprise me," said Karen, scanning the crowded auditorium for her husband. "See you later," she said, spotting him. "Enjoy the show."

Lucy made her way down the crowded aisle and slipped into the seat Bill had saved for her.

"Are the girls nervous?" he asked.

"More excited than nervous, I think. The squeaky-voice index is hovering around ninety-nine point nine."

Bill chuckled, and reached inside his pocket. "By the way, I found this in the mailbox." He handed her a letter.

Lucy fingered it curiously. She hadn't written or received a letter in a long time. She had had many correspondents when she was in college, but now she reached for the phone.

The return address was in Washington, D.C., but the sender had not included a name. Lucy opened the envelope and looked for a signature.

"It's from Louise Roderick," she said, and began eagerly reading the neat, round script.

"Dear Lucy Stone [she read]. There is no way I can ever express my great thanks to you. You saved my dearest friend's life, you protected my daughter, and you did all this despite real danger to yourself and your family. You must be a very rare and wonderful person.

"I have been granted custody of Melissa on a trial basis, supervised by the court. I know I have a lot of work to do if I'm going to be the good mother I want to be, and we're both seeing counselors.

"Oddly enough, I find I can deal with the things Philip did to me and maybe even to Melissa, but I cannot stand the fact that he hurt you and Caro. My constant prayer is that you will both recover completely, and that he will receive the punishment he deserves.

"Thanks to you and Tatiana and Caro I now have a chance for a new life with Melissa. I am taking things one day at a time, trying not to forget or deny the past,

but to accept it and let it go. What's done is done, to-morrow is full of possibilities. Thank you."

Amen, thought Lucy, folding the letter and tucking it into her purse. Perhaps someday she would meet Louise. She hoped so.

"Is this seat taken?" demanded Miss Tilley, nudging Lucy's shoulder.

"Not anymore," said Lucy, gathering up the sweater she'd put on the next chair so Toby could sit there. "I see Toby's sitting with his friends."

"How are you feeling?" inquired Miss Tilley, fixing her sharp eyes on the scarf Lucy had wrapped around her bruised neck.

"Pretty good," admitted Lucy. "Every twinge just makes me more determined to see Philip Roderick go to jail for a very long time."

Bill nudged her and she looked up just in time to see Franny appear. Accompanied by her mother, Franny looked relaxed and happy. One or two friends began clapping, and within seconds the entire crowd was welcoming her with applause. Stunned, Franny stood there, smiling and clutching Irma's arm while tears ran down her cheeks.

Finally, a gentleman Lucy recognized as the Smalls' neighbor came to their aid and led them to a pair of empty seats. People smiled and waved, and some reached for her hand as she made her way down the aisle. Lucy found herself grinning and brushing away tears at the same time. She felt the warmth of Bill's hand covering hers, and she leaned her head on his shoulder.

Observing this sign of affection, Miss Tilley humphed softly. "Did you see Kitty?" she asked.

"No. Is she here?" Lucy straightened up, followed Miss Tilley's gnarled finger, and found Kitty Slack seated next to a handsome white-haired man. The two were engaged in an animated conversation.

"He's Gerald Asquith, president of Winchester College," she hissed in Lucy's ear. "I told her he's just after her money, but she won't listen to me."

"She should," said Lucy, remembering the conversation she'd overheard in the post office. Then she added, "There are more important things than money. She looks awfully happy."

"Pah!" said Miss Tilley, so loudly that several people in neighboring seats turned curiously.

The lights dimmed, and Lucy felt the old woman's hand pat hers. "I always said you were one to watch," she whispered in Lucy's ear.

Then a spotlight revealed Tatiana, wrapped in a saffron cape, in front of the curtains. She was welcomed with a scattering of polite applause. The audience was restless—they'd waited a long time to see the children perform.

"I'm very happy to welcome you to our ninth annual show. I know the children are very excited about performing for you tonight. But before we begin, I want to thank two special people, Ann Douglas and Mitzi Crandell, for all their help."

She paused and the audience gave the expected round of applause for Ann and Mitzi. When it was quiet again, she resumed.

"Also, I would like to dedicate this year's show to a wonderful teacher, my mentor and also my friend, Caroline Hutton."

There was another round of applause, louder this time, and Tatiana disappeared behind the curtains. A second or two later the spotlight was turned off, and the audience sat in the dark waiting expectantly.

Music began to play, the familiar strains of a Strauss waltz filled the auditorium, and the curtain opened on seven pairs of dancers dressed in filmy pastel gowns and crowned with flowers. Lucy recognized the girls as members of Tatiana's intermediate class, none of them particularly talented. But in their beautiful costumes each was a star tonight. They whirled around the stage carried along by the sumptuous music, and the audience adored them. Friends and relatives pointed out their darlings, and cheered and clapped for them. This was what they'd come for and they applauded enthusiastically when the girls ran off the stage.

The older dancers, the high school girls, were greeted with shrieks of appreciation from the claques of friends and admirers. Tottering about on their toes, they remained cool and professional and never missed a step. No matter how much they were looking forward to the party afterward, or hoping for a bouquet from a certain someone, they didn't dare let Tatiana down while they were performing.

After a slight delay the very littlest dancers, the babies, tippy-toed on stage to be greeted with oohs and aahs. They looked very tiny, and absolutely adorable in their pink tutus. They also looked very much alike with their hair pulled back into identical buns, and Lucy had a difficult time picking out little Sara. All the babies looked slightly dazed, and some were so dazzled by their first stage appearance that they completely forgot to dance. Instead, they stood awkwardly, shifting their weight from foot to foot. Others, including Sara, performed like old troupers. The audience loved them, especially when the little girls held their tiny hands about six inches from their button noses and attempted to pirouette. That brought down the house, and the babies exited to the loudest cheers and applause of all.

When the curtain reopened, Tatiana stood alone, center stage, in her glamorous costume. Everyone watched attentively as she began the sinuous movements of a harem dancer. The audience was impressed. Tatiana was a hometown girl, someone they'd known forever, and she could dance just like someone on TV. They rewarded her with appreciative applause.

The grand finale was unforgettable. As each group of dancers appeared, and performed briefly, they were welcomed with a burst of applause. Soon the dancers were entering so quickly there was no break in the clapping. Lucy and Bill beamed with parental pride and slapped their hands together until their palms burned and their arms ached. Finally, everyone was on stage and Tatiana appeared; the clapping became a thunderous ovation.

Then, much to Lucy's surprise, Sara detached herself from the line of babies and took the center of the stage. Lucy recognized her anxious expression; it meant she knew she was supposed to do something but couldn't quite remember what it was. Responding to an offstage hiss, Sara turned and ran directly toward a disembodied beckoning arm. She disappeared offstage but soon reappeared, clutching an enormous bouquet of roses and trailing the ribbons. Nudged by the arm, she trotted across the stage, executed a perfect curtsy, and presented the flowers to Tatiana.

There was a final burst of applause, Tatiana took Sara's hand and bowed to the audience, the dancers all made a final curtsy, and it was over.

"Wow," said Bill. "That was better than a doubleheader!"

Epilogue

High in the cloudless blue September sky, a herring gull seemed to soar effortlessly, hardly moving its wings as it floated on unseen currents of air. Watching it through the window from her bed in the birthing room at the cottage hospital, Lucy wished she could change places with it.

This morning, when the contractions finally began to come five minutes apart, seemed eons ago. Had it been years, or just a few hours, since she stood at the kitchen sink? She had been counting off the minutes when she saw Caro and George on the path to the pond. It had been good to see them again.

Despite three months of convalescence, Caro was still not fully recovered. She was limping, still relying on a pair of aluminum crutches. None of that seemed to bother George. The golden dog held his tail high as he pranced ahead of his owner. Lucy could have sworn he was smiling.

Despite the crutches, Caro managed the path as gracefully as she handled most things. She took her time, and although she went slowly, she didn't appear to be straining or struggling as she made her way down the familiar route to the pond.

Lucy watched until she saw Caro return and get back into her car. The little Honda now had handicapped plates. Lucy guessed it had been modified in some way so Caro could drive it.

After she'd seen Caro safely gone, Lucy called Bill.

"They're about five minutes apart now," she told him. "I think we'd better get going."

"Okay," he said, fiddling nervously with the car keys. "Do you have everything you need? Pillows, lollipops, paper bag?"

"You make it sound like we're going on some sort of scavenger hunt," complained Lucy. "Whatever happened to the good old days when they clapped a gas mask on your face at the first sign of a contraction and you woke up with a brand-new baby?"

Bill chuckled sympathetically. His tone was hopeful as he asked, "Video camera?"

"Absolutely not." Lucy was firm.

"Let's go," said Bill, picking up Lucy's overnight bag.

Aside from the two of them, the house was empty. School had been in session for a couple of weeks, and all the children had left earlier that morning—even Sara, who was in kindergarten.

"Unnhh," moaned Lucy as a particularly intense contraction gripped her while she was getting settled in the car.

"Are you all right?" asked Bill, fumbling as he tried to put the key in the ignition.

"Oh, sure," said Lucy. "I feel like an idiot. I've been through this three times. How could I forget what it's like? But I did. I spent my whole pregnancy looking forward to this. Now it's started, I remember everything, and I don't want to go through it again. I just want to cancel the order, thank you very much."

"It's a little late for that, isn't it?"

"I suppose so. But this is absolutely going to be the last baby. I am *not* going to do this ever again. I'm going to remember every ache, every cramp, every contraction. This time I'm not going to forget."

Anticipating a quick delivery, Doc Ryder met them at the hospital.

"After all, Lucy, this is your fourth baby. You must have gotten the knack by now. Let's get this wrapped up by noon, okay? It's a real Indian summer day and I've got a one o'clock tee time," he told her as he escorted her to the maternity wing.

"I'll do what I can," promised Lucy, shifting uncomfortably in her wheelchair as another contraction began.

A cheerful nurse soon had her prepped and installed in the birthing room, where Doc Ryder and Bill joined her. They were both dressed in gowns and were wearing ridiculous paper shower caps on their heads. Bill pulled a chair up beside the bed and patted her hand encouragingly. The doctor settled himself in an armchair and took a nap.

The morning passed slowly, marked by the regular contractions, but the labor didn't seem to be making much progress. Bill had taped up a focal point for her, a photo of a baby clipped from a magazine, but Lucy preferred focusing on the gulls outside her window. There always seemed to be at least one; maybe they were attracted by updrafts produced by the sun beating down on the hospital's asphalt parking lot.

When she felt a contraction begin, she picked out a gull and fastened her attention on it. She concentrated on keeping her breaths light and regular, she concentrated on relaxing her arms and legs, she concentrated on the gull's perfect white shape against the clear blue sky. She wanted to scream.

"These contractions aren't very efficient," complained

Doc Ryder, peering at the ribbon of paper the fetal monitor was spewing out. "I think we ought to pep 'em up a little bit."

"What do you mean?" asked Lucy warily. She had heard horror stories told by veterans of the delivery room wars.

"I can give you a drip and you'll have better contractions. See," he said, waving the paper at her, "these kind of dribble along. They don't peak."

"These contractions seem just fine to me," said Lucy. "Won't a drip hurt?"

"No. It's just an IV."

"It'll make the contractions hurt more, won't it?"

"Hard to say," said the doctor, evading her question. "You'll have the baby sooner. You want that, don't you?"

"No," said Lucy. "I don't care if I have a baby. I want to die."

"There, there," said the doctor as he patted the back of her hand preparatory to inserting a huge needle in it. "You're just tired. I'll give you some glucose, too. That'll perk you up."

"Oh, thanks," said Lucy, groaning and gripping the bed rails as a force-ten contraction racked her body.

"I guess we'd better lower the dosage just a bit," conceded the doctor, fiddling with the IV. He nodded approvingly as the fetal monitor began graphing contractions with peaks.

Lucy was no longer watching the seagulls out the window. She'd given up looking for a focal point. She had retreated to a place within herself where the pains came one after another like waves on the rocky shore. She no longer cared where she was, or who was with her; she had given up the effort of remaining in control. She was aware only of the pains, and the periods of rest in between. She was entirely consumed by the process of giving birth.

"It's time to push," announced Doc Ryder. Bill and the nurse stationed themselves on either side of her and raised her shoulders.

"Tuck your chin against your chest and bear down. Work with the contraction," instructed the nurse, and Lucy did her best. The exhausting process was repeated many times, however, before she was rewarded.

"We've got a head," said the doctor, and with the next contraction the baby was born.

"That felt just like a slippery fish," giggled Lucy, relaxing back against the pillow. She might as well have been talking to herself, she realized. No one was listening. Doc Ryder, Bill, and the nurse were all clustered around the baby.

"That's one heck of a fat baby," said Doc Ryder.

"I've never seen such a plump, round little newborn," cooed the nurse.

"Wow, feel that grip," said Bill, smiling as the baby wrapped a tiny red hand around his index finger.

"Ten pounds, two ounces, and twenty-one inches," noted the doctor.

"Apgar?" asked the nurse.

"A ten. A definite ten. This is a very nice baby."

"Excuse me," said Lucy, raising her voice. "Do you mind if I ask a question? Is it a boy or a girl?"

"Well, Lucy," said the doctor, placing the blanket-wrapped infant in her arms. "It looks like you've got another ballerina."

Please turn the page
for an exciting sneak peek of
another one of Leslie Meier's
Lucy Stone mysteries:

VALENTINE MURDER

*Once upon a time there was a poor
kitchen maid named Cinderella . . .*

On the day she died, Bitsy Howell didn't want to
get out of bed. Her bedroom was cold, for one thing.
It was always cold, thanks to her landlady, Mrs. Withers,
who turned the heat down to fifty-five degrees every
night to save money on heating oil. It didn't matter
one bit to Mrs. Withers that it was the coldest winter
in twenty years.

And if the cold bedroom wasn't reason enough to
stay in bed, well, the fact that it was Thursday made
getting up especially difficult. Bitsy hated Thursdays.

Thursday was story-hour day at the Broadbrooks Free
Library, where she was the librarian. Just thinking
about story hour depressed Bitsy. She found it practically impossible to keep ten or fifteen preschool children focused on a storybook. Thanks to TV and video
games, they had no attention span whatsoever. They
fidgeted and wriggled in their seats, they picked their
noses, they did everything except what Bitsy wanted
them to do, which was to sit quietly and listen to a

nice story followed by a finger-play or song, or maybe a simple craft project.

This Thursday, however, happened to be the last Thursday in January. That meant the library's board of directors would meet, as they did on the last Thursday of every month. Bitsy would not only have to cope with story hour, but with the directors, too.

Bitsy had come to the tiny Broadbrooks Free Library in Tinker's Cove, Maine, from a big city library. One factor in her decision to leave had been her poor relationship with her boss, the head librarian. Little had she known that she was swapping one rather difficult menopausal supervisor for seven meddlesome and inquisitive directors.

Bitsy sighed and heaved herself out of bed. She padded barefoot around her rather messy bedroom, looking for her slippers. She found one underneath a magazine and the other tangled in a pair of sweat pants. One of these days, she promised herself, she would get organized and pick up the clothes that were strewn on the floor. Not today, of course. She didn't have time today.

On her way to the bathroom she raised the shade and peered out the window, blinking at the bright winter sunlight. Shit, she muttered. It had snowed again.

Arriving at the library, Bitsy studied the new addition, which contained a children's room, workroom, and conference room. It was undeniably handsome, and badly needed, but it had been a dreadful bone of contention.

When she had first come to Tinker's Cove the library was a charming but antiquated old building that was far too small for the needs of the community. Getting the board to agree to build the addition, and then raising the money for it, had been a struggle, one Bitsy wouldn't want to repeat. Now, if she could only get them to take the next step and buy some computers so the library could go on-line.

"Tiny baby steps," she muttered as she unlocked the door. Flicking on the lights as she went, Bitsy headed for her office. She had an hour or so before the library opened and she wanted to have her facts and figures straight before the board meeting.

Pushing aside a few of the papers that cluttered her desk, she set down a bag containing a Styrofoam cup of coffee, with cream and sugar, and a couple of sugary jelly doughnuts. She draped her coat over an extra chair and took her seat, flicking on the computer. Soon she was happily immersed in numbers and percentages, all the while slurping down her coffee and scattering powdered sugar all over her desk.

At ten minutes past ten she heard someone banging at the main entrance and realized she hadn't unlocked the doors.

"I'm so sorry," she apologized as she pulled open the heavy oak door. "I lost track of the time."

"No problem, my dear," said Gerald Asquith, smiling down at her benignly. Tall and gray-haired, dressed in a beautifully tailored cashmere overcoat, he was the retired president of Winchester College and one of the members of the board of directors. "I know I'm a bit early, but I want to go over the final figures for the addition before the meeting."

"Of course," said Bitsy. "I'll get the file for you."

Bitsy had hoped Gerald would seat himself at the big table in the reference room, but instead he hung his coat up on the rack by the door and followed her into her office. When she gave him the file he sat down at her desk, displacing her, and began studying it.

Bitsy gave a little shrug and headed for the children's section. She had to come up with something for story hour anyway; it was in less than an hour, at eleven.

She was leafing through a lavishly illustrated edition of *Cinderella* when she felt a presence behind her. Turning, she greeted Corney Clarke with a polite smile. Corney, an attractive blonde of indeterminate age, ran a busy catering service and called herself a "lifestyle consultant." She was also a member of the board of directors.

"Can I help you?" asked Bitsy, mindful of her status as an employee.

"No. I came a little early to see the new addition. It's a big improvement, isn't it?" said Corney, walking around the sunny area, admiring the low bookshelves and child-sized seating.

"It sure is," agreed Bitsy. "We must have been the only library in the state without a children's room."

"It must be fun doing story hour, now, in such nice surroundings," surmised Corney.

"Oh, yes," said Bitsy, attempting to sound enthusiastic. "Today we're reading *Cinderella.*"

"Oh." Corney wrinkled her forehead in concern. "I don't want to tell you how to do your job, but are you sure that's a good choice?"

"The children like it . . ." began Bitsy.

"Well, of course they do. But does it send the right message?"

"It's just a fairy tale." Bitsy bit her lip. Personally, she didn't think every story had to have a socially redeeming message, and she wasn't sure Corney was the right person to decide what was suitable for young children, either. After all, she was childless and never married, though not from lack of effort.

"Well, we don't want our little girls growing up and thinking life is a fairy tale, do we? We don't want them to wait for Prince Charming to rescue them from the kitchen—we want them to become self-actualizing, don't we?" Corney gave Bitsy an encouraging smile, and patted her hand. "I'm sure you can find something more suitable." She paused for a moment and came up with a suggestion. "Like *The Little Engine that Could,*" she said, turning and striding off in the direction of the office.

Bitsy rolled her eyes and replaced *Cinderella* on the shelf. Pulling out one volume after another, she dismissed them. Children's literature was so insipid these days. Everything had to have a positive, meaningful message. She wanted something with a little bite. Something exciting. She opened a battered copy of *Hansel and Gretel* and began turning the pages. This ought to keep the little demons' attention, she thought, admiring a lurid illustration of the tiny Hansel and Gretel cringing in terror as the grinning witch opened the oven door.

"Say, Bitsy, do you know where those figures for the addition are?"

Bitsy closed the book and turned to face Hayden Northcross, another member of the board of directors. Hayden was a small, neat man who was a partner in a prestigious antiques business that was known far beyond Tinker's Cove.

"Gerald's got them, in my office," said Bitsy.

"I'll see if he's through with them," said Hayden, turning to go. "Say, what's that?"

"*Hansel and Gretel.* For story hour."

"Oh, my dear! Not *Hansel and Gretel!*" exclaimed Hayden, throwing up his hands in horror.

"No? Why not?" inquired Bitsy, tightening her grip on the storybook and starting a slow mental count to ten.

"Not unless you want to traumatize the poor

things," said Hayden. "I'll never forget how frightened I was when Mumsy read it to me. I think it may have affected my entire attitude toward women." He cocked an eyebrow and nodded meaningfully.

Bitsy wasn't quite sure how serious he was. Hayden and his business partner, Ralph Love, had also been domestic partners for years. Hayden thought it great fun to shock the more conservative residents of Tinker's Cove by flaunting his homosexuality.

"It's just a story," said Bitsy, defending her choice. "I'll be sure to remind them it's make-believe."

"I'm warning you. You're playing with fire," said Hayden, waggling his finger at her. "That book contains dangerous themes of desertion and cannibalism—the mothers are sure to object."

"You're probably right," said Bitsy, putting the book back on the shelf.

"You know I am," said Hayden, flashing her a smile. "See you at the meeting."

The meeting, thought Bitsy, biting her lip. That was another sore point. The fact that the board met at the same time Bitsy was occupied with story hour was not coincidental. She was convinced it was their way of letting her know she was not a decision maker. She was just the hired help, allowed to join the meeting only for the last half hour to give her monthly report.

It hadn't always been like that. When she first took the job, the board had sought her advice, and had adopted her suggestion that the library be expanded. But as time passed they seemed to grow less receptive to her views, and began easing her out of their meetings. They'd also become increasingly intrusive, always poking their noses into her work.

Bitsy checked her watch and resumed her search. She had better find something fast; it was already a quarter to eleven and little Sadie Orenstein had arrived. She was slowly slipping a big stack of books through the return slot in the circulation desk, one by one, while her mother studied the new books. The Orensteins were ferocious readers.

Pulling out book after book, she shook her head and shoved them back on the shelf. It seemed as if she had read them all, over and over. Absolutely nothing appealed until she found an old favorite, *Rumpelstilt-skin.*

She smiled at the picture of the irate dwarf on the cover. The kids would like it, too, she thought. She would have them act it out and they could stamp their feet just like Rumpelstiltskin. Tucking the book under her arm, and telling Sadie she'd be right back, she hurried to the office. She'd just remembered that she had left a file open on the computer and wanted to close it.

There she found Ed Bumpus, yet another member of the board of directors, busy disassembling the copy machine. Ed was a big man and when he bent over the machine his shirt and pants parted, revealing rather more of his hairy backside than she wanted to see. She stared out the window at a snow-covered pine tree.

"We want copies of the addition finances for the meeting, but the danged machine won't work," explained Ed. He was a contractor and never hesitated to reach for a screwdriver.

"That's funny. It worked fine yesterday. Maybe it's out of paper. Or needs toner. Did you check?"

"What kind of idiot do you take me for? Of course I checked!" snapped Ed, growing a bit red under his plaid flannel shirt collar.

"We'll have to call for service, then," said Bitsy,

leaning over Gerald to ease open her desk drawer. "You can make copies at the coin machine by the front desk. Here's the key."

"Could you be a doll and do it for me?" Ed gave her his version of an ingratiating smile.

Still leaning awkwardly over Gerald, Bitsy reached for the mouse and clicked it, closing the file. Then she took the report from Ed. More children had gathered for story hour—she could hear their voices. They would just have to wait a few minutes. She was not going to risk being insubordinate to one of the directors, especially Ed.

When she returned she found him lounging in the spare chair, sitting on top of her coat, and joking with Gerald, who was still sitting at her desk. What a pair, she thought, annoyed at the way they made themselves at home in her office.

"Here you go," she said, handing him the papers and turning to go. She really had to get story hour started.

"So you're reading *Rumpelstiltskin* to them today?" inquired Gerald, who was still sitting at her desk. His tone was friendly—he was just making conversation. Now that he was retired he had all the time in the world.

"I think they'll like it," said Bitsy, eager to get out to the children. Unsupervised, there was no telling what they might get up to.

"Well, I don't think it's a very good idea. It's a horrible story," said Ed. "It used to make my little girls cry."

"Really?" Bitsy kept her voice even. She was determined not to let him know how irritated she was.

"In fact, I don't even think it belongs in the library. With all the money we spend on new books I don't know why you're keeping a nasty old book like that. Just look at it—it's all worn out."

"I guess you're right," said Bitsy, who knew the acquisitions budget was a sore spot with Ed, who favored bricks and mortar over books. His objection, however, reminded her of a box of new material that had arrived the day before but hadn't been opened yet.

"I'm just going down to the workroom for a minute," she said, more to herself than the directors. Grabbing the box of art supplies and taking a pile of red construction paper from the corner of her desk, she quickly left the office and hurried through the children's room, giving the assembled mothers and children a cheerful wave.

"I'll be right with you—we're making Valentines today," she called, opening the door to the stairs that led to the lower level. She rushed down, hearing her footsteps echo in the poured concrete stairwell, but caught her foot on the rubber edging of the bottom step. She fell forward, twisting her ankle and bumping her head painfully on the doorknob. The sheets of red paper cascaded around her; the coffee can containing child-safe scissors clattered to the concrete floor and crayons rolled in every direction.

Groaning slightly, she pressed her hands to her forehead and sat down on the next to last step, waiting impatiently for the blinding agony to pass. Using a trick she'd picked up in a stress management workshop, she concentrated on her breathing, keeping her breaths even. Gradually, the pain receded. She unclenched her teeth and blinked her eyes. Grasping the handrailing, she pulled herself to her feet, only to feel a stabbing pain in her ankle. Conscious that she was already late for story hour, she tried putting her weight on it even though the pain made her wince. The ankle held and she limped through the dark and empty conference room and on into the brand new workroom. The workroom, unlike the conference room, had windows and she squinted her eyes against the bright sun. She bent over the box, which was sitting on the floor, and yanked at the tape.

Hearing the outside door open, she raised her head.

"Oh, it's *you*," she said, recognizing the figure outlined against the bright light streaming through the windows. Of all the nerve, she thought angrily. This was just too much; the morning was spinning out of control. She'd had enough. She took a deep breath, preparing to give vent to the emotions she had been suppressing for so long, but she never got the chance to say what was on her mind.

Bitsy Howell's last words were rudely interrupted.

ABOUT THE AUTHOR

Leslie Meier lives with her family in Massachusetts. Her newest Lucy Stone mystery, WEDDING DAY MURDER, will be published in hardcover in November 2001, and she is currently working on the ninth, which will be published in 2002. Leslie loves to hear from her readers; you may write to her c/o Kensington Publishing. Please include a self-addressed, stamped envelope if you wish to receive a response.

More Mysteries from
Laurien Berenson

__**HUSH PUPPY** 1-57566-600-6	$5.99US/$7.99CAN
__**DOG EAT DOG** 1-57566-227-2	$5.99US/$7.99CAN
__**A PEDIGREE TO DIE FOR** 1-57566-374-0	$5.99US/$7.99CAN
__**UNLEASHED** 1-57566-680-4	$5.99US/$7.99CAN
__**WATCHDOG** 1-57566-472-0	$5.99US/$7.99CAN
__**HAIR OF THE DOG** 1-57566-356-2	$5.99US/$7.99CAN
__**HOT DOG** 1-57566-782-7	$6.50US/$8.99CAN
__**ONCE BITTEN** 0-7582-0182-6	$6.50US/$8.99CAN
__**UNDER DOG** 0-7582-0292-X	$6.50US/$8.99CAN

Available Wherever Books Are Sold!

Visit our website at www.kensingtonbooks.com

Get Hooked on the
Mysteries of
Jonnie Jacobs

Available Wherever Books Are Sold!

Visit our website at **www.kensingtonbooks.com**

Grab These
Kensington Mysteries

Available Wherever Books Are Sold!

Visit our website at www.kensingtonbooks.com